Sola

Sola

DAKOTA KNIGHT

URBAN BOOKS LLC
www.urbanbooks.net

Urban Books
74 Andrews Avenue
Wheatley Heights, NY 11798

ISBN 1-893196-51-8

First Printing December 2006
Printed in the United States of America

10   9   8   7   6   5   4   3   2   1

Submit Wholesale Orders to:
Kensington Publishing Corp.
C/O Penguin Group (USA) Inc.
Attention: Order Processing
405 Murray Hill Parkway
East Rutherford, NJ 07073-2316
Phone: 1-800-526-0275
Fax: 1-800-227-9604

To Denise
¡Tu Puedes Hacerlo!

To Lawrence
Vaya Con Dios, Mi Amigo

Acknowledgments

I feel so excited and blessed I don't know where to begin. Of course, I can't move forward without thanking God for giving me the gift of writing and so much more.

To my parents, who have given me so much. There are no words to describe the depth of love and gratitude I feel for you. You were there for me in my darkest hour and continue to show me unconditional love and support. Thank you for everything.

To my sister, who so graciously shared her light with me when I could no longer shine on my own. I am forever in your debt. I am glad I have you to look up to. You are a woman of exquisite class and grace.

To my aunt, thank you for supporting me when I needed you. From the prom dress (which I still have) to my favorite Bears jersey, you always come through. For my cousin, Di, and your two sons, you came through the storm and you continue to rise. Be Blessed. And for all my family members near and far, we may not get to see each other often, but there is a bond that will always hold together.

To Joylynn, thanks for giving my writing a chance and taking me on as your client. Your advice and support are invaluable. You have definitely helped me grow as a writer. To Carl and Urban Books, I truly appreciate the opportunity. Carl, you are taking African American Literature to another level. Thanks for taking me along for the ride. Earth, one day, I hope to show you the money. To Carol's Cakes and Mrs. Matthews, and The Art of Beauty Hair and Nail Salon and Denetria, thank you for opening your doors and showing your support.

To Xavier University of Louisiana, Dr. Norman Francis, Mr. George Baker, and Dr. Thomas Bonner, among others, we don't always know why things happen the way they do, but I know Xavier will continue to improve. Xavier has been a beacon of light for many, and I know that light will continue to guide students for many generations to come.

To my blogging friends, Bernita, Shawn, Emanuel, Hasina, Kell, and Erik, I enjoy communicating with you and wish all of you the best for the future. You've all made blogging fun!

Denise, your friendship means more to me than you'll ever know. Maybe I'll take that valium one day so we can go to Europe. (On second thought . . .) Keep doing your thing. Urielle, my favorite M.D., you've been through so much (namely putting up with me for so many years) and you continue to show a silent strength that amazes me. Hope to see you soon. Stephanie, we've been friends since middle school and I treasure our friendship. What happened to that McChicken anyway? I'm looking forward to celebrating your future success. Stefphanie, we've shared good times and bad, but the friendship remains. Let's keep in touch. Michael Hill, where are you? Fadi, my *habibi* forever, congratulations on your new life and your new wife. I'll be in Cali soon so we can celebrate. Larry, who read my work when no one else would, please know that your enthusiasm gave me the confidence to move forward with my dream. I hope that you continue to move forward with your dreams.

And to Elsie, my mentor, tennis partner, my friend. Your presence in my life has been a true blessing. I can't say thank you enough for everything you've done for me. I hope one day I can help others the same way you've helped me. See you on a court one day soon. (And be gentle on me, okay.)

For the countless others that have touched my life through the years, I offer my appreciation. And for those who will touch my life in the future, I'm looking forward to it.

Dakota Knight

dakotaknightwrites@hotmail.com

Sola

Prologue

*In order to be successful in the game of chess,
you need to have a strategic mind, be a quick-
thinker, be careful, and plan well.
Without these qualities, you are sure to fail.*
—The Qualities of Chess Masters # 101

March 30, 11:00 P.M.

It was a perfect night to take care of business. It was moon-
less and there were no stars illuminating the black sky.
Better still, there were only a minimal amount of potential
witnesses walking the streets. As the Brown Recluse looked at
her black classic Movado watch, she knew it was almost time
to go to work. She was glad the almost perfect opportunity
had presented itself; this particular assignment had taken
longer to finish than she first thought it would.

The Recluse stuck her head out of the driver-side window
and inhaled the cool spring air. She had waited in the old
Ford Econoline as long as she could. The smell in the vehicle was nauseating, a mixture of sweat, oil, gas, and something rotten she hadn't discovered and didn't want to. While
she was driving to the west side of Columbus, Ohio, the con-
tinuous airflow from the moving vehicle kept the smell at
bay, but now that she was parked, it was beginning to perme-
ate everything.

She gave herself a mental note to curse out Joe B., the man who had stolen the van for her. When she met with Joe B. to pick up the van, he told her with a toothless grin that it would "ride like the fucking wind." No wonder he left so quickly after she paid him, talking about how he had to get some food and diapers for his baby. *Ride like the fucking wind,* she thought. *He must have meant to ride it in the fucking wind.*

Of course, her first choice would have been to drive her own car, a 2002 black convertible BMW Z-3. She had taken it on some of her other jobs, but this particular occasion called for something more discreet. She hadn't been to the west side for a long time, but she knew that BMWs weren't the standard fare in the West Arms Apartment Complex.

She reached into her backpack and pulled out a pair of plastic gloves and a small spray bottle of bleach. She jumped out of the van and placed the backpack carefully on the ground. She sprayed bleach on the driver's seat, the wheel, and the inside and outside of the door. After she finished spraying the van, she poured the remaining bleach on the driver-side seat. There was no need to wipe anything down; the bleach would do the trick. If anyone ever decided to check out the rusty piece of shit, any evidence of her existence would be gone.

The Recluse walked slowly and took in her surroundings. In the black void of the night, the large brick apartment buildings stood like large barriers leading to another world. Although it was late, there were still people hanging around outdoors. An eclectic blend of tejano, salsa music, hip-hop, and R&B filled the air, reflecting the varied musical tastes of the apartment complex's inhabitants.

She made sure to note the faces of the people she passed by. The neighborhood was mostly Latino, but Blacks and Whites had a small presence. Mainly she wanted to make

sure nobody looked at her for too long. That spoke of famil-
iarity, which was dangerous.

She took pains to look like she belonged there. Her light-
brown, shoulder-length hair was pulled back into a ponytail,
which made the Hispanic features she inherited from her father stand out more than the African American features she
inherited from her mother.

She didn't wear any make-up, not that she needed any.
Her smooth caramel skin was flawless. She had deep, dark-
brown eyes that were highlighted with miniscule flecks of
amber. Her thick, black eyelashes were longer than store-
bought lashes. She wore non-prescription glasses and a fake
nose ring just to alter her normal appearance.

To complete her transformation, she picked up a knock-
off black Juicy Couture track suit from a street vendor on the
East Side. The outfit was nice, but it was gear that wouldn't
normally be a part of her wardrobe. At any rate, she didn't
think anyone around the complex would care. But it was
best not to take chances. Black Reeboks and a small black
backpack completed her outfit.

As she neared the entrance to West Arms, she passed by
several men speaking Spanish. They were probably Mexi-
cans, as were most Latinos living on the west side of Columbus. She didn't glance at them long enough to see their
faces, but she smiled slightly as she overheard a part of their
conversation. They were talking about her body. It wasn't
anything new. She had heard it all before and then some. In
her line of work, keeping in shape was a necessity. Years of
physical activity had kept her lean and toned, and she had
curves in all the right places.

She added a little switch in her step, knowing the men
were still watching her under the glare of the street lights.
She could almost feel their eyes trained on the curve of her

backside as it swayed gently with each step. It still amazed her how much power a female could wield over a man with her body.

"Buenas noches, morena," one of the Mexican men said, wishing her good night in a deep, husky voice. The Recluse smiled, but she didn't respond, didn't even look back. There was no time for idle greetings or conversation.

She reached the main street with no problem and began walking briskly. She wanted to get her heart racing. She knew that the increased blood flow would clear her mind and enhance her senses.

Fifteen minutes later, she reached her destination. She looked at the small one-story house in front of her. She had passed by the brick structure numerous times over the past couple of weeks and each time she saw the same thing: a neatly manicured lawn with pink tulips now in full bloom, a security door, bars on all of the windows, dim lights, and little traffic in and out of the house.

Each time, the particulars of the dwelling made her a little uneasy. She had been given the task of taking out a man who was supposedly trying to take over her boss's turf, and yet this man chose the least amount of security. There were no flood lights or motion detectors. He didn't even have any of his boys standing by the front door to watch his back in case anything went down. As she looked at her watch, she figured his reasons for choosing vulnerability wouldn't matter much in about twenty minutes. He just made her job a lot easier.

She walked along a concrete pathway that led into the backyard. Not even a pit bull to announce her presence. Once she passed the patio, she stopped, placed her backpack on the ground and crouched down. She knew the large barbeque grill and patio furniture would shield her presence from anyone inside of the house.

The Recluse pulled out the gun case that held her favorite gun and silencer. This was her last job, so she thought it was only fitting to use her favorite piece. She waited for a couple of minutes, using her senses to make sure everything was right. Hearing nothing out of the ordinary, she crept quietly towards the house. Her target was the bedroom she had identified just over a week ago as that of her prey.

It appeared to be dark inside of the bedroom, and she wondered how long she would have to wait until he turned on the light and met his destiny. She crept along the side of the house, running her hand along the course brick to keep her balance as she concentrated on the ground. She didn't want to trip on any wayward objects. Once she reached the bedroom window, she stopped. She stood at an angle so she wouldn't be in the line of sight of anyone inside.

When the Recluse looked through the bedroom window, she was pleasantly surprised. *There he is*, she thought. It was dark, but a television emitted a soft glow and allowed her to see him. She didn't know his real name, not that it mattered. She didn't like a lot of personal details about her prey. Her eyes continued to adjust to the dim light and she studied him carefully. He was sitting on the bed. Naked as the day he was born. She smiled at the irony. *He would go as he came*, she thought to herself.

Although the television was on, she couldn't hear any sound. Her prey wasn't watching it anyway. His head was tilted back, facing the ceiling. She figured he was watching a porno and getting himself off. *It figured*, she thought, shaking her head in disgust. A dresser and the television shielded a portion of the lower part of his body. Not that it mattered, because she was aiming for the two parts that mattered most, the head and the heart.

She had already figured it would take four rapid shots, two

to break the glass and then the kill shots. He wouldn't even know what hit him. If he was lucky, he'd finish his hand job before she took him out.

The Recluse closed her eyes, placed her hand on her stomach, and raised the gun into position. She didn't like to hesitate, so she fired the first shot. The glass shattered. She walked closer to the window and looked at her prey. He was staring at the window in a state of shock. She then fired three consecutive shots. She didn't have to look again to know he was dead. But then she heard the screaming.

The screams were coming from the bedroom. "Shit," the Recluse mumbled under her breath.

She knew immediately that the screams weren't coming from the television. She closed in on the window again and stared at the back of the naked woman standing in front of the bed. The woman was looking down and shaking her head wildly, presumably looking at the now deceased man. Acting on instinct, she raised her gun and fired three more shots. The screaming stopped.

The noise was unexpected and shook her concentration, but only for a second. She reached for her bag, placed the gun inside, and hurried back towards the street. Once she reached the sidewalk, she started to walk slowly to the bus stop. She didn't look back.

The COTA bus stop was six blocks away from the scene. While waiting for the public transportation, she glanced down the street towards the house she had just visited. No cops, no sirens, no nothing. That was a good sign. Within a couple of minutes, a bus rumbled towards her and stopped. She got on and smiled at the driver as she fed the meter with her fare.

Before sitting down, she made a quick assessment of the other bus passengers. First, there was a middle-aged man with an unkempt beard and a receding hairline. His mismatched clothes and hopeless expression told his story. She assumed he was homeless. She knew that sympathetic bus drivers sometimes let the homeless ride on the bus for a while.

Next, there was a black woman who sat in the back of the bus with a squirming young baby. The woman was rocking the baby back and forth and humming in an attempt to keep the baby calm. The last woman was a working type, she had on a uniform. She may have been a cleaning lady, but whatever she did, she was proud. Even though it was late, the woman's makeup was flawless, as was her pinned-up hairdo. The working woman was engrossed in a book, which she lifted into a position that covered half of her face. The Recluse shifted her head sideways to look at the title of the book. It was *When Souls Mate* by an author named Joylynn M. Jossel.

The Recluse sat in one of the hard metal seats, opened up her bag, and pulled out her iPod. Soon, Beethoven's *Ode to Joy* was filling her ears. Some of her associates laughed at her penchant for classical music, but she brushed the criticism aside. She loved her hip-hop, from the old school groups like NWA and Public Enemy, to the current popular acts like 50 Cent and Ludacris. But there was a time and place for everything. The classical music calmed her down, and for the first time in a while since she could remember after doing a hit, she really needed some calming.

She fiddled with the iPod until she found a more relaxing melody. Beethoven's *Moonlight Sonata* was mellow enough to relax her nerves a bit. She thought briefly about the woman she had just killed. She didn't like the fact that she had to take the extra shots. She should have known the woman was there. It was her job to know. But she had never seen her before, not even once in the couple of weeks she had been scoping out the house. She figured the woman must have been a hooker. *Oh well,* she thought, *the ho was in the wrong place at the wrong time.*

After about a fifteen minute bus ride, the bus reached Broad and High in the middle of downtown. The Recluse pressed on the long yellow strip that informed the driver a passenger wanted to get off. The bus traveled another block before stopping near the City Center Mall. She got off the bus and walked the short distance to her car.

The sleek black car shined under the glare of the street lights. She stared at the vanity plate, SASS N. Most people who met her thought it meant "sassin" because of her brazen personality, but the few who knew her best knew better. She normally favored discretion, but her vehicle was one of the few things she allowed herself to splurge on.

After she got into the car and started it, she grabbed her cell phone. She dialed the phone number to B.L., her boss's assistant. She had never really liked him, but he served his purpose. He was the man that doled out the money, and in the end, that was all that really mattered.

An automated system requested a pin number. Sola entered a four-digit number. The voice told her that her number had been accepted. After two rings, B.L. answered the phone.

"What up?" he asked. His voice was deep and gruff.

"The roach has been exterminated," the Recluse responded, her voice mellow yet overflowing with her trademark confidence. "But you know roaches, there's always more than one. So I had to bomb the whole show, if you know what I mean. I had to get rid of them all, but I won't charge you for the extra clean up." She snapped her phone closed to end the call and then pulled off.

She drove east on Broad Street, turning onto a side street that led to Franklin Park. She parked next to an old yellow mansion and got out of her car. She walked across the street to the park. The grounds were well lit, and during the day, the blooming flowers and park greenery were wonderful sights to behold. But she wasn't there to take a walk or enjoy the scenery. She followed a path to a small bridge that overlooked one of the many ponds in the park. She took out her cell phone and threw it into the pond. *Let the fish chew on that*, she thought as she returned to her car.

Five minutes later, she drove a couple of blocks west to the Parker Building on Broad Street. Like most buildings located on the historic street near downtown, the Parker Building was actually a converted brick, three-story Victorian mansion. It housed offices for several of her boss's operations. She drove around the building to the alley. A nondescript trash can stood by one of the exit doors. She got out of her car and went over to the trash can. She lifted its lid and to her surprise there was nothing there.

"What the fuck?" she said. She looked inside but didn't see anything that looked remotely like her cash. This was always where she collected her payment for her jobs. She closed the lid and lifted the trash can slightly off the ground. Still, there was nothing there. She went back to her car and drove to the BP gas station, located a couple of blocks west of the Parker Building. It was one of the few places left in the city that still had outdoor payphones. She dug around in her ashtray where she kept loose change and got money to use the phone. She dialed B.L. but he didn't answer the phone. He didn't have voice mail, not that she would have left a message anyway.

She waited for a bit longer and tried to call B.L. again. No answer. She drove back to the Parker Building and returned to the alley. She checked the trash can again. There was nothing inside but a few pieces of trash. She got back in the car and waited. No cars or SUVs drove up. She was concerned. Maybe the cops had put the heat on her boss already. It had happened before. Things had gotten hot and she had to wait for her money. She hoped that wasn't the deal this time. Getting that money meant the end of an era, the end of over a decade of playing with life and death. Unfortunately, it appeared she would have to wait. She knew not to press the issue too much. Her boss understood the nature of business. She didn't have to worry about getting paid.

She drove to Main Street and parked in front of the Kelton Market, one of the Arab-owned convenience stores that lined the street. In a neighborhood where most businesses closed before dark, the market stayed open to serve the needs of the drunks who wanted their fixes of alcohol and the kids who maintained diets of potato chips, cookies, and soda pop.

Once she entered the store, she headed past the cluttered masses of bootleg movies, cheap framed prints, and knock-off designer clothes and shoes, and headed towards the glass-enclosed counter. She glanced at the few items the Kelton Market thought were special enough to have a space behind the glass. All varieties of cigarettes, packs of condoms, and instant lottery scratch-offs lined the dingy wall behind the counter. The item she wanted was stuck in a dimly-lit corner next a small display table holding even more cigarettes.

She pointed toward the corner and nodded as the Arab store clerk picked up a small box containing a pre-paid cell phone and held it up so she could see it. Pre-paids were the perfect tool. Unlike the Pay-As-You-Go plans at places like Cingular and Verizon, pre-paids in the 'hood didn't require personal information. No names, no hassles, and very inexpensive. She waited patiently as the store clerk activated the phone. The phone chirped as it came online.

"It is all ready for you," the clerk said with a deep, accented voice.

When the Recluse returned to her car, she dialed B.L. again. He didn't answer. She knew her new phone number would register in B.L.'s caller ID, but she paged him anyway and entered her personal code so that he would know who was calling. She thought briefly about returning to the alley, but decided against it. She didn't want to take any chances, especially if the cops were involved. It was time to call it a night and head home.

Her ranch-style home was located on a quiet tree-lined residential street in a middle class area on the East Side of the city. She liked it that way. Her neighbors were all older retired couples with nothing to do but sit around all day. This meant they were all extremely nosy. It was almost better than having a burglar alarm. She entered her driveway and parked behind her house.

Once she opened the back door leading to the kitchen, sleepiness hit her like a brick. She had forgotten how much her profession took out of her. *Thank God for early retirement*, she thought as she closed and locked the door behind her. She walked down the narrow hallway to her bedroom and pulled off her shoes and took off her jacket before lying in the bed. She didn't even bother turning on the light. She just needed a little nap to refresh her.

She checked her cell phone again. No calls. She left her cell phone on just in case B.L. or one of his minions decided to call. *One last thing to do*, she thought with a sigh. The Recluse reached under the pillow on the empty side of the bed and felt the cold steel beneath it. She pulled her hand from under the pillow and smiled as she smoothed out the fabric on the soft cushion. *Everything will be straightened out in the morning*, she thought. And then she closed her eyes and let her dreams overtake her, completely unaware of the nightmare that reality had prepared for her.

Chapter One

Sola's Story, Part I – 1992

If someone wrote the story of my life, I wonder how they would describe it. On the outside looking in, some writers might say I'm a stone-cold killer, undeserving of any sympathy. And that's cool with me. I know it would be easy to paint the lines of my life in black and white, but truth be told, my world is full of gray.

No one cares about the small stuff because most people from my corner got the same story. Out of momma's belly with no daddy in sight. Momma living on assistance and food stamps and scraping to get by. A life of crime must be the only solution to the problem of a ghetto girl surrounded by the game, right? But in between my birth and my first kill at fourteen, a lot of shit happened. Some good, some bad, and all leading to what I am today.

So what do you want to know? That I grew up in the projects in a place called Sullivant Gardens where nothing grew but thugs and hos? The Gardens were located in the butt of

Columbus, Ohio. It was a shadowy enclave on the West Side. The townhouse buildings were located between a freeway and a cemetery.

People would say there were two ways out of the Gardens—on the road or in a box. The brick buildings were so far away from the main street that you would drive right by the Gardens if you didn't know where they were. It was a melting pot of broke folks from every corner of the earth. Blacks, Whites, Asians, and Latinos lived together in a warped version of Dr. Martin Luther King Jr.'s dream. Even though black and white kids were holding hands together, nobody was free at last because life in the Gardens was rough. But what can I say except there ain't nothing pretty about ghetto living?

What else? That I was stuck in gifted and talented classes at an early age? Only thing I can say about that is there was a lot of ass-kickings being dished out over fools calling me a nerd. Only reason I did my work and stayed in those classes is because I liked my teacher, who taught me the game of chess. I loved chess, which is a sport to us gifted and talented students, and I could hold my own in a scrap with any nigga or bitch. That's how it was. Yeah, I went to sleep hungry sometimes, and I didn't always have the best clothes, but that was life in the 'hood. The people who live it all understand one another, ya dig?

Well, things changed during the summer of my thirteenth year on this great green earth. That summer my momma, Synthia, hooked up with a drug dealer known in the streets as Rocky, because he dealt more crack rocks in the 'hood than Mickey D's cooks burgers. One billion addicts served, if you know what I mean. He was a hardened criminal with slick hair, gold teeth, nice clothes, and the standard gangsta Cady. I called him Iceman because the first time Momma brought him to our townhouse, I thought I would be blinded by all the diamonds on his neck and hands. You would think all the old school hustlers were more discreet with their shit, but they were just as flashy as some of the new school hustlers slinging today. They were just more smooth with it.

I still remember the first time Rocky spoke to me, when Momma brought him to our little two-bedroom townhouse in the Gardens. School had just let out for the summer, and I was still basking in that lazy glow of not having anything to do but sit around all day. She had been out all night and there was no doubt in my mind that Rocky was the reason.

I was asleep on the couch in the living room and the sound of Momma opening the front door woke me up. She was talking real loud and laughing. She was so happy to have a man in the house she almost forgot to acknowledge my existence.

"Momma, you bring anything home for me?" I said, the words spilling off my tongue. Once I opened my eyes, my stomach started growling like a rabid dog. I was so hungry I couldn't even think straight.

Momma looked at me. She had a young, pretty face with smooth, light-brown skin. Her shoulder-length hair was styled to perfection by her stylist at The Art of Beauty Hair and Nail Salon. She was thick, but toned as could be, like an hourglass of dynamic proportions. She was short in stature, but her out-going personality made her stand out in any crowd.

"Girl, why would I bring something for you?" Momma asked. Her voice had a tinge of 'watch yourself before you get slapped' attitude.

I got off of the couch and stood up. I put my hands on my hips and responded with a little attitude of my own. "'Cause I'm hungry, that's why."

Momma's happy expression changed to guarded annoyance. "Girl, you know there's food here." She looked toward our small kitchen. "You better get your ass up and cook something."

Momma started walking towards the stairs. She stared over at her new man and her happy expression returned. "Baby, I'm going to freshen up a bit." Her voice was like melted honey. "Have a seat and I'll be right back."

Momma started up the stairs and Rocky watched her backside until she disappeared into upstairs hallway. I heard her footsteps walking down the hallway towards her bedroom and a door close once she reached her destination. Rocky turned his attention to me. The sun beaming in through the living room window caught his bling and I had to put my hand up to my eyes to protect them.

"Dang, do you got to have so much ice on?" I asked.

Rocky laughed. I could tell he had a deep voice by the grumble in this laughter. "I can tell you act grown as hell," he said, his words muffled by his chuckles. I shrugged my shoulders but didn't say anything because he hadn't answered my question.

"So, what up, lil' lady? What's your name?" he asked.

People had to get up close to hear what he was saying because he had so much bass in his voice. But even though his tone was low, his speech was as smooth and gangsta as his look.

I was kind of mad because Momma didn't even think to introduce me to her man, let alone tell him my name. "There ain't nothing up but the sun," I replied coolly. "And my name is Sola." I spoke loudly as he moved closer to me. He smelled of some kind of thick, masculine cologne, mixed with the more familiar scents of cigarettes and liquor.

"Who you getting smart with, girl?" Rocky asked, looking at me like I was crazy. "I'm just trying to say hello."

Just as I was about to give Rocky a major piece of my mind,

I heard a door open upstairs, which meant Momma was coming out of her room. A second later she appeared at the top of the stairs, and floated down them like a fairy princess. She had changed out of her clothes into a long Victoria's Secret gown with a matching robe. She had purchased that outfit from one of the street vendors a couple of weeks before. She smelled like fresh flowers.

Momma gave Rocky a look I wouldn't totally understand until years later. Her eyes were hazy and she had a slight smirk on her lips. I looked at Rocky. He had the same gaze in his eyes. They were talking to each other without saying a word.

Momma walked to me, grabbed my shoulders and started pushing me to the door. "Why don't you go outside and play," she said, her voice more like frozen ice cubes towards me than melting honey.

"Play what?" I asked, snapping my head back. It was early in the morning and there weren't any other kids outside.

"Go on, girl, and don't get smart with me. Me and Rocky need to talk, don't we, baby?" she smiled at Rocky and walked up to him, circling her arms around his waist.

"Yeah, honey," Rocky said as he returned Momma's embrace. "We need to have a real serious conversation."

"Oh, please, do you think I'm still a baby?" I asked in pure disbelief. Come on, even *I* knew what was about to go down, even though the thought of Momma with Iceman gave me the chills.

Momma pressed hard on my shoulder until I felt pain. She bent down and I could feel her breath on my ear. "If you don't get your ass outside, I am going to hurt you. Don't mess this up for me. Vaya con Dios." I could tell by the tone of Momma's voice that she was getting annoyed with me again.

I rolled my eyes. She was telling me to 'Go with God' and

she was about to get her groove on. I knew she was just trying to impress Rocky by speaking Spanish, but she really only knew a couple of words, mainly the curse words. Her and my Puerto-Rican father weren't together long enough for her to fully learn his native tongue. They were together just long enough for her to get pregnant. I learned my father's language from my grandmother (my father's momma) when she used to take care of me while Momma was working. That was before my father married and his entire family moved to New York. He used to tell me he'd come back for me, but when the phone calls turned to a card every now and then, the cards turned to nothing, I knew he was gone for good.

Momma gave me a not-so-gentle push, and in an instant, I was outside on the porch. I heard the lock turn. Needless to say, I was pissed, but there wasn't a thing I could do about it. Before walking off the porch, I kicked the door. I wanted Momma to know I didn't appreciate being left outside.

I decided to walk up to Kelli's Deli. It was a hole in the wall convenience store located in the shopping center across from the Gardens. I didn't have a dime, but that didn't keep me from getting a Snickers candy bar and some apple Jolly Ranchers. I got a discount on my stuff at Kelli's—the five finger kind. Heck, if my pockets would have been big enough, I could have picked up a bottle of Snapple Kiwi Strawberry too. As I walked through the Gardens sucking on a Jolly Rancher and enjoying the tart taste on my tongue, I started feeling better.

And so it began. Rocky would come over to have his "talk" with Momma. He then started buying us things too. No more rent-to-own furniture that would end up repo'd in a couple of months anyway. Our living room was now decked out with a long, black leather couch and a panther print rug. The broke-down TV was replaced with a state-of-the-art audio-video system. I could finally watch HBO and MTV on cable instead of being stuck with the antenna channels. Where there were previously bare white walls, there was now beautiful African art prints hanging in their expensive frames.

And there I was with my Lady Cross Colours and Karl Kani, when all I had a month before was the hand-me-down special from Momma's closet. Rocky even got me a Nintendo (you couldn't beat Super Mario Brothers and Mortal Kombat back in the day) and an electronic chess game.

"This is for you to reach your potential," Rocky would say every time he gave me something. It didn't take me long to understand what he meant.

Like I said, things changed when I turned thirteen. The woman that had been hiding in me decided to wake up and take over. It seemed like overnight that I turned from a skinny, flat-chested, flat-ass girl to a five feet, ten inch Amazon with tits and ass galore. Boys started paying attention and so did Momma. She didn't hesitate before giving me the real deal about men. Fuck the birds and the bees. One day she decided to come into my bedroom and told me everything about sex in graphic detail. She ended her lesson in sex education by giving me a handful of condoms.

"I don't care what no nigga tell you when he trying to do his thing. You don't spread 'em if he don't wear 'em," Momma said as she pressed the condoms into the palms of my hands.

"I ain't thinking about no dudes," I replied, sucking my teeth as I tried to give the condoms back to her.

"Honey child, you may not be thinking about dudes, but they thinking about you. You're going to be having emotions flowing through you so much, you ain't going to know what to do," Momma pushed my hands away.

"Say no. That's what I'm going to do," I said in my know-it-all tone.

Momma chuckled. "That's easier said than done."

"I can't even imagine wanting no dude to stick his thing in me." I turned up my nose and cringed at the thought of some dude sticking his thing in my cat.

"Yeah, I said that too," Momma said.

"I'll say no and mean it," I said as I put the condoms down on the bed.

Momma stared at the condoms and then looked at me with a serious expression on her face. "Maybe you will. But remember one thing. Watch out for the man you trust. He is the one with the flower in one hand and the thorns in the other." Momma put her hand on my shoulder.

"What's that mean?" I asked.

Without hesitating, she answered. "He'll break your heart."

I scooped up the condoms from the bed and put them on my nightstand and mumbled out a fake, "Thank you."

Momma hugged me. "Well, see, that wasn't so bad, was it?" She asked, her voice oozing relief.

Just as I shook my head, hopefully to reassure her that I would make any dude trying to step to me wear a jimmy not only on his thing, but on his head, hands, and feet, there was a knock at my bedroom door.

"Yo, Synthia, I need you," Rocky yelled, calling for Momma, probably so they could 'talk.'

As Momma let go of me, I stared at the condoms. "You sure you don't need them?" I asked her jokingly, pointing at the condoms, raising my eyebrows, and smirking my lips in what I thought was a parent-like manner.

Momma pushed me playfully and laughed. "Girl, don't you be getting in grown folks business." She got off of the bed and straightened out her skirt with her hands.

"You going out tonight?" I asked.

Momma's eyes darted towards the door. "Yeah, honey child. Momma got to get her groove on sometimes. And I'll probably be real late, so don't wait up."

"That's cool," I said, nodding my head. I knew that she would be out all night again.

Rocky knocked on the door again. "Synthia, let's go," he said.

"Coming, baby," Momma responded. She gave me a kiss on the cheek and squeezed my shoulders before walking briskly to my bedroom door. When she opened it, I saw Rocky. He was standing there in a pinstripe suit that looked like it cost more than his Cady.

"It's about time," he said, peaking into my bedroom. "What are you doing in here?" He glanced at my nightstand and his eyes widened.

My cheeks started getting warm as I realized what he was staring at. I was so embarrassed I wanted to scream. My hands started shaking as I quickly opened my nightstand drawer and pushed the condoms inside. As I looked up with a forced smile, trying to hide my utter humiliation, Momma turned around.

"Don't you worry about us," she said, giggling like a school girl. "We were just having a little girl talk."

Rocky kept looking at me as Momma started pushing on his chest. "Let's go, baby, we don't want to be too late getting to the C & S Lounge," she cooed.

She turned around one more time and waved as she exited my bedroom. Rocky also waved, smiling and glancing at the nightstand one more time before Momma closed my bedroom door. I sat in my bed shaking my head. My cheeks were still warm from the uncomfortable experience of Momma's man seeing condoms in my bedroom.

I laid back in my bed and allowed some of Momma's words to sink in. "I'll never figure out why people don't practice what they preach," Momma included. She was so in love with Rocky, she didn't peep his true nature. And neither did I, until it was too late.

Chapter Two

Learn as much as you can about your opponent before the match begins. Never doubt that your opponent is learning about you.
—The Qualities of Chess Masters # 124

March 31, 6:00 A.M.

The call came just before sunrise. The Hunter was still asleep, but the Tupac *"How Do You Want It"* ring tone from his cell phone was like a rooster on a country farm. He bolted up from the bed and reached for the phone in the dark bedroom.

Instead of his phone, his hand bumped into soft skin. It was a woman's back. He shook his head and tried to catch his bearings. He squinted as his eyes adjusted to the darkness. He heard a faint voice saying hello in a feminine tone. He reached out again, slightly pushing the woman in front of him.

"Give me the phone," he said sternly as he gave her another push for emphasis.

"Uh, hold on," the woman said softly as she turned toward him.

He thought about warning her against answering his phone until her soft hair brushed his face. A soft and satisfying scent filled his nose. He recalled her name, Candy. Sweet and supple. She melted in his mouth and in his hands. Memories of their night together started to replay in his mind. He groaned inwardly.

"You don't have to be rude about it," Candy said before smacking her lips. He heard a slight thump and felt a wisp of air as the phone dropped in front of his face.

He reached for the phone and held it to his ear. "Yeah," he spoke into the phone. His voice was shaky, evidence of his previous unconscious state.

"Sounds like your hands have been in the cookie jar," A male voice with a James Earl Jones baritone said.

"My business is my own," the Hunter responded gruffly.

Laughter emanated from the phone. "Hey, whatever floats your boat," the baritone said. "But I just need to know if you're ready."

"Ready for what?" the Hunter asked as he gripped the phone tighter.

Just as the baritone voice started speaking again, Candy broke the Hunter's concentration by mumbling something about going to the bathroom. She pushed the bed covers over his body. The bed moved slightly as Candy got out of the bed. He tried to study her curves, but his eyes hadn't adjusted fully in the darkness and Candy's body looked like a shadow. The baritone had stopped speaking by the time his attention returned to the phone.

"What did you say?" the Hunter asked, pushing the covers down to his waist.

"It's time to step on the Brown Recluse," the baritone said. "You've got one hundred thousand reasons to make it happen fast."

He couldn't believe his ears. "What?" he asked, his voice rising slightly as he spoke into the phone.

"I won't repeat myself again," the baritone responded. "You have twenty-four hours."

"Are you sure?" he asked as he shook his head in an attempt to clear the fogginess of sleep. His voice flowed with pure disbelief.

Silence was the only reply, the man had already ended the phone call.

The Hunter lay in the bed for a couple of minutes, holding the phone to his ear. *It's time to step on the Brown Recluse,* the words played in his head. He had every reason to believe he was dreaming. The Recluse had been protected for a long time. No one could even look at her for too long for fear of some type of retribution. Named after the poisonous spider that embodied her personality, she was the ultimate death dealer, but now, her time was up.

He placed the phone back on the nightstand and looked toward the large window near the door. His eyes had fully adjusted to the dark and he could see the 40 Winks Motel sign just outside the window. It was still night, but he knew the sun would rise soon. He had twenty-four hours, so he had to start planning right away.

He switched on the lamp on the nightstand and squinted as the light filled the room. It was time to focus. He put his hands on the back of his head and pondered how the Recluse had fucked up. It must have been a pretty bad deal. Now he had the chance to offer her head on a platter, and he couldn't wait.

The thought of taking her out excited him in every way. He didn't know how he would do it, she would definitely be a challenge. She wouldn't go down without a fight. The Recluse had been the cause of many of what the media and cops called "drug-related" deaths. He wondered how the newspapers would write her eulogy.

He had studied her from a distance for so long, waiting for the moment he received the call to take her out. The huntress was now the hunted, and he wouldn't disappoint. His dick was throbbing now, as he thought of taking the Recluse's life. He heard a click behind the door on the far side of the motel room. The door handle turned. He reached instinctively for his piece but withdrew his hand as he remembered. Candy. The exotic dancer. Sweet and supple. In the thrilling moments after the phone call, he had almost forgotten her.

Candy opened the door to the bathroom and started to walk fluidly toward the bed. Her naked body was a sight to behold. Her long, straight, dark hair swayed over her large breasts, which giggled each time she took a step. He thanked God for the light as his eyes traveled down past her taunt flat stomach. His gaze lingered at the valley between her creamy brown, toned thighs.

"Damn, baby, I can see you're ready for some more of this sweet stuff," Candy purred as she stared at his arousal underneath the bed sheet. She looked at him and smiled. Her almond-shaped, dark-brown eyes could make a man forget his troubles.

The Hunter didn't argue as Candy pulled the sheet off of his body and joined him on the bed. She stared as his arousal and then looked him in the eyes again, licking her lips seductively as she moved closer to him. He groaned as she took him into her mouth. He felt himself swelling, getting harder. He groaned again and grabbed her head, guiding her up and down as she devoured him. She took every inch of him and held him deep in her throat. Candy was a master of oral gratification and the sensations she was giving him were almost overwhelming.

As the Hunter closed his eyes and his mind began to let

go, the Recluse drifted back into his mind. He wanted the physical contact with her, to feel her last heartbeat and her last breath. He imagined her eyes as she looked at him and realized her fate, witnessing her own death in his eyes.

He reached down and pulled Candy's mouth off of him. He grabbed her shoulders and pushed her down on the bed. He spread her legs and entered her, thrusting forcibly and rejoicing in the screams rising beneath him. He imagined the Recluse, bending to his will and his desires. He thrust harder, moved faster, as he thought of choking the life out of her.

The Hunter imagined the Recluse as the body struggled beneath him, fighting him. He heard the screams surround him, felt the heat rising in him, the fingers clawing at his back and the body thrashing underneath him. He heard his own ragged screams as his body released its lust.

He inhaled deeply as he opened his eyes. He gasped as reality came thundering back into his brain. His hands were wrapped around Candy's neck, and she was staring at him, her eyes wild and wide with fear. Her mouth was open slightly. He rolled off of her and stared. She didn't move. He wanted to reach out and touch her, to ask her if she was okay, but he hesitated. He didn't know if he would like the response.

The Hunter's chest tightened as he began to ponder what to do with Candy, but then something caught his eye. Candy's breasts were moving. She was breathing. He closed his eyes and exhaled, feeling a deep sense of relief. Then his head snapped back and he felt his right cheek sting. He opened his eyes and reached out in time to stop Candy from striking him again.

"What the fuck is wrong with you?" Candy yelled out as she struggled against him. Her voice was strained.

"Calm down," he said as he pushed her arms to the side of her body.

"What do mean, calm down? You're fucking trying to kill me!" Candy shook her head and tried to kick him.

He thought quickly about a way to diffuse the situation. Candy was glaring at him with murder on her mind. "Look, baby, I'm sorry. I just got a little rough, that's all."

"A little?" Candy spat out.

The Hunter released her hands and started caressing her arms. He looked her directly in the eyes. "C'mon, baby," he pleaded, "you know I wouldn't hurt you intentionally. You just made me want you so bad, I just couldn't stop myself."

Candy's eyes softened. "You hurt me, almost choked me to death." She coughed softly as she reached for her neck.

His hands followed Candy's own, and he touched her neck gently. His fingers traced the welts forming around her neck. He leaned forward and kissed her neck, using his tongue to sooth her discomfort. Her throat hummed as she moaned.

"I'm sorry," he mumbled against her neck. "It won't happen again."

"Apology accepted," Candy said, moving closer to him.

"Let me make it up to you," he said as he began to pleasure her to ease her further. He massaged her gently, kissed her softly, and stroked her core with his tongue until she shivered beneath him. By the time Candy reached her peak, the sun was shining through the window. As she basked in the glow of the ultimate pleasure, he excused himself from the bed and went to the bathroom.

As the Hunter leaned against the bathroom sink and turned on the faucet, his thoughts returned to the Brown Recluse—Sola Nichols. He had needed to relieve his sexual tension, but his zeal had cost him precious time. He splashed the water on his face, letting the cool water cleanse his senses. He had to have a clear head before he went to work. *One hundred thousand reasons to make it happen fast,* and he only needed one. He would have offered to take the Recluse out for free just for the memory of watching her die.

Chapter Three

Sola's Story, Part II — 1992

It's funny how your perspective changes over time. Back when I was thirteen, I still believed that someone could give you something without expecting something in return. Like I said, Rocky was giving me things and I was taking. I thought he was trying to get in good with Momma through me. It had happened before. Dudes treating me nice and buying me clothes and toys so Momma could tell them how nice they were. They figured if they can get in good with the kid, then they were in there with the momma. It never lasted for too long, though, and eventually, me and Momma would be taking our new-found goodies downtown to Uncle Sam's Pawn Shop on Main Street, for some much-needed cash.

I didn't even suspect anything when Rocky gave me a diamond and platinum tennis bracelet that must have cost more than Momma made whenever she wanted to work. "Dang, what's this for?" I asked as I let the bracelet fall into my hand.

"Hey, I like to treat my ladies well," Rocky responded, the bass in his voice rumbling like woofers in the back of a Chevy Blazer.

"I don't think Momma would let me have this," I said as I tried to give the bracelet back to him, even though I didn't want to. "Maybe you should give it to her." I could feel the sour taste of disappointment on my tongue.

"She has one that's even better," Rocky said as he took the bracelet and put it around my wrist. "This bracelet can be our little secret."

I looked at the bracelet and then looked up at Rocky. He smiled and winked at me. The bracelet would be out secret. And before too long, me and Rocky would have many more secrets.

Momma was right about one thing—boys were on me like white on rice. Men, too. I guess it didn't help that I was fond of wearing tight-ass designer clothes that molded onto my body like clay. I had never been really into fashion, but when Rocky started supplying me with all the latest gear, I couldn't help but to dress to impress.

With my height and looks, I would guess I could have passed for at least seventeen. Even older with make-up. I started hanging with the older girls from the Gardens. My PICs (partners-in-crime) were rough. They would jump other females and start trouble just for fun. People change when they deal with folks that take from others with no remorse. I figured my girls were that way because most of them were attached to drug dealers, gang-bangers, jailbirds, and other menaces to society. If you can't beat 'em, join 'em, right?

I can still remember my first real encounter with a guy. My girl Trina had invited the crew to her townhouse for a summer barbeque. Trina was the "it" girl in the Gardens and at her high school. She was ghetto, for sure, but she had that light that separated her from the pack. She had dark brown skin and she had a short hairstyle that reminded me of Nia Long's hairstyle in the movie, *The Best Man.* Trina was medium height and had tits and ass for days. She dressed in the latest fashions and her boyfriend was the best-looking dude on the West Side; a drug dealer named Chris.

Since Momma was gone on one of her Rocky-inspired trips, I figured I would spend the day at Trina's place. By the time I walked three blocks down to Trina's, her boyfriend and his boys were already rocking the grill with ribs, steaks, and hot dogs. Trina and a couple of girls I hung with were sitting on her porch, smiling and laughing. When Trina noticed me, she yelled out to me to announce my presence.

"Hey, girl, what's the deal-e-oh?" Trina asked, waving at me with her new set of airbrushed acrylics. She was well-versed in the street slang, and it showed in her fast, high-pitched, no-holds barred lingo.

"Nothing but the rent," I responded as I sat down on a white plastic chair on the porch and took my place among my PICs, the Gossip Girls.

Trina was the unofficial ringleader of the crew. Then there was LaKisha, another ghetto-fabulous diva who wore entirely too much gold. She was average height with medium brown skin. She wasn't naturally pretty but she cleaned up nice. Basically, she was covered in Fashion Fair cosmetics whenever she appeared in public.

Dee was a little pint-sized pack of kick-ass energy. She was small, but tough as nails like Jada Pinkett Smith. She even had those light eyes like Jada. Dee's only flaw was that her hair was real thin, an unfortunate by-product of trying to put white people's perm in her hair when she was younger. Her scalp never recovered and her hair wouldn't hold curl anymore. So she started sporting microbraids way before it became a major fad. She looked younger than me even though she was seventeen, the same age as Trina.

Netta was the enforcer of the crew. She was stocky and hard, and really looked more like a dude than a girl. If it wasn't for the fingerwaves in her hair and her tits, I would have still been guessing. I could swear she had a six pack and everything. She was always aiming to beat somebody down, I mean, she needed anger management classes and an overdose of Ritalin. The tripped out thing was that she was forever pulling dudes left and right. None of us could compete with Netta when it came to getting boyfriends.

"Hey girls, this is like the first great summer party of the year," Trina said in her animated voice.

I looked at all the teenagers and kids hanging out behind Trina's townhouse and nodded my head. "Did you have to invite the whole Gardens population?" I asked.

"Girl, you know how word spreads. When Trina does her thing, it gets done," Trina replied, holding up her hand and waving it like she was listening to a pastor preach at church.

I noticed Dee staring at my new tennis bracelet. "Dang, girl, where did you get that glacier?" Dee asked me with her soft, baby-like voice.

It was my first time wearing it out of the house. I had been shy about it at first and didn't want to show off too much, but barbecues were about showing off, so I had to wear it.

"A present from my momma's man," I responded.

Trina got out of her seat and walked over to where I was sitting to get a closer look. "Your Momma definitely hooked up with the right one. You know you would never have anything like this if wasn't for Rocky." she said, fingering the bracelet as I shook my wrist.

"If he's being that generous, maybe you need to ask him for some more stuff," LaKisha suggested. "He's in a buying mood, and we've all seen the home improvements at the Nichols household. Ms. Nichols must be putting it down real proper."

"Yo, Kish, don't be talking about my momma," I said, looking at her with an exaggerated frown on my face. I knew LaKisha didn't mean any disrespect. I stuck out my tongue and we all laughed.

Netta added her two cents. "You better put that shit up somewhere before some crackhead steal it. There's enough stones in that baby to keep an addict satisfied for the rest of his life."

I gripped the bracelet and turned my head in an exaggerated motion as if I was looking for crackheads. We all laughed some more, reveling in our jokes.

"Well, Netta, if any skinny rocks try to attack Sola," LaKisha interjected, "you can just stomp they asses." Skinny rocks was LaKisha's nickname for totally doped out crackheads. She laughed hard again and began holding her stomach.

I glanced at the grill. "I hope you got enough food." I said, trying to change the subject. I didn't want them to put too much attention on the bracelet. Despite our jokes about the crackheads, there were people in the Gardens that would make a kid jump out of his Air Jordans on threat of death. I imagined some crazy person trying to snatch my jewelry, holding a knife or a gun to my throat. I wasn't trying to be on anyone's hit list.

Trina laughed and said, "Chris got some food stamps from some crackhead he sell to, so we got enough food for an army."

We spent the remainder of the afternoon mainly talking about people. Trina had the latest dish on who was pregnant, who was strung out on crack, who was dealing, and who was killing. Listening to Trina talking was like watching *The Young and the Restless*, lip style.

By the time the barbeque was ready, half of the people who lived in the Gardens, and even the hungry fools that didn't live there, were standing in line with a plate. Trina was right about one thing, there was enough food for everyone and then some. After we smacked down on some grill, we cheered on the guys as they played spades and dominoes. We were just a bunch of teens without a care in the world.

When the sun went down, the party moved inside Trina's townhouse. Her momma worked three jobs and was never home, so it was the chill spot for all of the crew. Everyone would gather in the apartment to drink, smoke Chronic (name made popular because of Dr. Dre's CD), play video games, and whatever else came to mind.

On this particular night, Chela, a half-Black, half-Latino cutie, had been giving me the eye. He was fine, with caramel skin, hazel eyes, long eyelashes and good, curly hair that he wore in a ponytail. He was slightly taller than me. His full name was Juan Chela Martinez, but everyone called him by his middle name because they thought it sounded tight.

Chela's mother was from Mexico and came to the United States for a better life. She used to live up in Northern Ohio working as a migrant worker at some big farm until she ended up in Columbus. The word on the street was that she met up with some black, old-school baller who had a taste for Latina women. He left her after she pumped out a couple of kids. I don't know if life in the Gardens was what Chela's mother had in mind when she was crossing the border, but it's exactly where she ended up.

Funny thing is, I was in the same grade as his sister, Carla. The girls in my school crew would get mad at us because we would talk about people in Spanish. Some of my girls, with their smart asses, would accuse me of trying to act Hispanic. Most people thought I was just Black, but I didn't make too much of a deal about it.

When Chela stepped to me, I was glad that he was interested, but I tried to act like I didn't care.

"What's up?" he asked. He had a flat voice with just a hint of accent, I assumed he picked up from just talking Spanish at his house.

I nodded my head to let him know I was straight. "What up with you?" I added, trying to sound strong and confident, like I didn't have a care in the world.

"Nothing too much," he responded. "Come on," he said, nodding towards the couch. I stood there silent and nervous. There was a moment of uncomfortable silence before Chela spoke again. "Are you coming, or not?" he asked, pointing towards the tan sectional couch in Trina's living room. I then followed him over to the couch.

We sat down and started talking about general things. Somehow we just started talking in Spanish and it seemed natural. When I realized how we were conversing, I mentioned it and he laughed.

"I'm so used to it, you know. Mama acts like she don't know any English so that's the only way I can talk to her," Chela said.

"I'm just glad it still comes easy to me. I'm always afraid I'll forget how to speak Spanish. I mean, we only speak ghetto-fied English in my house," I said.

"You never forget your roots," Chela said seriously.

"Why you trying to be all smart and deep?" I asked.

Chela's beautiful eyes bore into me. It was like he was looking into my soul. "And what's wrong with being smart and deep? It's better than being dumb and dead, which is the fate of most of the people we know."

I shrugged my shoulders. He was right, and I wasn't even

trying to argue, so I changed the subject. "So tell me, Chela," I asked. "What do you like to do?" He threw me a sexy look. "I mean like for fun in your free time, a hobby or something."

Taking a deep breath, Chela thought for a moment. "Chess," he said. It was ironic to find out Chela had a love of chess, like I do. "If you know how to play chess," he said, "you can figure out most things in this world."

After thirty minutes or so, there was nothing more to say. Everyone else had coupled up and were busy in other parts of the apartment. We just sat there looking at each other and a weird silence hung over us like an umbrella. Chela moved in closer. At first, I was uncomfortable and tried to move away. Chela picked up on my actions and frowned.

"What's wrong?" he asked, his voice etched with concern.

I inched away from him. I may have been young, but I figured out what he was trying to do.

"I'm trying to figure out why you all up in my space," I replied. My voice was shaky because I was starting to get nervous.

Chela moved in even closer. "Oh, I think you know why." He started to kiss me.

Looking back, I realize that the kiss was a sloppy mess, but back then, I thought I was in heaven. Chela was kissing me deep, using his tongue and everything. I thought I would melt when he started feeling my tits. I didn't know what to do, so I kept kissing him back and letting him do what he wanted to do. That is, until he tried to undo my shorts.

"Wait," I snapped, pushing Chela's hands away. I was breathing heavy. I kept my eyes closed for a moment, then opened them and kept my eyes focused on Chela's white T-shirt. I didn't want to look him in the eyes.

"What's wrong?" he asked. He was breathing heavily too, and I could feel the warmth in his breath.

I knew I wasn't ready to go that far with anyone, so I said the first thing that came to mind. "You got a condom?" I asked, hoping and praying he would say no.

Chela sat up on the couch. "What?" he asked in an astonished tone.

"A c-o-n-d-o-m." I spoke loudly as I enunciated each letter of the word.

He responded by asking the age-old question that has left many a girl with diseases and babies. "What do we need one of those for?"

"'Cause I don't want no babies," I replied, rolling my eyes at him.

Chela started to caress my face and placed his fingers in between mine. He was making me feel good. Too good. My head was light and I really wanted to let go. It took a great deal of effort to pull away, but I did.

"So, do you got one or not?" I asked.

Chela looked irritated and replied, "Condoms mess me up. C'mon. You know it feels good. I'll pull out before I cum. I promise."

I knew I wasn't trying to have sex with Chela, but I also didn't want him to think I was a virgin, even though I was. I wished that we could have just kept kissing and feeling each other, but I knew he wanted more. I had to push him away before my brain melted into mush and my body decided to give up its innocence.

"The only thing I know is that I'm not going there with you." I said as I stood up and straightened out my clothes.

"You teasing bitch!" Chela snapped. "If you can't handle it, you need to go home and play wit' your dolls."

"I got your bitch," I responded as I moved away from the couch and started walking to the door.

Before I left, I turned around and stuck up my middle

finger at Chela. He grabbed himself and smiled, silently mouthing the words, "Suck my dick."

I put my finger in my mouth and acted as if I were gagging. I rolled my eyes one more time and then walked out the door. It was definitely time for me to go.

Little did I know that my little encounter with Chela would shape my life. Truth be told, everything we do leads to who we are. Sometimes I like to think that if me and Chela had finished what we started, I wouldn't be who I am today, but looking back, maybe it was just a catalyst to bring about a predetermined destiny.

They say people never really change, that they are who they are and who they will be at an early age. People don't change, only situations do. But it makes it easier sometimes to dream that I could have turned out differently, that I would have a normal life. But my reality, of course, is all I really have.

Chapter Four

Be prepared for your opponent's first strike;
a slow response could prove fatal.
—The Qualities of Chess Masters # 147

March 31, 11:30 A.M.

Sola slowly opened her eyes. Her body was on alert. Her skin was tingling and the hairs on the back of her head were standing up. She was hot and sweating like she had been on a five-mile run. Her head was throbbing as if she had been hit on the head with a brick. *Something's not right,* she thought.

She lay motionless for a moment, listening for any unusual sounds. A bird was chirping outside her window. One of her neighbors was mowing the lawn. Her bathroom sink, which she swore she would get fixed six months ago, was leaking. *Drip. Drip. Drippity. Drip.*

Nothing seemed out of the ordinary, she thought.

She wiped her eyes and looked at the clock on her nightstand. It was 11:32 A.M. She had slept longer than she wanted to. Maybe she had a nightmare or something. Although she couldn't remember for sure, it seemed the perfect reason for her heightened state of alert.

She picked up her cell phone to check for phone calls. None. She had gotten rid of her landline over a year ago, so she didn't have another phone to check. *The boys could have been late*, she thought, *maybe the money was now at the pickup spot.* The first task on her agenda was to be sure.

She lingered in bed a bit longer, enjoying the comfort of her 1000-count white Egyptian cotton sateen sheets. Another indulgence, as was her classic Henredon bedroom suite. She was in the class of people who believed the bedroom was the most important room of the house.

Something was still grating on her mind. She couldn't shake it. She hadn't felt so uneasy in a long time. She shook her head and prepared to get out of bed.

"Get a grip, girl," she mumbled. But something wasn't right.

As she rose from the bed, she felt lightheaded. She put her hand to her forehead and sat back down. She massaged her temples until the dizziness subsided. She hadn't felt as woozy since she had too much to drink at Adele's in New Orleans a few years before. That experience taught her to never drink another drop of alcohol.

She looked around her bedroom for a clue. Nothing seemed out of place. She got up again and walked around the bed. Nothing. She walked to the bathroom and peaked around the corner to look at the glass-encased shower and whirlpool tub. The bathroom light bounced off of the gold-plated tiles that surrounded the bathroom, giving the room a soft glow. Still nothing.

As she returned to the bedroom, she thought about taking a long soak in her tub, surrounded by her favorite Pink Passion aromatherapy candles by Dulces. After stressing about the mishap with last night's job, a good, long bath was just what she needed.

As she was getting ready to pull off her Juicy Couture track pants, something caught her eye. The white curtains covering her bedroom window were spread open and swaying from the outdoor breeze. That only meant one thing, her bedroom window was open.

As she dove for the bed, she felt her shoulder explode. She rolled onto the bed, grabbing her shoulder and grimacing in pain. *Fuck, I've been shot,* she thought as she instinctively reached under her pillow and grabbed her nine millimeter handgun. "Fuck, fuck, fuck," she said forcibly as she spun off the bed and positioned herself near the wall away from the window.

How fast the tables turn, she thought as she pressed her back against the wall. Less than twelve hours ago, she was shooting into a man's bedroom to take him out, and now, someone or some *ones* were here to return the favor.

She didn't hear a shot, which meant that the unknown shooter used a silencer. *Shit, maybe I underestimated my latest job.* Her boss had told her that the man she killed the night before was extremely dangerous. Then, factor in the collateral damage and now this. Even worse, her home was now compromised. Her bedroom window was open and she didn't know how. *Damn, I am truly slippin',* her thoughts continued. Someone had been in her house and could have easily taken her out. *Why hadn't he?*

He, she surmised, not them. If there was more than one person involved, she knew with absolute certainty she would be dead. When it came to killing, three was definitely a crowd. He, the shooter, was definitely male. No woman would have taken the time to break into her house, open the window, and wait outside until she had the perfect shot. That is, no woman she knew except for herself.

Her shoulder was hurting and the wet feeling against her skin told her she was bleeding. The wound wasn't fatal, but she didn't have time to access the injury. Someone was playing with her, and she didn't know if the game was over.

Her mind raced as she tried to process everything that had happened. She crawled to the foot of the bed and looked around. No one was there. The man she was dealing with had to be a professional. There were two possibilities: If he was sure of himself, like she was, he would mistakenly believe that he had taken her out. If so, the shooter was already gone. However, he could be a player, the kind of killer who liked to play around with his victim like a cat with a mouse. He might know that his job wasn't done. He could be just getting started. And if so, he could be prepared to do anything.

Her first goal was to get out of her house. That could prove difficult. She couldn't use her car. The errant shot could have been a ruse to get her to start her car and then— BOOM!! She had used that trick before with much success. Stealing a car also wasn't an option. Her senior citizen neighbors wouldn't take too kindly to watching her steal one of their cars. *Then again*, she thought, *she could always borrow one.*

She crawled to the other side of the bed, grabbed her sweat jacket, shoes, and her cell phone. She winced in pain as she put on the jacket and zipped it. She reached under her bed and pulled out a medium-sized gift box. Her backpack was lying near the bedroom door that was slightly ajar. She knew her car and house keys were in the kitchen, which was located at the rear of the house.

Given the situation, her best bet was to walk right out of the front door. She figured that some of her neighbors would be outside. There was less of a chance of the shooter trying to finish the job with witnesses around. True professionals, especially on residential jobs, tried to finish the job as quiet as possible so they could have enough time to flee the scene.

She stayed low to the floor as she opened the bedroom door. She learned some time ago that most people automatically assumed that individuals stood when they opened the door. Standing up could have exposed her to another shot. She peered out of the doorway and looked down the hallway. No one was there.

She reached into her backpack and pulled out two small round silver balls that resembled unpainted Ben Wa balls. She rolled them in her hands until she felt warmth emanating from them. *Her special little cajones.* The balls were special toys she received as a gift from one of her associates. She never thought she would have to use them in her own home.

She rolled one of the balls down the short hallway. When it stopped at the end of the hallway and hit the wall, it started emitting white smoke. She rolled the other ball in the opposite direction. The smoke made visibility difficult, but didn't trigger fire alarms or sprinklers. When the air was sufficiently filled with smoke, she started crawling towards the front door.

She listened for footsteps, stumbling, voices, or anything else that would signify the presence of the shooter. She heard nothing. When she reached the front door, she reached up for the lock and turned it. The doorknob turned and she opened the door. The bright light of the sun made her squint. She stood up quickly, grabbed her possessions, and closed the door. She scanned the street for unusual vehicles. Her immediate neighbor, Mr. Johnson, had just finished mowing his lawn. *Perfect*, she thought. She threw her backpack over her uninjured shoulder and walked towards him. She was glad she was wearing black, for it would conceal the bleeding from her shoulder. She checked to make sure no blood was on her hands or on the gift box.

Mr. Johnson was a kind old black man. He was medium height, with a handsome aged-face and bald head. He and his wife had lived in their house for at least thirty-five years. Through their conversations over the years, she learned that he was a retired Army vet. He had spent his life serving his country. But his duties left him scarred in a way nobody could see outwardly. Seems the bombs and deaths of war left his mind in shambles. He went to sleep frightened most nights because the nightmares of his previous life were almost too much to bear. Sola could relate to him perfectly.

As Sola walked closer to Mr. Johnson, he tugged at his blue overalls and white shirt. Sola walked to his garage, trying to hide her pain. *I must ignore the pain. Must ignore the pain. Must ignore the pain*, she repeated over and over again in her head. She feigned a smile.

"Good morning, Mr. Johnson. How are you doing today?" she said, managing a slight wave.

He wiped his forehead, looked her up and down, and then returned her smile. "I'm doing fine," he replied in a cheerful tone. "How about yourself?" he asked.

Mr. Johnson's eyes were boring into her and he was grinning sheepishly. She could never tell whether he regarded her as an adopted daughter or fantasized about her in some warped sexual way. Whatever his motivations, she knew she could use his affections to her advantage.

"Well, I've got a problem and I'm hoping you can help me out," Sola said as she frowned and looked back toward her house.

Mr. Johnson's smile widened. "What can I do?" he asked enthusiastically.

She sighed and raised the gift box in her left hand. "Well, I've got to get this present to my sister for her birthday and my car won't start. I was wondering-"

Mr. Johnson raised his eyebrows. "You mean that sharp, shiny foreign sports car?"

"Yes, sir. That would be the one," she answered. "I would really appreciate it if I could borrow one of your cars. It won't take me long to deliver this gift. I'm a good driver, and I won't even put a scratch on your car. I'll even fill it up, wash it, anything. I'll have it back in your garage in no time." Sola tried to express a genuine smile.

Mr. Johnson looked toward his garage. He had one black Cadillac Seville STS and a red Chevy Cavalier. "Well, I guess it'll be okay to take the Chevy. You know I don't drive much anymore. But you'll have to promise me something." His eyes narrowed but the playfulness in his voice told her he didn't want anything too serious.

"Anything," she said, grateful for the kindness of her neighbor. She smiled again, this time trying to shield a grimace as a sharp pain moved down her arm. *I must ignore the pain. Must ignore it. He can't know, so I must ignore it.* Sola wanted to yell out, but fought to remain silent.

"You'll let me take a spin in your fancy ride when you get it fixed." Mr. Johnson pointed in the direction of Sola's BMW.

Sola laughed. "Of course."

"Well, let me get the keys and I'll be right back." He turned around and started walking toward his garage.

Sola watched as the old man walked into his house. She turned around and walked backward until her backpack touched the Johnson's house. She scanned the street again, taking in the neatly manicured lawns and the spring flowers coming into bloom. Then her glance focused on her house again, her eyes traveling from the front of the house to the backyard. She wondered where the shooter had gone or if he had gone at all. She had an eerie feeling he was watching her.

"Well, here you go," Mr. Johnson said, coming up behind Sola. She jumped and then groaned loudly as pain shot through her arm. Mr. Johnson chuckled as handed the car keys to her. "Oh, I didn't mean to scare you."

Sola laughed nervously as she took the keys. "It's okay. I'm just a little jumpy this morning. I had a bad dream last night."

Mr. Johnson nodded. "You know I know about bad dreams." He handed her the car keys and then reached for the rake. "I got to finish this lawn, so I'll see you when you get back." His eyes drifted off and she could tell that he was thinking about more than his lawn.

Sola smiled. "See you soon, Mr. Johnson. Thank you so much," she said as she jangled the keys in her hands.

She jumped into the car and started it. As she backed out of the Johnson's driveway, she waved at the old man. He waved back. She almost hated the fact that she had to take his car. No telling what fine mess she'd get herself in with Mr. Johnson's car, but this was about survival. She stared at her house as she passed it. She knew she had to get back there. There were too many important things left behind.

For now, she had to worry about taking care of her shoulder. Greater still, she had to find out exactly who was trying to kill her.

Chapter Five

Sola's Story, Part III – 1992

I should have known the incident with Chela was going to be the talk of the Gardens. Thank God it was summer break or else my name would have been all over the whole school as well. I could hear the gossipers ringing in my ears, talking about something they really didn't know a thing about.

I was still asleep when the first call came the next morning. I bolted straight up in the bed when the phone rang. "Speak," I said groggily. That was my standard greeting.

It was my girl, Trina. She started talking so fast that I couldn't understand what she was saying. She ended by taking a deep breath and saying, "Girl, that ain't even right."

I wasn't really in the mood for extended conversation, especially when I didn't know what was up. "Girl, I don't even know what you're talking about," I replied.

"Don't front. I just can't believe you'd hook up with Chela." Trina's voice was filled with attitude.

That woke me up. I gripped the phone. "What?"

"It's all over the Gardens."

Okay, I knew she was tripping. Most people in the Gardens had to still be asleep.

"Me and Chela?" I asked, nervously twirling a piece of my hair.

"Yeah, girl. I would have never thought you'd suck his thang," Trina said.

I jumped straight up out of the bed. "I didn't do that!" I yelled into the phone.

"Tell it to God, 'cause He's the only one who'll believe you," Trina said, expressing that she didn't believe me.

I rubbed my eyes and started to pace around my bedroom. I didn't know exactly what to do. Back in the day, it was still really "taboo" for a black girl to give head. And I didn't get a *chupa* pass for being half Puerto Rican. My Latina side didn't exclude me from the doing the unthinkable. Hey, don't get me wrong, some girls were definitely doing it, but nobody told.

"I can't believe this shit." I raised my voice again. "Did he tell you that?"

"Naw. It was LaKisha. And she heard it from her boy."

"Well, I didn't do it. So you tell LaKisha and everyone else that Chela is a liar!" I screamed into the phone.

"Chill, girl. That's why I called. I just wanted to know the real deal." Trina's voice was calm.

"Well I didn't suck his dick or anything else. So now you know." I walked to my bedroom window and looked outside. I expected it to be gloomy and raining with the way I was feeling, but the sun was shining.

"Something must have happened. There ain't no way you was alone with Chela's fine ass and you just talked. So what went down?" Trina asked with her inquisitive ass.

"What did you hear?" I asked.

"That you was messing around, and he didn't have no condom, so you hooked him up with your lips," Trina replied.

"That is so foul!" I yelled, twisting my lips in disgust. "We did kiss, but that was it."

"Dang, don't bust my drums, girl." Trina said, referring to my screaming into the phone. "If you say nothing happened except some kissy-kissy, then I believe you. But you need to talk to Chela, 'cause—"

I interrupted her. "Don't worry, I'm about to check this shit right now."

I got off the phone and picked out some clothes to wear. I washed up quick, got dressed, and sat out on my goal to find Chela.

When I went outside there were a couple of guys hanging out. They looked at me strangely. I figured that they had heard the rumor. I looked away from them, tightened my lips, balled my fists, shook my head and continued on the path to Chela's place.

Less than five minutes later I was at Chela's place. I had to stop myself from knocking on the door too hard. I didn't know if his mother was home and I didn't want to be rude. I pressed the doorbell once, and waited. My heart was pounding and I tried to paste a smile on my face in case Chela's mom answered the door.

My fears were unfounded, because when the door opened I was staring at Chela's sleepy ass. My first instinct was to punch him, but I put my hands on my hips and started to curse him out.

Just as soon as he stepped out the door, I started on him. Respecting his mother went to the back of my mind. All I wanted him to do was admit he lied.

"Where the hell do you get off telling people I sucked your dick! You know it didn't happen!" I yelled at the top of my lungs for maximum effect. I wanted to make sure everyone in the Gardens heard the truth.

Chela countered with his own loud voice. "You know what happened, don't front."

I was really pissed. I stepped to him. "I didn't suck your dick!"

"If I was you," Chela said, "I would back up off me and go home. Don't step to me like you crazy."

I couldn't stand it anymore. Chela standing there right in my face and acting like he wasn't in the wrong was killing me. I pushed Chela—hard. He stumbled backwards but didn't fall. He regained his balance and started walking towards me. I was ready for him to hit me. I wanted to fight. I couldn't believe he would lie on me.

As Chela neared, I closed my eyes and braced myself for his fist. I felt him enter my personal space. Instead of feeling a punch, I felt his breath blowing against my forehead as he spoke. "Look, I'm going to go back into my crib before I do something I regret. But on the real, you need to chill," he said calmly.

I opened my eyes. Chela was in front of me. "You punk-ass lying nigga." I continued to bait him.

"Little girls shouldn't play grown up games." Chela smiled mockingly. "I'm sure your Mama told you about what to do if you can't stand the heat. And if she didn't, I suggest you go and ask her how to deal. Come back when you've got more to show than a loud mouth because, once again, all you've shown is that you know how to open wide." Chela turned his back to me and walked into his townhouse.

Tears stung my eyes but I wiped them away quick. I looked around. Nobody was outside but I knew people were listening. In the 'hood, even the trees have ears. They just know how to remain silent. I looked more stupid than I did before I went over there. I didn't stand there licking my wounds though. I held my head up high and walked home. Needless to say, I was in a foul mood, so I was glad Momma wasn't home. She had been spending more and more time away from home, but at least she was leaving me some money behind.

I stomped to my bedroom, slammed the door behind me, dived into the bed, and covered my whole body with my sheets, including my head. There was no way I was going to do anything that day. I wasn't about to show my face in the Gardens. All I wanted to do was sleep.

I don't know how many hours passed before the sound of the doorbell woke me up. It kept ringing and I tried to ignore it. If it wasn't Trina trying to gather all the info she could get so she could pass it along, then it was LaKisha, Dee, or Netta trying to get their news breaks, because they hadn't spoken with me yet. I didn't feel like dealing with any one of them. So I placed my pillow over my head and soon the ringing stopped. I was on my way to dreaming again when I heard a door open. Something told me it wasn't Momma.

I slid off the bed quietly. My heart was beating so loud that I thought it would jump out of my chest. The stairs squeaked and I looked around my room for a weapon, anything to hurt the intruder. I had a couple of pairs of sneakers and some high-heeled shoes that could maybe pack a punch. I picked up one of my black three-inch heels and prepared to do some damage. It was then I heard a voice calling my name. I realized the unwelcome visitor was Rocky.

Something stopped me from speaking right away. My heart was still beating fast and I felt a little scared. Rocky called out my name again.

"Girl, I know you're here. What are you trying to hide for?"

I could tell by the nearness of his voice that he had

reached the top of the stairs and was close to my bedroom door. By the tone of his voice, I wasn't really certain whether he was talking to me or if he thought Momma was home. But my gut told me he was looking for me. My feet wouldn't move. I forced myself to drop my shoe and move back toward my bed. I stood near the side of my bed holding my covers close to my chest. I stared at the doorknob as it started to turn. Rocky opened the door.

"What's wrong with you, didn't you hear me calling you?" he asked.

I struggled to speak because there was a knot in my throat. "I-I was sleeping," I said as I clutched my bed sheets.

Rocky walked closer to me and then sat on my bed. He was decked out in all black, his bling was shining as usual, and so was his hair.

"Why don't you sit down? I want to talk to you," he said, patting a seat for me next to him.

I was frozen. "Momma's not here," I said.

"I know that. I sent her and her friend, Nikki, to Cleveland to take care of some business for me. Now, come on, sit down." Rocky looked in my face and then his eyes traveled down my body. I still stood there frozen. "Sit down," he said in an authoritative tone.

Clasping my covers, I sat down on the bed. I tried to sit as far away from Rocky as I could. He was making me uncomfortable. He turned to me and moved a little closer.

"I heard some things about you today that I didn't like." he said.

Suddenly, I felt a sense of relief. I knew what he heard, and that wasn't a good thing, but I also knew that it wasn't true and I didn't want to give him the impression that what he heard was valid.

"You shouldn't believe everything you hear," I said.

"Oh, I didn't say I believed anything." He moved closer. I

moved to the head of the bed. My back was against the head-board and I couldn't move anymore.

"What do you want?" I asked, starting to feel uneasy again.

"Hey, why are you acting so scared? I just want to talk to you." He moved closer to me. Rocky's face softened and he reached out and put his hand on my shoulder. "So, is it true?" he asked.

"I don't know what you talking about." My heart was racing and I started thinking about how I could get off the bed.

He started caressing my shoulder. My skin was crawling and the knot that had been in my throat was now in my stomach.

"You should know by now that I hear everything that goes on around here. I'm not going to play games with you. Were you with Chela or not?" he asked.

I looked at Rocky's face. He was concentrating on his hand that was still caressing my shoulder. He started touching my hair, which flowed past my shoulders like Momma's. I reached up to remove his hand, but he stopped me. The covers fell into my lap.

"Tell me. Were you with him?" Rocky asked.

I felt my eyes water with shame and embarrassment. I knew what Rocky was thinking about me and I had to set him straight.

"I didn't do nothing but kiss him. He lied and told people I did something I didn't do," I replied, my voice trembling.

Rocky's hand moved off of my shoulder and slowly moved downward. He looked me in the eyes. "I can't have no nigga lying on my lady. I can make sure he sets the record straight."

His hand was near one of my tits. I started to shiver. "Please, stop," I mumbled, putting my head down. I tried to move again.

Rocky used his other hand to hold my head up. "I ain't trying to do nothing but make you feel better." His hand traveled lower. "I told you I'd take care of it for you."

"Momma won't like—"

Rocky moved quickly and started kissing me. I could taste the alcohol on his breath. His hand cupped my one of my tits. I tried to push him away, but it was no use. He was stronger and outweighed me. I started to struggle as he tried to push me down on the bed.

"Stop!" I managed to scream out. I started gagging and spitting out the taste of his alcohol and his breath.

"What's wrong with you?" Rocky asked.

"This ain't right. Momma—" I said as I tried to push him away.

Rocky interrupted me. "I'm not worried 'bout your Momma now. I'm worried about you." He looked down at my tits. "Your nipples are hard. I can tell you like it." He started to rub one of my nipples.

"If you don't stop, I'm going to have to scream." I raised my voice.

Rocky stopped rubbing on me and his expression changed from that of a man in control to that of a man whose hand had just been bitten by the mouth he was trying to feed with it.

"After all I've given you and your Momma, and you're gonna treat me like this. You give some half-breed nigga more than you give me?" I watched Rocky's face transform to a twisted mask of rage. I tried to get off of the bed. Rocky stopped me. "I wouldn't move if I were you," he said, gripping my wrist so hard that he cut off my circulation.

"You can have all of your shit back, the bracelet, everything. I'm not down for this." I yelled as I reached over to the nightstand to grab the bracelet from the silver box I kept it in. I would have pulled off the clothes off my back to stop him. I was really crying and the tears fell freely down my face.

"You look and act so grown, sometimes I forget that you don't know how things work." Rocky moved closer to me and started touching me again. "Your Momma understands and now it's your time, too. You're one of my ladies until I say differently. You need to understand that."

"I don't know what you're talking about. I think you might have had too much to drink and I think you need to leave." I turned my head away from him and closed my eyes.

"I'm not going anywhere." Rocky pulled me even closer to him. We were damn near face to face. "I thought I'd be able to wait for you. But with you looking all good and niggas coming after you, I'm going to have to take what's mine before it's too late."

I was weak. I wanted to scream, but I couldn't. I wanted to tell Rocky to get his old ass hands off of me, but I didn't. He took control and I couldn't fight him. He took off my clothes and did things to me he shouldn't have done. I lay there and let him do his thing. The pain I felt was more than what he was doing, it was knowing I couldn't do anything to stop him. He moved on top of me, grunting and moaning. I absorbed the pain and tried to remain silent. I hoped it would be over soon, but it felt like forever before it was.

After it was over, I just laid in the bed and closed my eyes. Rocky was putting on his clothes. "I got to take care of some business," he said calmly, as if what we did was natural, like he hadn't done anything wrong. I didn't respond. "I know you may be a little uneasy now, but you'll feel better later," he said in the most comforting tone he could muster up. I heard the zipping sound as he fastened up his pants.

I remained silent.

"Oh, and I'll take care of your problem with Chela."

Rocky walked over to me. I could feel his breath against my skin.

Please, just leave me alone! I screamed in thought.

Rocky grabbed my face. I kept my eyes closed. "If I were you, I would keep this our little secret. You know how ugly rumors get." I could still feel Rocky's handprints on my face after he released me.

As soon as I heard Rocky leave my room, and his footsteps as he descended the stairs, I opened my eyes and let the tears flow from them. When I heard the front door close, I jumped out of bed and went to bathroom and began puking in the toilet. I threw up what little food I had inside of me and I felt like I hacked up the entire lining of my stomach. I lay on the bathroom floor for some time, my body was hurting everywhere.

When I gathered my strength, I turned on the shower and scrubbed my body until my skin was raw. I didn't even stop when the hot water stung my skin and every inch of my body felt like it was on fire. I couldn't believe what had happened to me. I couldn't wrap mind my around the reality of my situation. Even worse, I didn't know what to do about it. I couldn't go back to my room, so I went to my mother's bedroom and laid down in her bed. I started to cry again, only this time I didn't hold back. Rocky had taken more than my virginity that day, he took my soul.

Chapter Six

Your opponent will surely make surprising moves. The key to success is making sure you retain the upper-hand.

—The Qualities of Chess Masters # 160

March 31, 11:50 A.M.

As the Hunter laid out in Sola's backyard and reflected on recent events, he pondered his next move. When he arrived at Sola's house just after dawn, he couldn't believe his luck. He parked a couple of blocks away from her street and walked the rest of the way. When he caught the first glimpse of her one-story ranch home at the edge of the cul-de-sac, his heart started racing. He quickened his pace until he reached her driveway, then he slowed down to assess his surroundings. Based on what he heard on the radio on the way to Sola's house, she could be waiting for someone to deal with her. He wanted to make sure he made the first move.

The Hunter walked to the back of the house. Sola's BMW was parked at the edge of the house near the back door. He felt the hood. It was cool to the touch. That meant she hadn't been traveling for a couple of hours. He reached into his pocket and pulled out a small, round, mechanical device. He knelt down beside the BMW and stuck the device under the driver's side car door. It was a tracking device, linked to a GPS satellite system. Sola wouldn't be able to get away from him even if she tried.

His heart raced again as he prepared to enter the house. He wasn't nervous. He was excited. He couldn't wait to see her. He was surprised to discover how easy it was to enter her house. He used his cell phone to link into Sola's wireless security system. She had a state-of-the-art system, and he had to pay good money to learn how to deactivate her code. As he punched in the numbers and received a response giving him the okay, he knew the cost for the code was worth every cent.

The Hunter entered Sola's house through the back door, which led to her kitchen. It was simple, yet elegant, with mahogany-stained wood cabinets and stainless steel appliances. He stood by the breakfast bar and reached for one of his guns, which was nestled in the small of his back. His other gun was located in the briefcase he carried with him. He waited for something to happen, but nothing moved, there were no footsteps, and no gunfire. It was as silent as the grave.

The Hunter walked from the kitchen through the dinette, then passed through an entryway that led to a hallway in one direction and the living room and front entrance in the other direction. He glanced at the front door before placing the briefcase on the floor. He opened up the briefcase and pulled out a pair of goggles and a small respirator mask. He also took out a pair of gloves and a small package that resembled a piece of gum. He stared at his other gun and silencer before closing the briefcase. He knew he wouldn't need it until later.

The Hunter walked quietly down the hallway to Sola's

bedroom. He had studied the blueprints of the house at the Franklin County Recorder's Office. It was a two bedroom house with two full bathrooms. The master bedroom was located near the end of the hallway. It was large and had a separate bath. It didn't take any effort to find it.

The bedroom door was ajar. He knew that at any moment a shot could ring out and he would be dead. It was a chance he was willing to take. He knelt down beside the door and put on the gloves, goggles and respirator. He carefully unwrapped the small package. As soon as the air hit the substance inside of the package, it started bubbling. He put the package and its contents on the floor and waited until the bubbling stopped.

He waited a couple more minutes before peeking inside Sola's bedroom. He heard heavy breathing. Sola appeared to be asleep. He pushed the bedroom door open until there was enough room to go inside. Sola didn't stir. He decided to keep on his gear because he wasn't sure that the gas had completely dissipated. Instead, he pulled out his gun again and aimed it towards the bed.

It would have been so easy to kill her now, he thought. But the time wasn't right. He had plans for the Brown Recluse. Planning her death was like a fine wine. He wanted to savor the taste as long as he could, not gulp it down and lose the prolonged satisfaction of the experience.

The Hunter moved silently, putting everything into place. As he worked, he kept looking over his shoulder to make sure she didn't wake up. Before he left the bedroom, he stared at Sola again. She was as fine as ever. He felt his dick rising. It was time to go.

He gathered his belongings, left the house, positioned himself in Sola's backyard and began the waiting game. He knew it would take some time for the effects of the gas to wear off, but he was a patient man. He could definitely wait.

He didn't have to worry about anyone seeing him in his current location. Sola's white privacy fence gave him plenty of cover.

After a couple of hours, the Hunter began to wonder when Sola would wake up. He had placed a listening device by her bed, but all he heard was Sola's heavy breathing. It seemed like forever before the familiar sounds of awakened movements vibrated in his ears. It took even more time for her to move into his crosshairs. His shot was perfect. By his calculations, she only suffered a simple flesh wound. It wouldn't even require a trip to the emergency room. He wished he could go inside the house to watch her squirm. He knew she was wondering who was trying to kill her and that made him smile.

Then, she surprised him. He was sure she would escape in her BMW. *What could she be thinking?* Smoke drifted out of her bedroom window. At first, he thought she started a fire, but the smoke didn't have that suffocating smell of smoke that accompanied fires. He knew she was full of tricks. He smiled at the irony. Only a couple of hours before, he was using his own tricks to make sure Sola stayed unconscious and didn't put a bullet in his head or in his back. They were similar beings, almost kindred spirits, he surmised. He watched the smoke as it rose up toward the sky. He concluded she was using the smoke as a diversion tactic. She must have thought he was still in the house. The smoke must have been some type of smokescreen.

Damn, the Hunter thought, *she's leaving out the front door.* After a couple of minutes, he heard her talking to her neighbor. Something about borrowing a car. He heard a car start. He knew she was gone.

He lay on the ground at least a half an hour after she left. The neighbor had put a wrench in his plans. It would be harder to track Sola since she wasn't using her car. When he heard the neighbor's garage door close, he stood up and gathered his belongings. As he walked around the house, a man's voice stopped him.

"Can I help you?" the voice asked.

The Hunter turned around and looked at the elderly black man. "I'm looking for Sola Nichols," he replied, trying to sound calm and natural.

"You here about the car?" the old man asked.

The Hunter glanced at Sola's BMW. He had to think quick. "No, sir. I'm canvassing the neighborhood following up with homeowners who are interested in purchasing new windows."

The old man stared him up and down. The Hunter was glad he picked out a suit for the occasion. After all, he was preparing for a funeral. *Two funerals, actually,* he thought to himself, remembering Sola. His pinstriped special from the Men's Warehouse was perfect for mourning, even if his sorrow wouldn't be genuine.

"Windows? You didn't come to my house," the old man said suspiciously.

The Hunter thought momentarily about pulling out his gun and shooting the old man between the eyes. But it was too early in the game to rack up a body count. He looked at the old man's house, squinting as he studied the white-trimmed windows that glistened in the midday sunlight.

"Well, sir, looks like your windows are pretty new." The Hunter hoped he was right.

"Yeah, well, there're only a couple of years old," the old man said proudly, nodding his head.

"Since Ms. Nichols doesn't seem to be available, I'll have to be on my way." The Hunter waved and started walking toward the street.

"She'll be back," the old man said.

The Hunter turned around and smiled. "I'll be canvassing

the neighborhood most of the day. I left a message for her. I'm sure she'll get it."

The old man walked toward him and stuck out his hand. "I forgot to introduce myself," he said. "I'm Cecil Johnson, Sola Nichols's neighbor."

The Hunter shook the old man's hand. "Nice to meet you," he said as he pulled back his hand.

Mr. Johnson looked at him strangely. "Do you have a card or something?" he asked.

"I'm sorry, seems like I'm fresh out," the Hunter replied, patting the pockets of his pants for emphasis. "But don't worry, Ms. Nichols will know who I am." He waved at Mr. Johnson again and began walking down the street, praying silently that the old man wouldn't call him back to ask for his name. The Hunter would definitely tell him, but then he would have to kill him.

The Hunter walked briskly, reaching his vehicle in record time. As he got into his SUV and started up the engine, he thought of Sola. If he was right, she would first try to find out what was going on. The fact that she was still at her house when he came meant she didn't know what she had done to bring about her fate. She would soon find out just how grave her situation was. And then she would try to run; he was sure. And he was definitely ready for the chase.

Chapter Seven

Sola's Story, Part IV — 1992

It's still difficult to explain what happened to me after Rocky started raping me. I became an empty shell, a zombie. I was ashamed because I felt weak, I was ashamed because I was scared, and I was ashamed that I was silent.

Rocky didn't spend as much time at the townhouse when Momma was home. He wanted me all to himself, so he started sending Momma away more often. Momma didn't have a clue as to what Rocky was doing to me. She fancied him as some father figure, or maybe my savior, protecting me from the darker elements of the Gardens' life. Every time he would send her off, he would come over to the townhouse and lead me upstairs to do his thing. I cursed them both.

At first, I would protest. "This is wrong," I would tell him. "You're hurting me," I would say. My attempts to save myself fell on deaf ears. So I became silent, a lifeless participant in my own slow destruction. My body was a grave for a once vibrant soul.

I blamed myself, of course. I knew it had to be something I did to make Rocky do the things he did to me. I stopped wearing the designer threads that I used to love. I tried to hide myself in sweats and baggy clothes. My hair, which was usually well-kept, turned into a wild mass of curls that I couldn't control. That made Momma take notice.

I was sitting on the couch in the living room, staring off into space, when Momma came back from one of her trips. I rarely ventured upstairs anymore, except when Rocky came. She was all smiles and happiness, decked out in an expensive Donna Karan pants suit. As usual, her hair and makeup were flawless.

"Hey there, sweet Sola," she said blissfully. When I didn't respond to her delightful greeting, she sat next to me on the couch. "What's up with you, honey child?" she asked, raising her eyebrows and pressing her lips tightly together in a look of concern.

"Nothing," I responded, shrugging my shoulders.

"Something's up. You think a mother don't know? You ain't been yourself lately, all moping around and dressing like a dude." Momma pushed my curly hair away from my face with her hand. "And look at this hair," she exclaimed.

Maybe that would have been the perfect time to tell her that her man was raping me. Believe me, it was at the tip of my tongue. But as much as I tried, I couldn't get it out. Instead, I focused on the part of myself that blamed her for bringing that child-molesting freak into my life.

I mustered up all of the attitude I could and said, "Maybe if your ass was here more, I would be myself."

My face stung as Momma's hand struck my face. I stared at her as I absorbed the pain. Maybe I should have cried, but I didn't have anymore tears. They had all dried up in my bedroom.

"Where do you get off cursing at me?" Momma screamed. "I'm trying to provide you with a good home and good things and you're spitting back in my face. You need to get a grip." I didn't have the energy to argue. I remained silent. "Oh, so you're trying to give me the silent treatment, huh? Go ahead and mope around like you don't got no sense. We'll see how much money I leave you when I go back to Cleveland tomorrow." She got off of the couch and started pacing the room.

Rocky was sending her off again to do God knows what. I didn't know everything, but I knew she was somehow involved in Rocky's drug business. But that knowledge was paled by the fact that I didn't want her to leave again. The thought of Rocky coming over and putting his hands on me made me cold.

"Do you have to go, Momma?" I asked in a pleading voice.

"Yeah, if you want me to keep bringing money home," Momma replied. "Honey child, we got a good thing going on here. Look at all the stuff we've been able to get. We got new furniture, a new TV, new clothes, and new jewelry. And there's more to come. I might even have a new car soon. Maybe even a Mercedes or a BMW," she said excitedly.

I couldn't share Momma's excitement over the material things we possessed. I knew I would have been the first one screaming up and down in the past, but all I worried about was my survival.

I was staring off into space when Momma walked back to the couch. She rubbed the cheek she had just slapped a minute before. "Look, I don't like hitting you, but you can't disrespect your Momma," she said apologetically. I remained silent. Momma sat back down. "And if anything is going on, you can talk to me about it." She stared at me, waiting for me to pour out my soul.

I nodded and stared at her as she rose from the couch again and walked towards the stairs. "Well, honey child, I got to get some rest. Me and Rocky are going to the Frankie Beverly and Maze concert tonight. You know it's going to be nice. Then it's off to Cleveland again in the morning."

I closed my eyes so Momma wouldn't see me roll them. *So what else was new?* I thought. Momma was so distracted by her trips, clothes, and nighttime activities, she didn't have the time or the inclination to see what was going on under her own roof. Our townhouse had become Momma's Holiday Inn and Rocky's brothel. I was the only one sentenced to the hell of staying there.

I laid down on the couch and thought about a way out. I didn't have any family in Columbus other than Momma, and nobody I knew had room for another teenager. I thought about running away, but where would I run to? I heard about the dirty homeless shelters and there was no way I was sleeping out on the streets. I also thought briefly about taking some of the money Momma gave me, taking a taxi to the Greyhound station downtown, and hopping on a bus to New York to see my father. But I knew he had a new family and I also knew I couldn't handle any sort of rejection from him. It was almost like I was an orphan.

I could've called the police and told them what Rocky was doing to me, but he'd probably tell them I was asking for it and they'd believe him. A part of me believed he had some of the cops on his payroll anyway. No one slung as much crack as he did without having someone in blue personally protecting and serving him.

I was just about to fall asleep when the doorbell rang. My heart jumped at first, thinking it was Rocky. But then I remembered that he didn't even bother with the doorbell anymore because he had a key.

I walked to the door and looked through the peephole. It was Trina. I opened the door and she burst in.

"Hey, girl, I thought you were on the back of a milk carton. You need to get out," Trina joked as she flopped down on the couch. "I know you heard the news."

I scratched my head and sat down beside her. "Heard what?" I asked.

"'Bout Chela." Her voice was animated.

My heart sunk. "What about him?" I asked. My first thought was "now what this nigga said about me now." But I wasn't quite prepared for what Trina told me.

"Girl, they found him by I-70 beat up real bad. Chris told me that one of his leg bones was sticking out like someone had snapped it like a twig or something." Trina was talking so fast she had to suck in air when she finished talking.

You only get out of the Gardens on the road or in a grave.

I could hardly speak. "Is he dead?" I managed to ask.

Trina exhaled. "Not yet, but he's in critical up at Children's Hospital."

I knew immediately that Rocky was behind Chela's injuries. As much as I was mad at Chela for spreading that rumor about us, I never wanted him to get beat down like that. My heart raced as I wondered if anyone else had made the connection I made so easily, that I was the cause of Chela's injuries.

And what about Chela? Did he know who had done this to him? Did he know that whoever beat him down did it because of me? And if so, what retribution would I face?

"Damn, that's messed up," I said nonchalantly, trying to mask my fears.

"I know, girl, everybody's trying to figure out who did it. It's not like Chela was going to join no gang or nothing, and even the bangers leave your limbs intact, if you know what I mean," Trina said, shaking her head.

My stomach was knotting up and I knew I was about to throw up. I couldn't let Trina know how much Chela's situation bothered me. She was like a police dog on a car full of drugs. Once she sensed trouble, she would let everyone know. "I can't think of anyone who'd want to jump him," I said.

Trina tilted her head and studied my face. *The dog was sniffing.* "Well, y'all were arguing not too long ago," she said.

"Please, don't bring me into this, Trina. We hang with the same crew. If I had anything to do with it, you'd know," I said in my own defense.

Something told me I was looking guilty as hell, so I looked away from her so she couldn't see how nervous I was. I could feel Trina's eyes glaring at my back. I knew she wished she had X-ray vision so she could look into my soul, or ESP so she could read my mind. Thank God for small favors.

"Even if you did know something, would you tell me or would you keep it a secret? I mean, we all have secrets, don't we?" Trina asked, giving me a knowing smile.

Did she know about Rocky? I thought.

I tried my best to keep my poker face. "Are you trying to get on my bad side or what? I haven't even been thinking about Chela, and I definitely wouldn't try to beat him up or kill him." I stood up in front of Trina.

I looked down at Trina. The look I gave her told her that it was time to go. She understood me perfectly. She rose up from the couch. "Girl, I know you wouldn't do nothing like that," she said, laughing nervously.

"I'm glad you know." I walked to the front door. Trina followed behind me.

"I'll keep you posted if I hear anything." She looked at me as I opened the door.

"You do that," I said as Trina walked out the door.

It was hard for me to sleep that night. I kept thinking about Chela, battered and broken and fighting for his life. I tossed and turned on the couch until I went to sleep. But even then, I didn't get any true rest. I had nightmares of Chela screaming and begging for his life.

The next morning, I rushed to get dressed so I could get out of the townhouse. I decided to spend the day in City Center downtown. I really wanted to avoid Rocky if I could.

I hopped on a COTA bus and got off near Broad and High, downtown. I walked to City Center Mall, which at the time, was the best mall in Columbus. I hoped the sight of shoes, clothing, and jewelry would take my mind off of my life. It didn't.

Instead, I thought about Chela again, at the hospital fighting for his life and hooked up to all sorts of tubes and machines. I took the escalator to the third floor of the mall and walked to the payphones that lined the walls near the public bathrooms. There were no yellow pages in sight, so I had to call Information to get the number to Children's Hospital. Once I had the number, I called the mainline. A woman's cheerful voice answered.

"Children's Hospital, how may I direct your call?" she asked.

"I need to find out about a patient; my brother," I said, gripping the phone and hoping my voice didn't sound too shaky.

The woman's voice changed. It was soft and consoling. "Is he a patient?"

"Yes. His name is Juan Chela Martinez." My voice was trembling and my stomach was in knots.

I heard a few clicks on a computer keyboard. "Hold, please," the woman said.

After a few moments, another woman picked up the line.

Her voice was husky, and she sounded like she was having a bad day. "Can I help you?" she asked.

"I want to find out how my brother's doing, Juan Martinez," I responded.

There was a slight pause. "And who are you?" The woman's voice had a questioning tone.

"I'm his sister, Carla," I mustered, trying to sound as real as possible.

Another pause. "Well, *Carla,*" the woman said, stressing the name Carla, "your mother is here and—"

I was busted. I slammed the phone down before she finished her sentence. I knew I would probably have to rely on Trina's gossiping ass for information. I couldn't concentrate and I couldn't eat because my stomach was hurting. I walked around some and then left the mall. I dreaded going back to the Gardens, but it was the only place I knew.

Upon my return to the Gardens, I immediately knew I made a mistake. As I reached the street that led to my townhouse, I saw Rocky's Cady. My first instinct was to turn around, but he was in his car and had already spotted me. "Sola!" he called out in my direction.

I walked slowly to Rocky's car. There were several people outside, kids playing and such, but I still didn't feel safe.

"Hey, lil' one," Rocky said. "Synthia had to go out of town again and she wanted me to look after you." He held up a bag in his hand. "I got food for you."

I passed by his car and went to my townhouse. The bastard was trying to keep up appearance with that "she wanted me to look after you" shit. I opened the door and walked inside. Rocky followed close behind. I stood by the wall near the kitchen while Rocky placed the food on the table.

"I'm not that hungry," I said.

"I didn't buy all this food for it to go to waste. You need to sit your ass down and eat, because we got things to do and I don't have a lot of time." He slammed his hand down on the table, which caused the bag to rise and then fall over.

I sat down at the kitchen table and opened the bag. There were a couple of cheeseburgers and some fries inside of it. I unwrapped one of the burgers and started eating it slowly. I figured the slower I ate, the longer I could hold Rocky off. My grand plan didn't last too long.

At first, Rocky sat on the couch, watching TV and drinking a Forty. It must have taken me twenty minutes to finish off the first burger. I ate my fries one at a time, taking small bites and chewing slowly. As I started unwrapping the second burger, Rocky got up off of the couch, walked over to the kitchen table, and stood over me. I stopped eating.

"What's taking you so damn long?" Rocky asked.

"You told me to eat," I replied sharply, lifting the burger to my mouth.

Rocky slammed his empty Forty bottle on the table. "Well, you're taking too long. I ain't got time to watch you eat."

Rocky grabbed my wrist and the burger fell out of my hand and onto the table. My mind was racing. I didn't want to go upstairs. I had to think of something to say; something to give me more time.

"Rocky, I'm not really feeling too good. I think I'm sick. My stomach is—"

"I don't want to hear the 'I'm sick shit'," Rocky interrupted me. "You wouldn't be trying to eat if your stomach was sick. Now I guess you can save the rest of your food for later. Let's go upstairs." He motioned towards the stairs.

I got up from the table. I knew the routine. Before I started walking up the stairs, I stopped and looked at Rocky. "Why did you do it?" I asked.

"Do what?" Rocky asked with a puzzled look on his face.

"Chela," I responded.

Rocky smiled. "Don't ask about grown folks business. I told you I'd take care of the problem and it's taken care of."

"I never told you—"

Rocky reached for me and grabbed my hair. "You should be thanking me." When I didn't say anything, he pulled my hair even harder. "You should be thanking me," he repeated.

I couldn't stand the pain so I gave in. I said what he wanted to hear. "Thanks," I muttered.

He released his grip on my hair and grabbed my butt. "You're so welcome. Now let's go upstairs."

Again, I gave in. I did what he wanted. I walked upstairs and he followed close behind me. The familiar blend of alcohol and cologne that made my nose hairs stand and my skin crawl, drifted past my nose. Before we even made it to the top of the stairs, I heard Rocky unbuckling his belt and unzipping his pants. I closed my eyes and wondered if there was a God.

Chapter Eight

Unknown elements can shape the outcome of your match.
Prepare wisely.
—The Qualities of Chess Masters # 187

March 31, 12:05 P.M.

Sola drove onto the freeway and headed west. She pulled out her cell phone and began making calls. No one was picking up the phone. Something bad had gone down, and she had to find out what was going on. Her other concern was her money. Given the situation, she didn't want to return to the pick-up location without knowing for sure that the money was there. Whoever was trying to kill her might know how she got paid. She couldn't do anything routine.

She tried her boss's assistant again. After she entered her code, the phone rang four times, which meant B.L. had to have his cell phone on. She heard something click. *Finally,* she thought, as she heard B.L.'s gruff voice.

"What up?" he asked.

"Man, am I glad you answered the phone. What's going down?" Sola asked, sighing with relief.

"Where are you?" B.L. asked. His voice was solemn.

He's got some nerve questioning me like a schoolgirl. "The better question is, where's my money?"

"Yo, I think we need to meet up," B.L. replied.

Sola didn't like the tone of his voice. Her shoulder started throbbing again. "There's some crazy shit going on and—"

B.L. cut her off. "Ain't that the biggest fucking understatement of the year?"

"Look, you sound like you got a major attitude problem right now, but I've got some major shit I need to deal with." She thought of telling him about the shooter, but hesitated. "The bottom line is that, I don't even want to know what your problem is, I just want to know when I can get my cash."

"Hold up." There was a slight pause. "Why don't we meet up by Timken and we can settle accounts?"

Timken. The barren piece of abandoned property on the north side was not the best location, but *oh well.* If that's what she had to do to get paid, then so be it.

"Okay. Give me a couple of hours. I've got something to take care of." Sola grimaced as her shoulder started throbbing again.

"I'll bet you do," B.L. said. "And you're 100 percent sure you want to meet?" he asked.

"What is this, *Jeopardy* or something? I want my damn money," Sola said.

"Always the smart-ass, aren't you?" B.L. replied coldly. "I'll be there at three-thirty."

"See ya," she said, "and I'd rather be smart than just an ass," she concluded, but B.L. had already hung up.

Sola took the Hillard-Rome South exit off I-70 West and headed to Smith's Gas Station. Smith's really should have been called Abdul's, because it was owned by an Arab man, but he kept the Smith name because of the whole terrorism/9-11 deal. Seemed some fool had totally destroyed his previous business in Michigan.

Some ignorant folks blamed every Arab person in the United States for the hijacked planes, fallen towers, and lost lives on that unforgettable September day. Anyone who looked like or whose name sounded like they prayed to Allah was feeling America's wrath and Abdul was no exception. He told Sola how much he hated discrimination. "Shit, join the fucking club," she told him.

The gas station was pretty nice, with state-of-the-art pumping stations, a car wash, and a convenience store. Not half bad for a man who came from Palestine with a few coins in his pocket. Sola parked her car in one of the spots reserved for the convenience store and studied the people pumping gas and walking in and out of the store. She saw white people mostly, with the occasional Latino. It was lunch time, and people from the various factories and plants in the area were taking their breaks. It was busy, considering the hour, but no one looked familiar, and no one looked like they were looking for her.

Sola got out of the Chevy, taking her belongings with her. She walked quickly to the convenience store, keeping her head down. The doors opened automatically and she felt a cool blast of air as she walked inside.

She walked towards the back of the store near the commercial refrigerators, which contained beer and soft drinks. She found some bottled water and reached inside one of the refrigerators to grab a couple of bottles. She walked up an aisle with overpriced health and beauty items, looking for a bottle of rubbing alcohol. There were two dusty bottles on the bottom of a shelf, and she took one. She also picked out a bottle of aspirin to help with the pain. Before going to the service counter, she glanced around again, looking for anything out of the ordinary.

A young Arab man was checking out customers. He had

olive skin, thick dark hair, and an over-abundance of facial hair capped off with a unibrow. He was wearing a plain blue shirt and a pair of khaki pants that looked like Dockers. He didn't wear a name tag.

Sola kept her head down as she waited in the checkout line. When she finally walked up to the counter, she placed her items near the cash register. She smiled brightly and asked, "Is Abdul here?"

The clerk stared at her briefly and looked her up and down before his eyes rested on her backpack. "Who wants to know?" he asked with a thick accent.

By the look in his eyes, she knew she had the answer to her initial question. Abdul was in the building somewhere. "Tell him his Nubian friend from the East is here," she said, winking.

The store clerk ignored her playful jest, picked up the phone and started talking in Arabic. She didn't even try to understand him, although the tone of his voice revealed concern. A woman behind Sola huffed impatiently. Sola wanted to turn around and tell the woman to chill out, however, she figured it was best not to respond at all. She assumed the woman had to return to work, but she seriously doubted the woman had a bullet in the shoulder for breakfast and her life in danger for lunch. The woman would have to wait.

After the clerk hung up the phone, he looked around the convenience store. His action caused Sola to look around too.

"Go, back there," the clerk said, pointing to a steel door near a coffee stand.

Sola nodded her head and paid for her items. The Arab continued to look at her strangely. After he bagged her items, she gave him a slight wave and walked to the door.

There was a small peephole above a white sign with black letters telling would-be readers "Employees Only." She heard a click, and then she walked in.

Abdul's office was plain, with bare, white walls, no windows, and the minimal amount of furniture. Sola knew that Abdul kept his safe under his desk, as well as a twelve-gage shotgun. Four television monitors were perched on a hutch behind him, keeping track of the inside and outside of the store.

Abdul was sitting in a black leather chair behind his medium-size oak desk. His crisp white shirt highlighted his brown skin and curly dark hair. In contrast to his clerk, he was clean shaven and thankfully, had two distinguishable thick eyebrows. He had broad shoulders and well-developed arms, molded from years of working out. Overall, he was a handsome man, and even Sola had to admire his attributes. He shuffled some papers on the desk as Sola entered the room and closed the door behind her.

"Keef Ha-lock?" Sola asked Abdul how he was doing in Arabic. He had taught her a couple of words when they first met, and she always greeted him in his native tongue.

Abdul nodded his head and replied, "I am doing better than you, my friend." He raised one of his hands, directing her to sit down.

She placed her backpack and bag on the chair. "I hope you don't mind if I stand." She pointed to her shoulder. "Someone tagged me this morning and I've got to keep the blood flowing as much as possible."

Abdul looked concerned. "I am sorry to hear it," he said.

Sola walked to the desk. "Look, let's cut out all the bullshit. I know you have ears all over the city and I need to know what's going on."

Abdul raised his eyebrows. "You mean you do not know?"

Sola sighed. "Look, I had a job last night. I completed it. Today, someone's trying to put a bullet in me." She touched her shoulder for emphasis. "Have you heard anything or what?"

"I must say, I am surprised that you are so ignorant. The woman I know would be on top of her game." Abdul shook his head slightly.

Sola gripped the side of the desk. "I'm not really worried so much about the game. I'm worried about my fucking life. If you know something, I need to know it too."

Abdul rose from the chair and walked towards the door. "I will have your answer in a minute."

After the door closed, Sola picked up her backpack and held it in front of her. She opened it and lightly fingered the nine millimeter. She considered Abdul as a friend, but he was a businessman first and foremost. Whatever had gone down, and because of it, someone was after her. She wouldn't blame Abdul if he made a call and informed interested parties as to her whereabouts. Especially if a big payday was in order. She probably would do the same thing if the situation was reversed. She positioned her index finger around her gun's trigger. Her piece was like her MasterCard, she never left home without it because she never knew what to expect.

Less than a minute later, Abdul returned to the office with a newspaper in his hands. He stared at her backpack as the door closed behind him.

"I know what you are thinking, my friend, but I am a neutral party," Abdul said as he backed up to the door.

"Don't blame me for being cautious," Sola said as she closed the backpack and placed it back in the chair.

Abdul returned to his chair and laid out the newspaper on his desk. He looked worried. "Are you sure you do not want to sit down?" he asked.

Sola shook her head. Abdul motioned for her to come closer, and she walked to the desk with an impending sense of dread. Abdul turned the newspaper over. Her eyes widened as she read the headline on the bottom fold of the newspaper. DAUGHTER OF SUSPECTED CRIME BOSS GUNNED DOWN

Chapter Nine

Sola's Story, Part V – 1992

As time went on, the days began to blur. I became more and more withdrawn. School started back, but I didn't feel like going. I should have been excited about starting high school, dressing in new clothes and meeting new people. Although being a freshmen wasn't the best of circumstances for most, my ninth-grade blues were cured by being one of the best friends of the most popular girl in school, Trina. But I didn't care about being on the A-list or about education. Some days, I thought about escaping, but I still hadn't figured out where I would go. My life had become a double-edged sword. My survival and my destruction were both linked to the last place I wanted to be.

It's hard to say it, but things ended up being "routine." I stopped complaining and did what I was told. Rocky basically had his way with me. I stopped believing in the light at the end of the tunnel. All feelings I had for anyone and everything, I hid deep inside of me. Rocky wouldn't be able to take them away.

Trina and my other PICs would still come by my townhouse every now and then or call me to keep me updated on Chela's condition. Trina told me that Chela had to have a couple of operations. She said he would never walk straight again. His smooth, handsome face was marred with a jagged scar on the left side of his face. The doctors also suspected brain damage, but they weren't sure, yet.

"I feel so bad for him," I said sadly into my cordless phone after hearing one of Trina's reports on Chela. I was sitting on the couch in the living room and MTV was providing the background sound.

"You should," Trina said sarcastically.

"You test our friendship every time I talk to you, don't you, *puta*?" I snapped. I couldn't stand it when Trina acted like a smart-ass.

"Don't be trying to call me names in Spanish. Even I know what *puta* means, Trina responded. "And you know what I have to say about that—you the bitch." Trina was getting loud. I could imagine her putting her hands on her hips and her neck swaying.

Trina continued, "A real friend tells the truth, and the word is you told your Momma's man to take him down."

"Why would I do that?" I asked innocently.

"Why does the Earth travel around the sun? Shit, I don't blame you for wanting revenge." Trina was still sniffing.

"Girl, I don't know what you talking about. And I don't really care. I know what I did and didn't do. I'm about to break, so I'll check you later." I hung up the phone without saying goodbye.

I sat there for a moment with guilt eating away at me. Chela had no right to lie on me, but he still didn't deserve the beating he got. Looking back, I realize he was a teenage boy doing what teenage boys do; exaggerating his exploits to make himself look more like a man. I won't pretend like I had that kind of understanding at thirteen, but I still felt bad about the situation. I knew I had to do something for Chela.

I got dressed in my standard sweat pants and extra-large T-shirt, then I walked up to the Sullivant Shopping Center. The Center was the poor man's mall, with a dirty grocery store, a drugstore, a check-cashing business, several clothing stores, and a post office. I usually went to the center to visit Kelli's Deli, although I didn't pay for my stuff every time. The owners let their teenage kids run the cash register, and they never paid attention to what was going on in the store, so I got the five-finger discount when it was necessary.

Next to Kelli's Deli was a flower shop named Gatherings. There were so many plants and flowers inside that it looked like some kind of exotic jungle. It was run by a blue-haired old, white lady. Everyone in the Gardens knew her as Mizz Petals, although I never did figure out if it was her real name. She took the flower thing to the next level—she even had a collection of flowered shirts and pants that she wore every day; well every time I saw her. She made a lot of money serving the Whitmore & Sons Funeral Home near the Greenlawn Cemetery up the street from the Gardens. Truth be told, Mizz Petals was arranging a lot of flowers for brothers in the Gardens who died before their time.

When I walked into the shop, my nose was introduced to the pleasant smell of blooming flowers. Colors exploded in front of my face. It almost looked like the movie *Little Shop of Horrors* that Tisha Campbell sang in before she was on *Martin* and with Damon Wayans on *My Wife and Kids.* A door chime sounded. Through all of the foliage, I almost expected to hear a deep, animated voice say "Feed me, Seymour." Instead, Mizz Petals, dressed in her usual flowery attire, came out of the back room and walked to the counter.

"How can I help you?" she asked. Her voice was the mixture of school teacher and grandmother.

"Do you send flowers to hospitals?" I asked, quickly glancing at the various flower arrangements.

"We sure do," she answered.

"What do you need in order to send the flowers?" I asked.

"The name of the hospital, the name of the patient, and the room number." Mizz Petals walked around the counter with a spray bottle and sprayed a couple of house plants.

I frowned. I didn't know Chela's room number. "What if I don't know the room number?" I asked.

"Well," Mizz Petals reached up to scratch her blue hair, "I don't know."

I tried to look as pitiful as possible. "Something really bad happened to one of my friends. He's up at Children's all messed up. I feel so bad and I just want to send something to him."

Mizz Petals seemed like she was trying to console me. "Oh, dear, I think we can do something for him. What's his name?"

"Chela. Juan Chela Martinez," I responded, still sounding pitiful.

Mizz Petals frowned. "You don't mean that young man they found up the street?"

"Yes, ma'am," I said, nodding my head as I responded to her question.

"He's still in the hospital?" I nodded slowly. She shook her head. "Horrible situation, that is. I don't know why anyone would want to hurt someone like that. The things people do to each other. Do you know his family started up a collection to help with his medical bills?" I nodded my head even though it was the first time I'd heard about it. "It is so nice you would think about the young man. Of course I'll help you out. I should have his hospital room number at my desk." Mizz Petals grabbed my hand and led me to a large array of flowers.

Mizz Petals helped me pick out an arrangement. When she told me the price, I almost screamed. "Forty dollars? That's a lot of cash."

"Good flowers cost money," Mizz Petals said, holding out her hand.

I reluctantly pulled two twenty-dollar bills out of my pocket. "Here you go."

Mizz Petals went to the cash register and put the money inside. She came back to me with a card. "Do you want to write anything to him?"

I held the card in my hand. I didn't really know what I could say to Chela. My hand shook as I scribbled "Sorry" and my initials, "SN." I gave the card back to Mizz Petals.

"There we go. We'll have it to him by tomorrow." She smiled and held out her hand. I held out my hand too and she shook it.

I thanked her and started to walk out of the door. Before I left, I took the rest of the money out of my pocket. I didn't even count it. "Mizz Petals, do you think you can add this to Chela's medical fund?"

She smiled as she took the money. "Of course. God Bless you."

I left Gatherings and started walking back to the Gardens, feeling better than I had for a long time. Mizz Petals's last words to me played over and over in my head. *God Bless You*, she had told me. I hoped that He would, and soon.

Chapter Ten

Sudden moves may throw you off track.
Use instinct to regain your balance.
—The Qualities of Chess Masters # 199

March 31, 12:45 P.M.

Sola stared at the headline again. DAUGHTER OF CRIME BOSS GUNNED DOWN. She started to feel faint and stumbled. Abdul stood up and grabbed her arm to support her.

"I know you are a strong-willed woman, but maybe you should sit down," he said.

Abdul led Sola to the chair on the other side of his desk and placed her belongings on the floor. Sola sat down and shook her head in disbelief.

"I can't believe this," she said. "I've met her. I should have known." She buried her head in her hands. "I told B.L. I took out a roach. Please tell me I'm dreaming."

"I am afraid you are very much awake, my friend." Abdul kneeled down beside Sola's chair. "You know I do not like to bear bad news, but the situation is grave. Blood calls for blood. There is a hit out on you."

Sola's shoulder throbbed again. Now she knew why someone had tried to end her life this morning. She began to feel nauseous.

"There must be some mistake. Give me the paper," she demanded.

"There is no mistake," Abdul said gravely.

"Just give me the damn paper," Sola repeated, pointing at the newspaper on Abdul's desk. "I need to read it, see what's going on. What options I have," she said, her voice trailing off as she focused again on the headline.

Abdul took the paper from the desk and handed it to Sola. She scanned the article, picking out the important parts. *West Side shooting. Two dead. Female, Black, identified as Denise Ann Monchats (pronounced mon-shah), age 20. Daughter of Pierre-Henri "Dennis" Monchats, reputed crime boss under federal investigation for racketeering, drug offenses, and involvement in various criminal activities. Male, Black, identification withheld pending notification of his immediate family. Autopsies performed today. Drug-related killings. Professional hit suspected, no witnesses.*

Sola let the paper drop out of her hand. "I can't believe this shit," she said incredulously.

Abdul held her hand. "It may be worse than you think," he said.

Sola looked up at him. "What could be worse than killing Monchats's daughter?" she asked incredulously, not knowing if she wanted to hear the answer.

Adbul released her hand and leaned against the desk. "The paper says the dead man is unidentified, but that is not entirely true."

"Just get to the point," Sola said.

"Your hit, the man you dealt the losing deck to last night, he worked for the Feds. He was an undercover agent. I think he was involved with the Monchats investigation." Abdul replied.

Sola felt her heart sink. "This is bullshit. Why would Monchats's daughter get caught up with a Fed? It doesn't make sense. Monchats kept his daughter away from his businesses. Even I've only met her maybe three or four times and I've been working for Monchats for over fourteen years." Sola slammed her hands on Abdul's desk. "This is shit I really don't need to deal with right now. Are you sure he was a fucking federal agent? I was told he was a dealer."

Abdul held up his hands and shook his head. "I do not want to know anything. This is not my fight. You know I am like the Swiss, I am always the neutral party and I like peace and making money. I will only say that experience should have told you not to always believe what you are told."

Sola bristled at Adbul's matter-of-fact tone. "Oh, right, like you don't have any blood on your hands?" Sola mocked him. "And your little comment is supposed to make me feel better how?"

"It is only a statement; nothing more, nothing less," Abdul said as he stared at the steel door. "I wish I could help you, but you are a dangerous commodity. I regret to tell you that you can not stay here."

Sola looked into Abdul's eyes and could tell he was concerned. "I understand. It's business, not personal."

He looked down at the floor. "You need to take care of that wound, too," he said.

Sola followed his gaze. Drops of blood were on the floor. For the first time in a long time, she didn't know what to do.

"Let me clean that up," she said.

"That will not be necessary. I will have Muhammad do it. You should leave now. If someone is looking for you, they will come here. I have not seen you today."

Abdul walked to his set of television screens and pressed on a button beneath one of the sets. A tape emerged from a video cassette recorder on the far side of his desk. He opened one of his desk drawers and pulled out another tape.

"I will destroy this tape after you leave," Abdul assured her.

Sola smiled slightly. Abdul knew the type of people he would be dealing with.

"Do you think I have time to clean up?" Sola asked, glancing at her shoulder.

"I think you should start preparing to leave." Abdul's eyes shifted towards the door. "You never know and I—"

"You don't have to explain a thing." Sola interrupted as she started gathering her things. "I'll be on my way."

Abdul reached out his hands. "If there was anything I could do to help you, I would."

"Since you are being so generous today, there are two things you can do actually," Sola said as she slung the backpack across her uninjured shoulder.

Abdul shifted uneasily in his chair. "What?"

"I need another car and I need another cell phone. I've got to keep flowing until I find out what's going on."

"I do not think it will be safe," Abdul said, shaking his head.

Sola hated to play her trump card with such a trusted friend, but she was playing a game of survival. She walked towards Abdul and looked him in the eyes. "You know I've risked myself for you, *my friend.* Yeah, I understand the nature of the business, but I'm sure you can find some fucking way to let me take one of your old broken down cars and give me a pre-paid cell phone. Believe me, I won't take it as a personal gesture," Sola said, trying to mask her irritation.

Abdul returned her ominous gaze. When he first set his eyes on Smith's Gas Station, another buyer, some Columbus, Ohio hotshot, had almost sealed the deal. Abdul believed his dream of prosperity would come true if he could acquire Smith's. Of course, the other buyer had to be taken care of. Through his connections, Abdul found Sola. She normally didn't do independent work, but they discovered a mutual connection. He gave her valuable information and she decided to take care of his problem. She told him to consider it a favor. Less than one month later, he was the proud owner of Smith's Gas Station.

After Abdul acquired the gas station, his business empire grew. He had convenience stores, check-cashing places, pizza shops, and car lots all over the city. His businesses were mainly located in low-income neighborhoods, but he still made tons of cash, and all because Sola helped him when he needed it most; when he had nothing at all. She got paid for the job, but there was really no repayment for the riches she had given Abdul because of her work for him. It was time to settle accounts.

"There is a blue Honda Accord on the far edge of the car lot near the ice machines. It runs pretty good. Take it." Abdul opened another desk drawer full of keys. When he found the correct set of keys, he gave them to Sola.

"And the phone?" She asked.

"I will have Muhammad take care of you," Abdul responded as he closed the desk drawer.

Sola smiled. "I appreciate your assistance."

"How can I turn down someone who has done so much for me?" Abdul said, returning her smile with one of his own. His response was more of a statement than a question. Sola searched for sarcasm in his tone.

There was an uncomfortable silence. "Well, I guess it's time for me to go," Sola said, rising from her chair.

"And where will you be going?" Abdul asked.

Sola stared at the door. "I don't think you want to know." She opened the door and prepared to leave.

"Mas Allah Ma," Abdul said, telling her goodbye in his native tongue.

She turned around and looked at him. His eyes were sad and filled with hopelessness. For all intensive purposes, their *friendship* was over. She knew she would never see him again. She wanted to respond, but she didn't know what to say. Instead, she nodded her head and walked out of his office door. As she neared the automatic doors, she looked back toward the steel door. Abdul was watching her leave. She nodded and gave him a weak smile. As she exited, she turned her head and didn't look back again. It was time to plan her next move.

Chapter Eleven

Sola's Story, Part VI – 1992

God works in mysterious ways, isn't that how the saying goes? I've never heard a statement more true. In the midst of my despair, something happened to me that should have made me sad. However, it filled me up with hope and I believed in life again.

It all started when I returned to school. I had been cutting class, thinking I would get some peace during the day. However, I had to start going back because Rocky found out I was staying at home and decided to start coming over. Anything was better than him. Even high school.

Trina decided to have a birthday party for me at her townhouse to celebrate my fourteen years on Earth. For a couple of hours, while dancing and partying, I forgot all about my troubles. It turned out to be the most fun I had that year. The whole crew was there, LaKisha, Netta, Dee, and a small army of soon-to-be gangsters. Chela wasn't there, and I thought of him, but it still almost felt like old times.

Since I had no choice but to go to school regularly, I joined the school chess club to keep busy. I hung with my crew, partied a bit, and went to football games when I could. I found any reason I could to stay away from home. Basically, I was trying to find some meaning to my life.

Then, I started getting sick. It would happen in the mornings, mainly. I was late to school a lot. I didn't think much of it until one of my girls told me how thick I was getting.

"Damn, girl, what you eatin' at home?" Dee asked me one day, poking me in my slightly bulging tummy with one of her childlike fingers.

I dismissed her curiosity, joking around about how I needed to stay away from fast food and stop stealing sweets from Kelli's Deli.

I had stomach problems, a lack of appetite, and two missed periods. It didn't take me long to figure out what was going on. One day, I cut school and picked up a pregnancy test from a drugstore near the Gardens. Thirty minutes later, the pink lines on the white pregnancy test stick confirmed what I had already suspected—I was pregnant.

I was scared, of course. The realization that there was a little life growing inside of me terrified me. I asked all of the questions: How would I take care of my baby? Where would I live? How would I tell Momma? It occurred to me that I never thought about having an abortion. I knew I was young, but I wanted my baby more than anything. No reason in particular. It's just that I had been trying to find some meaning to my life to no avail, and I figured a baby would be just what I needed to make my existence on earth worthwhile.

Deciding that I wanted the baby was a piece of cake, but figuring out how to tell my Momma about the new addition to the Nichols family was hard. Thinking about Rocky's reaction made it even harder. How could I tell Momma that her man was my baby's daddy? And what would Rocky do when he found out that he was the father of a teenage girl's baby? I didn't want to think about their reactions, so I tried to hide my pregnancy as long as I could.

One day, I went to a bookstore in City Center Mall downtown to buy a book about pregnancy. I wanted to take good care of myself while I was pregnant. I had even thought of names. Kayla, if I had a girl, and Josiah, if I had a boy. According to a book called *Amazing Baby Names*, Kayla meant "crown of laurels" or "pure," depending on whether I wanted a Hebrew or Greek name. Basically, I just liked how Kayla sounded. Josiah meant "fire of the Lord" in Hebrew. I thought the name Josiah was strong and powerful, just like I would want my son to be.

I started saving up any money Momma gave me. I hid it in the bathroom and in my bedroom. I knew I couldn't waste money anymore because I would have to buy baby items such as diapers, baby formula, clothes, and toys.

I learned about government programs that would help me out, like WIC. I even checked up on welfare and Section 8. I felt a sense of relief when I discovered the MOVE Program. The Moms' Organization for Valuing Education provided support and funds for teenage mothers who wanted to continue their education. Based on the information I picked up from the MOVE office on the East Side, I would be able to go to school and get assistance paying for childcare. They offered night classes and everything. MOVE even provided college money for mothers who graduated from high school. I planned on a good future for me and my child. I wanted to make sure all of my bases were covered.

I still wore my baggy clothes. It was the only way to hide my bulging belly. When Rocky came over, he didn't really notice I was pregnant. His ignorant ass thought I was getting fat. He told me to lay off the fried chicken. *Fuck him.* I convinced myself that I wouldn't let him get near my baby.

My friends started noticing my glow, the lightness in my steps, and the hope on my face. As usual, Trina was the first one to ask me about it. She came over to my house one day and just came out with the question, "Girl, you pregnant or what?" she asked. Trina was never one to mince words.

"What you think?" I asked.

"All I know is that you're getting big." Trina was nosy, and she had a big mouth. But I was so happy, I almost told her.

Something made me hesitate. This was my baby. My secret treasure. I didn't want anyone in the world to know, especially not the gossip box.

"Maybe I need to lose a little weight," I said, looking down at the floor.

Trina looked at my stomach. "You sure?" she asked. "You can tell me. It ain't like you would be the only girl around here having a baby."

Trina was right. Two other girls from the Gardens were pregnant. One was even a year younger than me.

"You always trying to start some drama and gossip," I smacked my lips and rolled my eyes. Trina was really getting on my nerves. "Stop worrying about me and find somebody else to talk about."

Trina frowned. "You've really been having a lot of attitude lately. We supposed to be girls. If I can't worry about one of my PICs, then who can I worry about?"

I felt bad about giving Trina grief, but I wanted to end our conversation or at least change the subject. Trina may have been my girl, but our bond didn't extend to her tongue. "Like I said, I just need to lose weight," I told her. "Maybe I'll join the basketball team or something."

My denials did nothing to stop the gossip. Even I heard the whispers. I still kept my head up and I thought my secret was safe. That all ended when Trina's mother told Momma that I was pregnant.

I can still remember when Momma stormed into the house. I was lying on the couch watching music videos on BET. She was always the picture of perfection, and today was no different.

"We need to talk," Momma said. Her voice was hard and concerned.

"About what?" I asked, feeling an impending sense of dread.

Momma pointed at the TV. "Turn that off. I don't want any distractions."

I pushed the power button on the remote. "So, what's going on?" I felt a lump forming in my throat.

Momma sat down on the loveseat. "I'm going to ask you something and I need you to be straight with me."

My heart started beating fast. I couldn't say anything, so I just stared at her. She reached over and put her hand on my shoulder.

"Are you going to have a baby?" she asked.

I couldn't speak and my silence answered her question. Her lips started trembling and a tear slid down her cheek. I sat up on the couch and lowered my head.

"After all I told you about condoms and men. How could you let this happen?" Momma said with such disappointment. She started crying and put her head in her hands.

I got angry. How dare Momma assume I just spread my legs for anyone. *If only you knew*, I thought.

"Why it got to be my fault?" I asked, fighting back tears of my own.

Momma stopped sobbing, wiped her damp hands on the couch, and reached out her hand. I thought she was going to slap me, but she placed her hand on my knee. "I'm not going to argue with you. We got some decisions to make, and quick." She said, looking at by stomach and frowning.

I placed my hand on my belly. "*I* already decided that I'm keeping my baby."

Momma jumped up off of the loveseat and stood in front of me. "What do you mean? You just turned fourteen. You can't even get a work permit. What makes you think you can handle a baby?" She was looking down at me.

I felt like she was scolding me. After all of the reading and studying I did, I thought I knew something about raising a child, even though I had just turned fourteen. I stood up and looked down at Momma. I was at least four inches taller than her.

"I want to have my baby." I said.

Momma looked at me in a way that sat me right back in my seat. "And how are you taking care of it, because I'm not."

"I already know that," I said, sticking out my chin. "I know how I'm going to take care of my baby, so you can keep doing whatever you doing."

"Girl, you smart. You can do lots of things. Don't mess it up-" Momma paused. She knew what I was about to say.

"Oh, so did I mess up your life?" I asked.

More tears started to fall from Momma's eyes. She reached up and touched my cheek.

"Please don't ever think that," she said sincerely. "I love you and want the best for you. But I'm not going to act like it's not hard to raise a child. I mean, is the baby's daddy going to help you?"

So there it was. The baby's daddy question. The perfect time to tell her about what Rocky had done to me. To tell her that my baby was the only thing giving me hope. But I couldn't tell her so I shook my head.

"I know it's going to be hard, Momma. But I looked at the programs for young mothers and everything I can do to give my baby a healthy life."

"And what about school?" Momma asked. "Don't think you going to be sitting around here collecting a welfare check. You have to go to school."

"My baby shouldn't stop me from going to school," I told her. "In fact, I've never wanted to go to school more." I sat back down on the couch and Momma sat next to me.

"Have you been to the doctor?" Momma asked, staring at my stomach.

I shook my head, feeling slightly stupid. I was so focused on keeping my baby all to myself that in all of my planning, I didn't even go to the doctor, let alone the free clinic.

"So you don't know how far along you are?" Momma asked.

In all honesty, I really didn't know. In all my so-called preparations, I overlooked some of the most important things when it came to insuring the health of my baby. I shook my head again.

Momma stared at my stomach. "Can I see?" She asked, her voice trembling.

I hesitated at first, but as I looked at Momma, I knew I could show her. I slowly lifted my shirt and then pulled down my sweat pants over my bulging belly. I moved closer to Momma. Her hand shook as she reached out and touched the shadowy line that marked me from my chest down the length of my belly. She started crying again.

"Honey child, you look like you're so far along. How could I miss this?" she cried, her voice a mixture of pain, disbelief and frustration.

I didn't say a word, but we both knew that she "missed it" because she was never around. Instead, I started rubbing my belly.

"Sometimes I think I feel him moving," I said.

Momma raised her eyebrows. "Him?" she asked.

I smiled. "Yes, him," I responded. "I don't know why, but I

really think I'm going to have a boy. I'm going to name him Josiah. It means the 'fire of the Lord.' I thought it sounded strong and I want to raise a strong man. I haven't thought of a middle name yet, but it'll probably be something Hispanic."

"You have a name? Josiah?" Momma stood up and started pacing the room and mumbling to herself. She turned around and looked at me. "We can deal with this," she said. "We can get through this. And we're going to do this together."

"That's what I want," I replied truthfully.

"Look," Momma said as she wiped her eyes. "I know you want to keep this baby. I can see it in your eyes. But we got to look at all the options, you understand?" She said, patting me on the head like I was five years old.

I nodded.

Momma looked down at my stomach again. Her tears were still flowing. I was happy that she finally knew. The truth was liberating. My head was in the clouds until she brought me back down to Earth. "Well," she started. "I know Rocky's going to be disappointed when I tell him." Then she reached to pick up the phone.

Chapter Twelve

Seemingly bad moves by your opponent
may mask a stunning blow. With an attentive mind,
you can turn missteps to your advantage.
—The Qualities of Chess Masters # 213

March 31, 1:15 P.M.

Campbell Donovan stared at the building in front of him, shaking his head. He studied the structure's bright red paint and the contrasting dark tinted windows. The blue neon sign sparkled in the sun. The sign was still on, and he could hear the faint crackling of a busted light. The neon light illuminating the S on the huge DOLLHOUSE sign had gone out, and he would have to replace it. But that was the least of his worries. For the past couple of minutes, he tried his best to tune out the man speaking behind him, but it was unavoidable. He didn't turn around, but mentally began to focus on what the man was saying.

"Look, I hold Mr. Monchats in high regard, as you know," the balding white man said in an annoying nasal tone. "But we've been receiving a lot of complaints from the neighbors about this strip club."

Campbell turned to face Mr. Fogelman. "Gentlemen's club, Mr. Fogelman," Campbell corrected him.

"A gentleman's club," Mr. Fogelman repeated. "If you insist." He fumbled with his blue and white stripped tie. "But my hands are strapped." He handed Campbell a sheet of paper.

Campbell took the paper in his hands and noticed the big red letters at the top of the page that spelled out VIOLATIONS. He lowered his hand and felt the paper graze the top of his leg through his pants. He used his other hand to wipe his eyes. He turned back around and faced the Dollhouse again. After last night's activities, he was thoroughly drained. Two exotic dancers decided not to show up and the bartender ran out of Alizé, which was hard to purchase during the weekend.

Then Campbell got the news that really shook him up—Monchats's daughter was dead. The news traveled through the club and the whole mood changed. No one felt like partying, stripping, or drinking anymore. Less than an hour after the news came out, the club was basically empty and the dancers were ready to head home. He didn't get much sleep the night before and had planned to rest most of the day before getting out of bed. But just when his eyes were getting heavy, he received Mr. Fogelman's call to meet him at the club. So much for a day of rest.

"Look, it's only for a couple of days," Mr. Fogelman said stiffly. "If we don't do something it's going to look suspicious. One week, the neighbors feel like the city is on their side and then you can open back up with no problem."

Campbell turned to face Mr. Fogelman. He could tell the code enforcement officer was nervous. His face was covered with sweat and turning red.

"A week is a long time. Time equals money. And you and I

both know that Mr. Monchats doesn't like to lose money," Campbell said.

Mr. Fogelman cleared his throat. "Well, I thought he wouldn't mind a couple of days with the unfortunate situation he has to suffer through."

"Let me stop you right there," Campbell replied. "I'm sure it's a painful blow to the heart and mind to lose a daughter, but there's a big difference between a personal life and a business operation. I'm sure you know Mr. Monchats keeps his private life and his business dealings completely separate."

Mr. Fogelman reached up and gripped Campbell's shoulder. "Oh, I'm sure of it." He was a red as a beet. "But as I said before, my hands are tied. You people have been very good to me, but the pressure that will be on Monchats if he doesn't shut down the strip club or gentleman's club or whatever you want to call it, will cost more than a week of closed doors," he said stiffly.

Campbell turned his neck and stared coldly at the pale, thick fingers curled around his shoulder. Mr. Fogelman must have felt Campbell's growing anger. He slowly released his hand and laughed nervously.

"Look, I am sure this situation will work itself out. This week will pass by before you know it," Mr. Fogelman said as he wiped the stream of sweat from his forehead with the hand that had moments ago been on Campbell's shoulder.

Campbell kept staring at Mr. Fogelman's hand as he shook the sweat from it, feeling a sting and heat on his face as though he had been pimped-slapped, but knowing there was no mark to verify the blow. He had the eerie feeling the code enforcement officer was taking some sort of twisted pleasure in wielding his limited power to close down the club. Mr. Fogelman had always seemed like a nice man, but now Campbell recognized that he had a major superiority complex. It was time to remind him who truly had the upper hand.

"Well, I'm going to hate to have to break it to Mr. Monchats that one of his most profitable clubs will be closed down because of some misunderstanding," Campbell said, deciding to return the favor and put his hand on Mr. Fogelman's shoulder. The smaller man stepped back for a moment, and Campbell noticed a slight glimpse of fear.

"But knowing Mr. Monchats like I do," Campbell continued, "I know he'll wonder why a man who has enjoyed the immense wonders that the Dollhouse has to offer would be so willing to terminate that relationship. Even for a short time. And the dancers. Especially the ones you've dealt with privately, it's no telling what they'll do if they don't get their money. Because if they don't work, they don't get paid. I've worked with them for some time now, and I really don't know what they'll say, or who they'll say it to." Campbell slowed down the last part of his sentence for emphasis as he slowly released his hand from Mr. Fogelman's shoulder.

Campbell watched with pleasure as the color drained from Mr. Fogelman's face. In almost an instant, Campbell had reduced him from a confident asshole to a blithering idiot. Fortunately for him that Mr. Fogelman made the universal mistake of doing things in the dark he didn't want in the light. Because of that, he would always have an extra shadow following him. Campbell was glad to help remind him it was there.

Mr. Fogelman cleared his throat. "I've never thought about it like that," he stammered out.

"I figured you hadn't. I just want to be able to clear up this misunderstanding so that we can continue our wonderful relationship. I think closing down the club for one day will be sufficient. Today, in fact, will be perfect." Campbell handed the violations summons back to Mr. Fogelman.

Mr. Fogelman took the sheet of paper. "With these new developments, I'm sure we can work something out. I'll take care of this on my end." He began to crumble the paper in his hand.

Campbell sighed with relief. Now he had another thing off his plate today. He didn't really like having to deplete Mr. Fogelman's ego, but unpleasant things were sometimes necessary.

"Great." Campbell said, looking down at his watch. "Well, I know we're both busy today, so I'll let you go," he said dismissively as he reached out his hand.

"Right. I do have to go," Mr. Fogelman said softly as he shook Campbell's hand weakly.

Mr. Fogelman turned towards the parking lot and proceeded to walk slowly towards his car. Campbell watched him for a moment and almost felt sorry for him until he remembered the "you people" comment. That really struck a nerve. He had to give just one more passing shot.

"Hey, Fogelman," Campbell yelled out.

Mr. Fogelman turned around to look at him. "Yes," he responded.

"Make sure to stop by sometime. I'll make sure you get a drink and a lap dance on the house," Campbell smiled widely as he stated his offer.

Campbell laughed as Mr. Fogelman looked left to right to see if anyone else who was in earshot heard Campbell even though the parking lot was empty, with the exception of Campbell's black Navigator and Fogelman's gray Volvo. Mr. Fogelman started turning red again, but he didn't respond. Instead, he turned around quickly and continued to walk briskly to his car.

Campbell continued to watch Mr. Fogelman until he sped out of the Dollhouse's parking lot. He then proceeded to his own vehicle, thinking of the bed awaiting him back at his

North Side apartment. He needed rest. He planned for a couple of hours in the bed to reenergize him for his night activities. Just as he deactivated his car alarm and started the SUV with his remote ignition key, his cell phone rang.

"God, I hope this isn't another mess I have to deal with," he mumbled as he pulled the cell phone out of its holder. When he looked down at the caller ID, his heart almost stopped cold. He took a deep breath before flipping his cell-phone open. He didn't even wait for the caller to speak.

"How dare you call me here," Campbell said harshly as he gripped the phone and pressed it against his ear.

"You will have to admit that this call is totally necessary," the voice said, cold and sharp.

Campbell leaned against the Navigator, feeling the slight vibration of the SUV as its engine idled. "Look, make it quick. I have things to do, and the last thing I need is another complication."

"Of course. But then you know what happened last night. And you also know what's going down today. You know the players and the pieces. I think it's time for us to meet."

Campbell sucked against his teeth as he responded, "Don't you think that's a bit dangerous? I'm not trying to get involved right now."

"But you already are involved. But while you're off the radar for a bit, I think we can safely arrange a meeting."

"What could we possibly need to meet about?" Campbell asked.

"That is something we can't discuss right now. However, I suggest you meet me at the rendezvous point in an hour."

Campbell looked at his watch. "Do I have a choice in the matter?" he asked, already knowing the answer.

"Do I have to respond?"

"No," Campbell replied.

"So, I'll see you in an hour?"

"Yes."

"Oh, and Campbell, have you found her yet?"

That was the one question Campbell didn't want to respond to. "I went to her house. She wasn't there. Her neighbor said she was gone."

"Wait," the voice interrupted him. "Give me a full report when we meet."

"Fine," Campbell said flatly as he ended the call by closing the phone.

Campbell got into his Navigator and turned west on Livingston Avenue. *Well, I guess I'll have to wait to get some decent rest*, he thought as he headed into traffic. Then he thought of her. The Brown Recluse. His intuition told him that at the conclusion of his upcoming meeting, finding her would be his number one priority.

Chapter Thirteen

Sola's Story, Part VII – 1992

As Momma spoke into the phone, I felt an impending sense of dread. I wanted to scream out to tell her not to tell Rocky, but I couldn't.

Momma looked at me the entire time she talked to Rocky, frowning and nodding her head. When she got off the phone, she rose from the couch and headed towards the stairs.

"By the way," Momma said before going up the steps, "Rocky is coming over." She reached for her hair and started patting it as if Rocky was already at the door. She then began up the steps.

"For what?" I asked.

Momma was at the top of the stairs and spoke loudly. "He wants to talk to us. I know he's been like a father-figure." she said.

At that point I had had enough. I had to tell her the truth

about Rocky and what he had done to me. Before I knew it I began shouting.

"He's not a father figure to me, Momma. I don't like him and I don't want him here. He's been—"

Momma quickly walked back down the stairs, walked towards me, and grabbed my shoulders. "Don't you start with the attitude and drama. Rocky has been good to both of us. Where do you think this nice stuff comes from? Money don't grow on trees," she said.

I had to tell her before he came over. I was scared because I didn't know what he would do. I needed to stop him, to protect my baby.

"Momma, you don't know what he's been up to when you're gone. He's been—"

She interrupted me before I could finish my sentence. It was almost as if she didn't want to know what I was going to say. Maybe her intuition was telling her she couldn't handle the truth.

"I don't want to hear it," Momma said as she glanced around the room. "You best get this living room together and fix yourself up. You look a mess." She touched my wild mass of curly hair. "Just because you're pregnant don't mean you have to let yourself go."

She turned away from me and walked back up the stairs. My heart was beating fast. I knew I had to get away. I could no longer stay at my townhouse. I knew that my baby was in danger. I knew there was no way Rocky would let me have my baby. My son. Josiah.

I ran upstairs and went to my bedroom. I was in survival mode. I grabbed a bag and threw a couple of outfits from my closet inside of it. The old Nikes I wore would have to do. I scanned the room to see if there was anything else I needed.

Next, I went to the bathroom. I wrapped up my toothbrush in a clean hand towel and gathered a few toiletries. I kept a stash of money beneath the sink. I took it and put it in my bag. As I readied myself to leave, I felt a sense of freedom I hadn't felt for a long time. I didn't know where I was going or how I would get there, but I knew that Rocky no longer held power over me. I walked out of the bathroom and walked into something solid. I closed my eyes, not wanting to look at what was ahead of me. But I smelled the familiar cologne and alcohol. I had collided with Rocky.

"What do you think you're doing?" he asked, filling up the hallway with his tall frame.

I stood there, silent. I looked past him, to the stairs. For a second, I wondered how he got to the townhouse so fast, but my thoughts quickly returned to my freedom. He grabbed my bag, but I held on. He released it and grabbed my shoulders.

"I said, what do you think you're doing?" he yelled.

Momma came out of her bedroom. "What the hell is going on out here?" she yelled.

"I think your precious little Sola is trying to go somewhere. What do you say, Sola?" His grip on my shoulders tightened but I didn't say a word.

Momma walked up to him, grabbed his arm and yelled, "Don't grab her like that, you might hurt her and the baby."

He didn't release me though. All he did was yell back at Momma. "Oh, there's not going be a baby." he looked me in the eye. "You let some nigga knock you up and you ain't got no money to take care of yourself, let alone a baby. I hope you don't think I'm gonna take care of some little bastard."

"Don't front like you don't know what's going on," I said angrily. "It stops, now—today."

Momma let go of Rocky's arm and began trying to pry his hands off of me. "Let off of her Rocky," Momma said to him. "We all need to calm down and get it together. We can talk about this downstairs."

Rocky pushed Momma off of him. She stumbled. "Don't fucking touch me right now, Synthia. I'm dealing with Sola." He looked at me and I backed away. His eyes were wild and he looked like he would kill me if he could.

I glanced at Momma. She was staring at Rocky in stunned silence. I'd like to think she had finally begun to understand Rocky's true nature. I wanted to talk, I wanted to scream, but the silence that kept me company for so long wouldn't allow me to speak. Rocky grabbed me again and started shaking me.

"How could you, you little bitch?" Rocky shouted. "We're going to a clinic first thing in the morning." He shook me even harder and I started feeling lightheaded.

Momma grabbed Rocky again. "How dare you call my daughter a bitch? What's gotten into you?" She was screaming and pulling on him, but he was too strong and determined.

Rocky released me and turned his attention to Momma. "Look, we can't have no babies running 'round here," he said.

I didn't wait for Momma's response. I saw a clear opening to the stairs and it was time to take it. I started to run towards the stairs. I heard Momma scream something, but I was worried about my freedom. I was running towards the light at the end of the tunnel. As I neared the stairs, someone reached out for me. I knew it was Rocky. I fought him; I couldn't let him hold me back. I had to save myself and my child.

I struggled and freed myself from Rocky's grip. The stairs were right before me. Rocky grabbed my bag as I took the first step and then he released it quick. I lost my balance and fell forward, landing hard on my stomach. From there, I started tumbling downward. I tried to break my fall but I couldn't grab ahold of anything. I felt pain as I tumbled over the stairs, and I finally stopped at the bottom step. I laid there for a second before sharp pains daggered my stomach. I was in total agony. I heard Momma screaming. And then, well, then the darkness overtook me.

Chapter Fourteen

A strong opponent will not back down easily;
he will attack without mercy.
—The Qualities of Chess Masters # 225

March 31, 2:30 P.M.

Pierre-Henri Monchats was a man not to be fucked with. Those who knew him best called him Dennis, as in *Dennis the Menace*. He was born in the Big Easy, New Orleans, Louisiana. Monchats wasn't born poor, but his deadbeat father left his mother when Monchats was still a baby, leaving her penniless and desolate.

Monchats spent the better part of his youth living with his family in the Florida-Desire Projects. He learned the game at an early age, and spent his teenage years honing his skills of kicking ass and selling drugs. He had four older brothers. All of them decided to make their fortunes as street pharmacists. Instead of amassing riches, they became statistics of the ever-growing violence in the land of Mardi Gras. All of them were dead before Monchats turned fifteen.

Monchats's mother died just before his seventeenth birthday. He took her death extremely hard, but he kept doing his thing. His big break came when one of the city's biggest drug dealers, Moth, took him under his wing.

He learned all the ins and outs of the business. After his first stint in jail and because of an escalating New Orleans drug war with a kingpin named Lamb, the powers that be decided to send him to New York. There, Monchats learned how to mix his drug dealing with semi-legitimate and legitimate businesses. As his bank account grew, he vowed never to live on scraps again. "By any means necessary" became the motto for his existence. He had skills unmatched in his circle of associates, a ruthless nature and an entrepreneurial spirit second to none.

Dennis Monchats was a good looking man in the prime of his life. He was six-feet, one-inch tall, with smooth caramel skin and light hazel eyes. He had a lean, muscular build and kept in shape by a steady regiment of lifting weights, basketball, and sex. Men respected him and ladies loved him. As he grew in power, the more merciless he became. He didn't let anything or anyone stop his rise to the top. His work was appreciated and his prize was Ohio.

Taking the state was easier than baking a frozen pizza. He had more men and more money on his side than anyone else in the state. And he had the backing of New York. His biggest challenge had been Columbus, but Sola, the cold-hearted bitch, had taken care of many of his problems. Things had been relatively calm for the past two years, only a situation here, and an issue there. Then, of course, the Feds came down on him like Antonio Tarver did on Roy Jones Junior. They knew they couldn't shake him when it came to his business affairs, so they tried the next best thing, his family. For years, it had only been him and his daughter. Now, there was only one Monchats left in the world, and someone was going to pay.

Years before Monchats settled in Columbus, he never thought he would fall in love. So many beautiful women threw their panties in his face, he never thought there would be a rose among the thorns. Then he met Ann Baptiste during a business trip to his hometown of New Orleans. When he first saw her, he knew she was the one. Ann was a beauty of Haitian descent, with smooth, chocolate skin and a full voluptuous body. Monchats was sprung before they even shared their first kiss.

Monchats wasn't deterred when he found out Ann lived a straight and narrow existence. She attended Dillard University and had dreams of becoming a nurse. But he tempted her with his riches.

"Why live a life working for somebody else, when you can live like a queen and have people serve you?" he asked her one day during a stroll in the French Quarter.

Monchats found out that he had some things in common with Ann. They were both parentless and didn't have any siblings. They both grew up poor and they were both stubborn. Ann was a strong-willed woman, and she resisted as long as she could. Monchats enjoyed the challenge of wooing her. Other women had thrown themselves at him at the first opportunity, ensuring at the most, a couple of dinners and sex. But Ann was more demure. She made sure Dennis knew she was interested, but she always made it clear that she demanded respect, and she wouldn't accept anything less than his full attention.

In the end, it wasn't the high-priced jewelry, high-fashion clothes, or exotic vacations that won Ann over. It was Monchats opening up to her, telling her his pain. He remembered it as if it were yesterday. He took her on a trip to Hawaii and they spent the entire time talking in their hotel room. He told Ann about his absent father, and how his family had to move from a decent house in New Orleans East to the crime-ridden and rat-infested projects.

Monchats shared things with Ann that he never shared with anyone else. He told her about his mother and brothers, about their lives and deaths, about how he held one of his brothers and screamed as blood squirted out of his brother's chest. He told her about how he watched his mother take her last breath. As Ann held him in her arms, Monchats knew that he would love her forever.

If there was one thing Monchats learned from his experiences with Ann, it was that all good things come to an end. One month after their trip to Hawaii, Monchats presented Ann with a five-carat engagement ring and asked for her hand by bending down on one knee. His heart almost exploded in pure joy when she gave him a tear-filled "yes."

Two months later, Monchats and Ann were married. It was an impromptu decision, made after having a good day at the craps table in a Las Vegas casino. Monchats paid cash for some platinum wedding bands and ran back to the hotel, convincing Ann to marry him that day.

"We don't need all the fancy stuff," he told her. "I want to be your husband today."

They exchanged their vows at a small, white wedding chapel where wedding ceremonies occurred twenty-four hours a day. That night, they shared their bed for the first time. Ann had wanted to wait until they were married, and he had respected her choice. It was exquisite to be with a woman who had never been touched by another man. He treasured her most sacred gift, and looked forward to their life together.

At first, it was hard for Ann to adjust to the lifestyle of the rich and infamous. Monchats had been quite candid about the personal details of his life, but he kept information about his business life close to his chest. Ann didn't like the hustle and bustle of New York, but had to admit that living in an upscale Harlem brownstone was better than living near the polluted canals of New Orleans. But the glitz of the drug life wore off over time and Ann began asking questions, too many questions. Telling her to mind her own damn business and keep out of his almost ripped his heart out, but he knew it was necessary.

Ann became withdrawn and distant, and Monchats did everything to cheer her up. But true bliss didn't come until Ann found out she was pregnant with Monchats's child. The pregnancy made Ann blossom, and Monchats again began to dream of a life of pure happiness. But he should have known he would never be truly content. His life was rife with hardship.

Ann's pregnancy was a hard one, and ended suddenly when she went into labor prematurely. Ann fought the hard fight, basically giving her life for the life of her child. Ann passed away with her child in her arms. With her last words, she gave her daughter a name—Denise. But Monchats wasn't even there to share in the joy and sorrow. He was on a business trip in Ohio, and returned to New York after receiving the frantic call to return. He arrived at the hospital fifteen minutes after his wife took her last breath. He never truly forgave himself.

Instead, he left New York a couple of weeks after Ann's death and made Columbus, Ohio his hone. He poured all of his love into Denise. She became the shining light in his life. Just as he had done with Ann, Monchats tried to shield her from the worse parts of his business. In Denise's world, Monchats was a social entrepreneur, making his riches on property development and urban improvement. He even kept her away from the people who really made the wheels of the Monchats empire turn. Denise blossomed in the world Monchats had created for her.

Denise grew up looking almost just like Ann. When Denise was angry or lost in thought, she was the spitting image of her mother. Monchats considered that a rare gift from God. Denise was medium height, about five-feet, five inches tall and a bit on the thin side. She was dark-skinned and had thick, black hair. The only hint of her father was her hazel eyes, which stood out because of her chocolate skin. She was a straight A student at the private school she'd been in since kindergarten, and when she decided to remain in Columbus to go to State College, he couldn't have been happier. Then she met Jonathon Stewart.

When Denise started talking about John, Monchats knew she was falling for him hard. He could see the light in her eyes when she mentioned him. Monchats had to meet the young man who was stealing his daughter's heart.

Monchats arranged a nice dinner for Denise and John at Monchats's home on Columbus's east side. Denise was so excited she could barely contain herself. During the dinner, Monchats studied John carefully. The young man seemed nice enough but Monchats knew there was something wrong about him. He had played the Game for a long time, and his instinct about the young, handsome pre-med student was that he wasn't who he appeared to be.

Monchats ordered an investigation. At the same time a private detective told him that Mr. Stewart's past didn't hold up under scrutiny, his lawyers told him that the Feds were investigating him again. The lawyers warned him the evidence the government had against him was strong. He had to prepare for anything.

The next day, Monchats was front page news, and his daughter was upset. Denise ran into his office crying and asking him if the charges were true. He hugged her and felt no remorse when he told her that the charges were false. He told her that the government didn't want black folks to have anything. The latter statement was true enough for some and his lies were only meant to protect her.

Further investigation into John's past revealed a new name and a different life. John Stewart's real name was Kenneth Washington, and he was an undercover narcotics agent from California. Monchats didn't even blink twice before ordering *Ken*'s immediate termination. The Feds must have thought they were messing with a lightweight. Monchats could handle interference with his associates and his businesses, but his family was off limits. And Mr. Stewart would have to learn that most painful lesson.

Taking the pig out was a perfect job for Sola. She had developed a reputation for delivering clean work with absolute discretion. He nicknamed her the Brown Recluse because she was adept at killing and thrived on being alone. He made sure to keep her well-paid and satisfied. He never wanted her to have a reason to work for anyone but him. Monchats knew she did a couple of jobs on the side, one of which almost got him in a lot of trouble, but he put the word out that Sola was not to be touched. *Until now.*

Monchats knew something was wrong before B.L. told him the news. Something in the pit of his stomach told him that his daughter was dead. When B.L. confirmed his fears, he went on a rampage, breaking everything in sight. He knew that the chickens would have to come home to roost someday, but he never thought his daughter would have to bear the brunt of his chosen lifestyle.

B.L. had to identify Denise's body, although it had been hard because half of her face no longer existed. The butterfly tattoos on her stomach confirmed Denise's identity. Monchats wouldn't even be able to have an open casket funeral. He wanted Sola dead before his daughter was lowered into the ground.

B.L. had the perfect solution. He knew a man just as skilled as Sola who wanted her dead. It didn't matter to Monchats, just as long as she was in a morgue before he finished eating breakfast tomorrow.

"Mr. Monchats," a soft female voice broke his concentration. It was one of his housekeepers, Maria. He hadn't even heard the doors to his home office open.

"Yes," he responded, his voice dry and strained.

"A man want you," Maria said in her deeply accented voice.

"Send him in."

Maria hurried out of the office and Monchats straightened up in his chair. Less than a minute later, a man with dark skin, a baby-smooth face, shiny bald head, and expensive pinstriped business suit walked through the doors. Monchats had already known he was coming, it was one of B.L.'s men. A newbie, just learning the ways of the Monchats organization.

As he walked closer, Monchats noticed that the man really looked more like a boy. He couldn't have been more than twenty. Before the young man could speak, Monchats thought it best to set the parameters of their upcoming conversation.

"This place is like a library and you know what they say about librarians," Monchats said sternly. He decided to remain seated at his desk.

"The library's operations were explained to me," the young man responded as his eyes shifted left to right. He was trying to take in his surroundings, but tried to give the appearance he didn't care about where he was and the significance of what he was doing. Monchats could tell he was nervous.

"So what do you have?" Monchats asked.

The dark-skinned man walked up to desk and placed a folded white sheet of paper on the edge of the desk. He then stepped back into his original position.

Monchats took the note and opened it slowly. He read the note carefully.

There will be more things cold at Timken than the concrete.

Monchats crumpled the letter in his hands, closed his eyes. He was lost in thought and almost forgot the man was standing in front of his desk. B.L. had trained him well. The man knew better than to disturb him or speak before he had been spoken to.

"Thank you for coming to visit. I enjoyed our conversation," Monchats said, pointing towards the doors.

The young man nodded his head and replied, "Thank you for the opportunity." He turned around and walked out of the door.

After the man left, Monchats began thinking about Denise again. He tried to remain strong, but his daughter's death wore on his heart. He didn't want to accept the fact that he could have been partly to blame for her death. In an unprecedented move, he ordered everyone out of his home, a large, brick mansion on the Near East Side of the city. The maids, groundskeepers, and even his chauffer were given the rest of the day off. He directed guards to stand outside the entrance of his home. There were also guards at the front gate. When he was sure the house was empty, he walked up the large circular staircase in the front hallway and went to his bedroom to do something he hadn't done since he watched his mother take her last breath. He cried.

Chapter Fifteen

Strive to take the lead at all times.
A follower will eventually be led down
the wrong path.
—The Qualities of Chess Masters # 235

March 31, 2:45 P.M.

Bailey B.L. Langston sat in the back of his black Cadillac Escalade, mind racing as the vehicle traveled to the north side of Columbus. Even though he didn't drink coffee anymore, he felt jittery and anxious, like he had been injected with a dose of caffeine. He knew the cause of his current state—the Brown Recluse—Sola Nichols.

He was surprised when she agreed to meet him after what she had done. He knew Sola had guts, in fact, he always thought she harbored deep mental issues, but she must have known she wasn't getting a dime. This time, there was no reprieve for the Brown Recluse.

He pondered for a moment whether she knew the extent of her misfortune. Could she be that ignorant? It was a fleeting thought. There was no way Sola didn't know about Denise's death. The headline blazed on the newspaper like a guiding light and the television and talk radio stations were providing up-to-date coverage. The deaths hung in the air and lingered on the tips of wagging tongues all over the city.

B.L. knew Denise's death should have upset him, but he was indifferent. He didn't even blink when he identified her lifeless body. His lack of emotion wasn't a mark of disloyalty. He had long ago displaced the most human emotion he could muster. For all intensive purposes, he was an animal. Above all, he relied on instinct, and the primal need to survive by any means necessary.

"Hey, B," his driver, Cole, said. "Phone for you." Cole reached back with one hand to give B.L. a cell phone while keeping his other hand on the wheel.

B.L. took the phone. "Who's calling me on your phone?" he asked. B.L. knew Cole wouldn't just give anyone access to him, but he had to be sure.

"It's Ruben," Cole responded.

Ruben was a newbie, trying to get his feet wet. When B.L. first met him, he was still doing low-level slinging on the North Side. At first, B.L. suspected that Ruben was just some wannabe teenager, but he soon found out he was twenty-three years old. A baby face went a long way.

B.L. thought Ruben had potential, so he had him cleaned up for the management side of the business. No more late nights on street corners dressed in baggy pants and XXXXL T-shirts for Ruben. B.L. gave him some money for some nice suits and shoes and sent him to his personal stylist. Ruben wondered why B.L. chose him, and B.L. told him to never ask questions, just accept the hand he was given. Yes, B.L. had plans for Ruben, and he recently discovered he had been right about his young, handsome, dark-skinned apprentice. B.L. sighed and put the phone to his ear. "What up, Rookie?" he asked.

"I didn't know if I should call you on your cell, so I

thought I'd reach you through Cole," Ruben replied, his voice wavering. "I just met with Monchats."

B.L. smiled. He still marveled at how grown men shook in their shoes when they first met the Menace.

"Did he go for your throat?" B.L. asked, stifling a laugh.

"What?" Ruben asked.

"Nothing. You just sound scared. You need to relax."

"Oh, I'm cool," Ruben's voice sounded more sure.

B.L. relaxed in his seat. "I just need to know about your conversation. Nothing more, nothing less."

"I, um, just gave him what you told me to and then he thanked me for visiting and then I left."

"You did good, Rookie," B.L. said.

"Thanks." Ruben sounded calm.

"I need to take care of some things on the street, but maybe you can hook up with me and the crew later on."

"I know you told me earlier that you wanted to meet at your place at 8 P.M., but I—"

"Don't get shaky now, Rookie," B.L. said. "I know things may be moving a little fast for you, but now that you're on my team, you've got to understand that everything is going to be different."

"Oh, don't get me bent," Ruben responded. "I'm looking forward to getting together."

B.L. interrupted him. "Remember whose line you're towing." B.L. had to remind Ruben they were talking on Cole's phone. He didn't want Ruben to get too excited and mention things better left unsaid. He knew Cole couldn't overhear what Ruben was saying, but he never took chances.

"I understand," Ruben said mechanically. "I'll meet you at your place, 8 P.M, so don't be late," he teased.

"Later then." B.L. closed the flip phone and tossed it over the front seat.

"Rookies," Cole said. "Can't live with them, but can't shoot 'em because you need them." he laughed.

B.L. returned the laughter. It was easy to joke around with Cole, the only man he trusted behind the wheel of his Cady other than himself. B.L. directed Cole to turn on the DVD player so he could watch a movie before the meeting with Sola. Columbus Auto Customs had recently installed the latest in plasma screen technology in the backs of his SUV seats. B.L. had a wide choice of movies to choose from, but he was feeling a bit like *Scarface*.

"Cole, start it up," B.L. said. "But don't drive off the road trying to watch Al Pacino do his thing," he warned. He also had a screen installed in the steering wheel because he knew Cole liked to watch movies and play video games from time to time.

As the movie started playing, B.L.'s thoughts returned to Sola. Would she show up? He really didn't know. But it was worth the traveling to make sure. He had told the boys to be ready for anything. He knew Sola was dangerous, and she wouldn't hesitate to kill, especially if she knew what was waiting for her.

He remembered when Sola was young, before she lost the rest of her innocence at the hands of Monchats. B.L. and Sola had never really been close friends. At best, they were associates working toward a common goal. But there was a time when he felt slightly sorry for her, even taught her a few things.

As the years passed and Sola became more ruthless, their fragile bond moved towards its breaking point. They argued constantly, became like oil and water. B.L. used to think Sola was just going through the last throes of her teenage years, but he learned there was more going on with the Brown Recluse.

At first, he thought she was betraying Monchats. He

started following her, watching her every move. Sometimes she would sit around in Franklin Park staring at the sky. Other days, she would drive around the city for hours. She was acting like someone with a lot on her mind, maybe the Feds were trying to get to her.

B.L. told Monchats about his concerns, but Monchats dismissed them. He thought the world of his young ingénue.

"I will never have to worry about Sola," Monchats told him. "Each time she takes a life, the more she becomes like us. Ruthless and beyond reproach."

Over time, it seemed that Monchats had been right. Sola became a true soldier. But B.L. had never been able to get that nagging feeling out of his head. He knew Sola was never meant to be a cold-blooded killer. She was like a wild lion that Monchats tried to tame. One day she would turn on him.

B.L. wanted to destroy Sola, but Monchats was behind her all the way. And when Sola found out about B.L.'s attempts to have her removed from the organization, she set out on her own mission. Eventually she discovered B.L.'s greatest secret, and with it, a sense of protection from him.

"I think I'll let you live," she told him coldly one day after she informed him of her knowledge of his extracurricular activities. "The suffering you'll face from always wondering if I'll open your closet is much more satisfying than watching you die."

Since that day, he worked behind the scenes to end her life. He had knowledge of his own, and he knew it would shake her to her core. He told the right people, and made sure it got back to Sola. And when she slipped just over two and a half years ago, he was sure he would help her complete the fall. He made the preparations, and rejoiced in the thought of Sola's death. But once again, the tide turned in her favor. He hated her for her luck.

"B. We're here," Cole said, interrupting B.L.'s thoughts.

B.L. looked up. They were parked on a side street right next to the old Timken plant. "Tell the boys to be on their guard," B.L. told Cole.

Cole reached for the door. "And what about you?" Cole asked.

"Oh, I'm staying in the EXT," B.L. responded. "I'll let the rats do the dirty work," he joked.

Cole opened the door and stepped out the car. "Sure thing," he said as he started to close the door.

B.L. thought of Sola once again. Knowing her, she would come bearing gifts, as in bullets wrapped in the barrel of a gun.

"And Cole," he said, "after you get done talking with the boys, I suggest you return to the truck."

Cole nodded and closed the door. B.L. looked at his watch. It was almost time.

Chapter Sixteen

Sola's Story, Part VIII – 1992

When I woke up, I was lying in a hospital bed. My brain was foggy, but an unusual blend of disinfectant, medicine, sick folks, and whatever else was in the hospital air cleared my senses. I felt . . . empty. Lost. Something was missing. I could feel it in my core.

I glanced at the tubes sticking in my arms to fill me up with fluid and then I let my eyes travel slowly down to my stomach. I didn't want to believe what happened to me, but I knew. The emptiness I felt inside was more than the fogginess of regaining consciousness. My baby was gone. Josiah. My "fire of the Lord" was extinguished.

Momma was there when I woke up. She was asleep. Her head was nestled on the side of the bed and her hand held my tube-free hand. My right leg was bound in a white cast and I felt a dull pain coursing through my body.

Momma seemed to sense that I was awake. Her head rose

and she rubbed her eyes. "Honey child, you okay?" Momma asked, her voice thick from resting.

I stared at her and then slowly shifted my eyes to my now empty womb. Then I looked at Momma again. She was staring at my stomach.

"Is he—" I started to ask, already knowing the answer but not wanting to accept the truth. My hands started traveling to my stomach.

Momma didn't let me finish my question. "Please, don't worry about that now, honey child. You just need to get your strength back. People have been asking about you," Momma said.

I didn't care about *people*, I cared only about my child, the breath of life that my body had exhaled. My son. I knew I was going to have a boy. It was a feeling. And now my son was dead. Josiah. Tears started to fall down my cheeks. Momma reached up to wipe them away.

"You may not want to hear this now, but the doctor says you'll be able to have more kids. Maybe it just wasn't your time," Momma said as she reached for a tissue and continued to wipe tears from my face.

I stared at the ceiling, the tears still flowing down my cheeks. "My time was now," I said, my voice cracking as I spoke. "We both know why my baby is gone."

Momma looked into my eyes, but her gaze quickly lowered. Maybe she saw the emptiness inside of me. I followed her eyes as they settled on her hands, which she had intertwined with one of mine. "You don't know how sorry he feels, Sola. He's been torn up-"

I interrupted her. "I don't want to talk about it," I said flatly, trying to mask the hate that was welling up inside of me. Once again, the perfect opportunity presented itself. I could have exposed him, let Momma know her man's true nature. But my mind was beginning to work. Plans were forming in my brain. I felt it best not to disturb the water before my ship sailed.

"I know. It's hard for you now. Maybe we can talk about it later." Momma paused and then changed the subject. "You know Trina and your other girlfriends have been wanting to see you," she said, displaying a pained smile in what I figured was her way to try and comfort me.

I turned my attention once again to the tile ceiling. I didn't want to talk to Trina's nosy ass, or anyone else for that matter.

"I just want to be left alone," I said softly as I blinked away the remaining tears in my eyes.

"I understand, honey child. I just wanted to let you know that your friends have been asking about you," Momma said, stroking my hair.

I closed my eyes and acted like I was asleep. Soon, I heard Momma get up and leave the room. I opened my eyes and stared at the ceiling again. I placed my hand on my stomach and the tears started to flow again. I forced myself to stop. *"Now is not the time for tears,"* I told myself. It was time for revenge. *An eye for an eye and a tooth for a tooth.* At that moment, I knew that a life would be taken for my baby's life. Rocky was going to die.

Chapter Seventeen

In order to maintain your advantage,
it is sometimes best to take a step back
and assess your opponent's strategy.
—The Qualities of Chess Masters # 251

March 31, 3:15 P.M

A honking horn jolted Sola out of her daydream. She was in the parking lot of Abdullah's Fish Market on Joyce and Woodland. She had been there for a couple of hours, stopping there to refuel and assess her options.

After arriving at the Market, she picked up a fish sandwich and a bottle of water, and then she returned to her car. She felt fairly safe on Woodland, as there wasn't much activity there during the day. She didn't realize how hungry she was until the smell of the sandwich reached her nose. She was normally a careful eater, but she woofed down her sandwich like she was feeling the effects of some of Monchats's weed.

When she finished her meal, she started the Honda and drove to the side of the building near the employees' cars. She unzipped her jacket and tried to view the wound the morning gunshot inflicted. Instead, she was greeted with a mass of dried blood and its accompanying metallic smell. She could tell she had lost a fair amount of blood, but at least the bleeding had stopped. Not knowing when one of Abdullah's employees would come outside, she decided to wait to clean and examine the wound.

She thought briefly about aborting the Timken meeting and returning to her house, but that was out of the question. By now, her house was nuclear. There was no telling who was inside or outside. She couldn't risk that. Timken was the better choice. She knew B.L. was too stupid to plan anything well, especially her death. He liked to display an explicit show of force, instead of the discreet strength of a true warrior. Since the fools under him thought he was God, they would follow his lead. And Sola didn't suffer any fools.

The horn honked again. She heard a man yelling, "Hey, you're in my space. Employees only!"

Sola raised her hand and really wanted to give the man the finger, but she waved instead. She started the car and backed out of the parking space. She noticed the time on the dashboard of the Honda. Timken was only five minutes away from her current location. She didn't want to be early, so she decided to take the long way so she would make it to Timken just in time.

Sola drove down Joyce to Seventeenth Avenue. She turned and kept traveling west until she reached the freeway. She was happy the Honda Abdul gave her rode smoothly. She merged into the highway traffic moving onto I-71 South and proceeded to take the 11th Avenue exit. She drove past the Linden Café and turned right onto Cleveland Avenue.

On another day, she might have taken the time to marvel at the changes taking place in the Linden Corridor at the four corners of Cleveland and 11th. She could remember a time when the Linden area, home of the former Windsor Terrace Projects, was considered the roughest part of Columbus. Now, there was a state-of-the-art COTA bus station housed in a modern brick building, a police substation, and several businesses.

People who wouldn't even drive past Linden only seven years ago were now purchasing some of the newly-built homes a couple of blocks away from the corridor. The only thing that reminded people of Old Linden was the Columbus Metropolitan Housing Authority Building on 11th, the only place in Columbus to apply for Section 8 Housing. But all of the misery and stress of poor folks trying to get government assistance was hidden inside of a brick building that shined like a new penny.

Like any unfinished plan, the freshest of renewal was replaced by the reality of inner city life as Sola drove past Camden Avenue, headed towards 5th Avenue. There were several boarded up homes and businesses in various states of decay. As she neared the congested intersection of 5th and Cleveland, several fast food restaurants and gas stations came into view. The smell of chicken from Bland's Chicken Shack made her stomach stir. She couldn't believe her stomach was grumbling again. She had just eaten a couple of hours ago.

As she waited at the red light, she stared at the great concrete graveyard of the once famous Timken factory. At one time, the factory was one of Columbus's biggest employers, but now it only served as a garden for the weeds that broke through the concrete with mindless abandon. It reminded her of a desert: dry, desolate, and inhospitable for humankind.

As Sola stared at the fence-enclosed property, she knew it probably wasn't the best idea to go there, but she had to know what she was up against. The light turned green. She knew she would only have one pass. She had to make it count. She pressed the Honda's accelerator, quickly achieving the thirty-five mile-per-hour speed limit. She already held her nine millimeter in her hand. The passenger-side window was down, allowing a soft breeze to circulate the air in the car.

Her eyes focused on the great expanse of concrete and weeds. Construction materials wrapped in large, white bundles were stacked on a small portion of the huge lot. On the edge of the lot, another two blocks further, stood three one-story windowless gray buildings, only accessible by a side street. She turned on her signal light and began to slow down. If the street was blocked, it would take a great deal of effort to escape. But it was worth the gamble.

As she turned onto the side street, she immediately noticed B.L.'s black Cadillac Escalade EXT. She also recognized the smaller Ford Explorer painted with custom crystallized purple and spinners. It belonged to Sizzle, one of B.L.'s thugs. She didn't recognize the third vehicle, a black Lincoln Navigator with tinted windows. She wondered who it belonged to. Two men dressed in dark suits stood outside of the vehicles. She caught a glimpse of silver in one of the men's hands—a gun. She couldn't make out their faces, but it didn't matter. They wanted to embrace her with a coat of lead. It was just as she thought. Monchats was not taking any prisoners. And neither was she.

She sped up quickly, pressing the accelerator almost to the car floor and straining the Honda for all it was worth. The men noticed her, but it was too late. She drove past them, aimed her gun and fired off shots until her clip was almost empty. She jerked the car onto a smaller cross street and headed back toward Cleveland Avenue.

She sped to the highway, returning to I-71 and heading north. *Damn*, she thought, shaking her head. Her intuition told her she didn't capture the prize she wanted most—the man who was trying to kill her. Sola also knew she didn't kill B.L., and she had no shame in admitting to herself that she would have been overjoyed to see his body lying out on the road. Over the years, they had both benefited from a shaky truce. They kept it strictly business. But now B.L. had crossed the line, and his heart was still beating. It would have to stop soon, and permanently.

She picked up her cell phone and dialed B.L.'s number. She punched in her code. She knew B.L. would answer the phone, even if it was only to threaten and try to intimidate her.

The call connected. Sola heard B.L. breathing heavily, but he didn't speak. She decided to speak first.

"I see you're still alive, that's unfortunate," she said. Her tone was crisp and unsympathetic. She wanted to bait him, make him angry.

"You fucking bitch! You're done," B.L. said harshly. It sounded as if he wanted to do some baiting of his own.

"I promised you before that you'd be taking your last breath before me, and I like to keep my promises," Sola said.

"Well, why don't you come and show me how good you are, bitch?" B.L. asked angrily.

"Does calling me outside my name make you feel good?" Sola was caught up in the moment, wishing that B.L. was standing in front of her so she could show him just how much of a bitch she was. "I mean, I could call you a fat ass bastard, but I choose not to. But don't worry, you'll feel my wrath soon enough, believe that."

"The only life you need to worry about is your own."

"I'll keep that in mind." Sola had enough of B.L. She knew his time would end soon. "I'll see you in hell," she said coldly.

"Not if I see you first," B.L. spat out.

Sola ended the call. The conversation got her juices flowing and gave her perspective. B.L. had always underestimated her, from the first time they met until now. His attitude always struck a nerve—her last one. She dialed another number and listened as the phone began ringing. After the fifth ring, she got anxious. She didn't want the phone to go to voicemail.

"Pick up, dammit," she mumbled to herself. As if on cue, the phone clicked. Someone picked up the phone.

"What up?" a man asked.

"I need to keep this short, okay," Sola responded, silently sighing with relief that her associate answered her call.

"There would be only one reason why you'd be calling me," the man said inquisitively.

"Right, take care of him as soon as possible," Sola advised.

"And what about my ends?" the man asked.

Sola smiled. In the end, it was all about the money. "You will be paid as we agreed."

"I'm glad to hear it. I'll get on it right away. Should I contact you when I'm done?"

Sola shook her head as she talked into the phone. "No. Don't call me. As I'm sure you know, I have some real heat on me right now and being available for conversation is not my top priority right now. I'll know when the deed is done. And I trust you'll be a total professional."

"I learned from the best." The man's voice was suddenly animated, excited from anticipation.

Sola felt an ironic sense of pride. "Well then, do me proud," she said before she ended the call.

Sola looked in the rearview mirror several times, but it didn't appear she had been followed. She thought briefly about acquiring another car, but didn't know if it was worth the risk. She had to remain mobile as long as possible.

As she continued north, she felt a tinge of pain in her shoulder and felt slightly lightheaded. She didn't know if it was due to hunger or the loss of blood. She would have to take care of her injury soon. She turned on the radio and tuned into the classical music station. The mellow tones of string and wind instruments calmed her nerves.

Within ten minutes, Sola reached the Polaris exit off I-71. She drove to Capps and ordered a donut and an iced cappuccino. She generally avoided sweets to keep her body in check. She tried to stay away from caffeine, too. She knew she would pay for it later, but she needed the sugar rush. It wasn't long before she felt more alert and began to feel better.

She parked in the large lot of the Polaris Mall and thought about her options. For once, she almost hated the fact that she had no one to turn to—*well, almost no one.* She reached for the gift box and fingered the small bow on the lid. She didn't have many options, and she didn't like being forced to play her hand so soon. But decisions had been made before she finished the job that ended Monchats's daughter's life.

She started the car and headed down the Parkway until she reached the Polaris Park Executive Arms Apartment Complex. She glanced at the gift box, which she had placed in the passenger's seat of the car. She began to feel nervous. *I have to do this,* she thought. She then parked the car and stared at the huge expanse of impressive brick buildings surrounded by immaculate landscaping.

Sola grabbed her belongings and prepared to get out of the car, until she saw a couple walking in her direction. The windows of the Honda were darkly tinted, so she knew the couple wouldn't see her, but their presence made her hesitate. She let her seat back and stared at the sky through the windshield. Despite her misgivings, she knew she would have to get out of the car. She heard a car start up nearby and she thought briefly about the couple. She closed her eyes, convincing herself it wouldn't hurt to wait a while before she reached her destination. She knew it was almost time.

Chapter Eighteen

Sola's Story, Part IX – 1992

Even though I wanted Rocky to die, I didn't know how I would do it. It was like a seed ready to burst. I just needed the right conditions to make my plan grow. I spent three days in the hospital, and another five weeks on bedrest. Since my leg was broken, I spent more time sitting around the house until the cast was taken off.

Momma didn't make me go to school, not that I would have gone even if she insisted. Too many people thought they knew what went down with Rocky, and I didn't want to hear the questions or the whispers. Based on Trina's gossip, most people thought me and Momma got into a fight over my now revealed baby. Rocky was running interference to stop a family confrontation. The result of our supposed argument was a fall down the stairs and a trip to the hospital. Trina had the nerve to be mad at me for not telling her about the baby.

"I thought we was better than that," Trina told me.

"Look, I'm not trying to be rude, but I didn't want the whole west side of Columbus to know I was pregnant," I replied.

"Well, I guess your plan worked," Trina said sarcastically.

I think I would have punched her in the mouth if I would have been able to stand up. I couldn't stand her sometimes, but eventually we were cool again. We were more like sisters than friends.

I shied away from my other friends and stayed to myself. Momma was nice enough to borrow some books from the library for me. She chose the romantic stuff, but it satisfied. She started staying home more and buying things for me. I guess she was trying to let me know how bad she felt.

As for Rocky, he was nowhere in sight. Momma never talked about him and I never saw him. I knew that Momma was still dealing with him, and still traveling for him to do business. All she saw was the dollar signs. For her, Rocky was the path to never being broke again. And if that meant she had to look past what happened and believe his lie that he didn't mean for me to fall down the stairs, then so be it.

I knew that I would see Rocky again. I figured he had to wonder what I said about him—if I would rat him out to Momma or the cops. He had to wonder why he hadn't been arrested yet. I would use his uncertainty to my advantage, to nurture the seed.

As the days went on and I continued to heal, the depths of my longing to end Rocky's life grew stronger. Every time I thought about my baby, my son, and his death, I thought of Rocky dying by my hands. After exploring my options, I finally decided that shooting Rocky was the best choice. After all, there were so many gun deaths in the Gardens and other projects that it wouldn't seem out of the ordinary. And getting a gun was easy. There were so many pieces in the 'hood and they all came from one place. I didn't have to worry about a thing.

I sought out Truth, a dark-skinned brother from Jamaica who dealt guns in the Gardens and other areas on the west side. He was in his early twenties and well entrenched in the game. I knew him from hanging out over Trina's because he was friends with her boyfriend.

Truth lived in the last townhouse building in the Gardens. As I walked along the path of broken concrete and badly mowed grass to Truth's place, people were staring and whispering but I didn't care. I knew I was the soap opera of the moment.

I knew everyone knew about the fall, but of course, that was "accidental." But when did I get pregnant? And the even greater question, who was the baby's father? Those were the big questions for the gossipers and the know-it-alls. It was the classic *Maury Povich Show* scenario. I could hear it now: "And Rocky, the blood test shows with 99.9% accuracy that you are the father!" Wouldn't the nosy people be surprised to find out?

I knocked on Truth's door. A dark-skinned woman answered the door. She wore a dingy, white T-shirt with the words 'Black African Princess' imprinted on it and cut-off jean shorts. Her blonde-dyed, short relaxed hair stood up on her head like she was playing in a light socket with a hairpin. Her dark legs were ashy and she smelled of sweat and weed. Her eyes were bloodshot and I could tell she was higher than a kite.

"Watchyu want?" she asked, her words slurring.

"I'm looking for Truth," I responded.

"Ain't we all?" The woman asked.

She obviously thought her little joke was funny, because she tilted her head back and began laughing hysterically, exposing her bad breath and a set of jacked up teeth. I wasn't in the mood for The Original Crackhead Queen of Comedy, but I didn't want her to think I was being uppity or rude because, for the time being, she was literally standing in the way of me and Truth. I smiled widely and nodded my head.

The woman kept laughing, holding her stomach and bending over slightly. She finally regained some composure and looked at me.

"C'mon in," she finally said, her chest heaving up and down as she caught her breath.

I thought Truth's place would be a mess by the look of the woman who answered his door, but despite her unkempt look, Truth's townhouse was very neat. He had the ghetto standard black leather couch, a love seat and chair. Incenses were burning, but they couldn't block out the smell of weed. I hoped I wouldn't get a contact high.

The woman disappeared upstairs and a couple of minutes later, Truth came down. He was tall and skinny with well-kept dreads that flowed down his back.

"How 'er doin' gurl?" he asked with a thick Jamaican accent.

"I'm cool," I replied.

"I 'erd 'bout yo illness."

I lowered my eyes. "I'm cool," I repeated. I was sure I sounded like an old stuck vinyl record.

"Well, watchyu need 'ere?" He motioned for me to sit down on the couch. He sat down in a plaid chair next to the couch.

I didn't want to waste time, so I just came out with it. "I need a gun."

Truth's eyes widened. "Did I 'ere you right, gurl?"

"I didn't stutter, did I? I need a gun." I had to be stern so Truth would understand I was serious.

Truth continued to stare at me, and I could tell his mind

was working. He wanted to ask me questions, but he knew that it was better not to. He only needed to decide to let me have a gun or turn me away.

He looked at me for what seemed like thirty minutes, when it was probably more like five. "Yo know 'ow to shoot a piece?" he asked me.

I hadn't thought about that. "No," I replied.

Truth shook his head, presumably in disbelief. "Yo don't tink yo should learn 'fore yo go off wit a gun?"

I couldn't believe it. He was going to turn me away. I knew that if I didn't get a gun from Truth, my chances for finding another one were slim. I didn't know anyone else to get a gun from. Anyone who needed a piece in the Gardens came to Truth.

"Can I trust you?" I asked, quickly thinking of a story to tell.

"Yo can't trust no one, gurl."

"But you know how to keep things quiet?"

Truth's eyes widened again. "Why?"

"Look, Truth, I need that gun. You're the only one I know I can get one from." I pulled out a wad of money from my pocket. "You can have all of this. But if I don't get a piece, I think someone's going to take me out."

I dumped the money on the glass coffee table. It was at least nine hundred dollars. Truth glanced at the wrinkled money and put up his hand.

"I don't want to 'ere yo story. Watchyu do is watchyu do." He rose from the chair and grabbed the cash. "I'll be back." He walked up the stairs.

Once he left, my hands started shaking. Could I really do it? I put my hand on my stomach. *For you, yes.* After a couple of minutes, Truth came back down the stairs carrying a brown paper bag. I got off the couch and met him at the bottom of the stairs.

"This 'ere is a small piece, not so much po'er fo yo." He handed the bag to me.

"What's a gun worth if it don't got no power?" I asked.

"It'll do what's it meant to do, gurl. It's loaded, no safety, so yo bet be sho when yo aim it."

I stared at the bag and began to open it, but Truth stopped me. "Do dat on yo on time, gurl." He walked to the door and opened it.

I walked to the door. "Thanks," I said as I stepped outside.

Truth looked at me strangely. "Don't mention it." His command was clear and lacked his leisurely Jamaican tone. I knew exactly what he meant.

I walked back home quickly and couldn't wait to close the door. I reached down into the bag and pulled out the small, black gun. It almost looked like a toy, but it was too heavy. Truth was right, it was loaded. I could see the tiny bullets in the six circular chambers near the base of the gun.

I went to my bedroom. Momma had bought me a whole new bedroom set, mattresses and everything. I decided to hide the gun under my bed. I lay down, thinking about what I would do next. Now that I had my weapon, I needed my prey. I would have to lead Rocky to his doom.

Chapter Nineteen

A successful player must always be willing to sacrifice.
—The Qualities of Chess Masters # 302

March 31, 4:00 P.M

The Hunter turned into the gas station and smiled slightly. Sola had been here, he thought. It was almost as if he could smell her scent. Once he had a minute to analyze the situation, it was easy to find out where she had gone; too easy in fact. He wondered if Sola was truly on top of her game.

HotPhonz, a pre-paid cell phone company, was known for the first three digits of the phone numbers that came with each phone: 614. The same three numbers were the city's area code. When B.L. told him that Sola contacted him from the number 614-614-5476, he couldn't believe his luck. There were only five locations in Columbus selling pre-paid HotPhonz phones. All of the locations were Arab-owned and four of the stores were on Main Street on the city's East Side. The fifth location was Smith's Gas Station on Hilliard-Rome Road.

Normally, the Hunter would have dismissed the far west

side location and focused on Main Street, but then he remembered Abdul. It was well-known that Sola assassinated one of Abdul's rivals so Abdul could purchase the gas station. She had slipped then, too, using the same nine-millimeter handgun linked to a murder one of Monchats's men had taken the fall for. The cops put so much heat on Monchats's businesses that he couldn't operate at full capacity for months. Despite the trouble, Monchats forgave Sola because he knew her skills were otherwise unmatched.

He got out of the car and headed toward the convenience store located past the filling stations. He had to act quickly because the employees from the businesses surrounding the gas station would be leaving work soon. For now, the store was almost empty. *Perfect*, he thought.

The Hunter milled about until the last customer left the store. He grabbed a pack of gum and some potato chips and went to the counter. A young Arab man checked him out. After he received his change, the Hunter asked the man about Abdul. The Arab looked at him strangely, picked up a phone and started speaking in Arabic. *He's been asked this question before today*, The Hunter thought.

The Hunter heard a door swing open behind him and hard footsteps. He turned around slowly.

"May I help you?" Abdul asked him.

"Abdul?" The Hunter asked.

"Yes, May I help you please?" Abdul nodded and smiled.

The Hunter placed his gum and chips back on the counter. "Yes, I need to speak with you about a personal matter," he said.

Abdul regarded him for a moment, looking him up and down. Abdul extended a hand toward the door that he had just exited from and replied, "Of course."

The Hunter followed Abdul into the room. Before Abdul could walk behind the desk, he pulled out his gun and said,

"I prefer you stand up." Abdul turned around slowly and his eyes widened as he stared at the Hunter's gun. "Raise your hands, slowly," the Hunter commanded, "but don't make any sudden moves or sounds. If you do, I'll be forced to kill you. Do you understand?"

Abdul nodded. The Hunter could see the lump forming in the Arab man's throat. He motioned his gun to the wall, and Abdul stood against it. "I'm going to ask you some questions. I strongly suggest that you give truthful answers. If I find out you're lying, it will be difficult for you."

Abdul nodded again.

"I'll start with something easy. Do you know Soledad Nichols?" the Hunter asked. Abdul nodded. "I'm not into sign language. I'm going to need to hear you speak," the Hunter said as he moved closer to the Arab. "Once again. Do you know Soledad Nichols?"

"Yes," Abdul responded.

"Good. Question Two: Has she purchased a pre-paid phone from you recently?" He positioned the gun toward Abdul's head.

"No." Abdul shook his head as he answered the question.

The gun clicked. "Do I look like I'm playing with you?" the Hunter asked, raising his voice. He felt himself getting angry and knew he had to relax. Allowing his emotions to take over could lead him to make a mistake.

The Hunter continued. "Presume I know everything and I just need you to confirm. Has Soledad Nichols purchased a phone from you?"

"Not purchased," Abdul stammered. "I gave it to her."

"And when was that?"

"I can not remember."

The Hunter was irritated. He couldn't believe Abdul still had the nerve to lie to him. He obviously didn't take him seriously.

"Do you really want to die because of that bitch?" he asked Abdul. The Arab man opened his mouth to respond, but the Hunter raised his other hand to stop him.

"You don't have to answer that one," the Hunter said. "But I need you to tell me the truth for your own good. Question Three—and think carefully: Was Soledad here today?"

Abdul's eyes shifted to the floor by his desk. He followed Abdul's glance, and noticed dried blood by one the black chairs.

"I don't have your answer," the Hunter said sternly.

"I saw her, yes," Abdul said, his lips trembling.

"And you gave her a phone?" He glared at Abdul, feeding off of the Arab's fear of not knowing what was going to happen next.

"Yes," Abdul said softly.

"And what is the phone number?" He asked. He was finally getting somewhere.

"I do not know," Abdul responded as he closed his eyes.

The Hunter walked up to Abdul and pressed the gun against his cheek. "Who the fuck do you think you're dealing with?" he yelled. "I know you keep the records of phone numbers from the company. You have one more chance. What is the number?"

Abdul swallowed hard. "My clerk, he set it up. He will have the number."

"Good. Now I'm going to pick up the phone so you can talk to your clerk and get the number. Don't make any sudden moves. Do you understand?"

"Yes," Abdul said.

The Hunter reached over the desk and picked up the phone with one hand, while keeping his gun trained on Abdul with his other hand. "What do I dial to get your clerk?"

"Just press one," Abdul replied.

The Hunter pressed the number and handed the phone to Abdul. Abdul started speaking Arabic into the phone receiver. The Hunter pressed the gun to Abdul's lips and he stopped speaking. "English only," the Hunter ordered.

Abdul was sweating now, tiny beads of salt and water were streaming down his face. He spoke cautiously, asking the clerk for the number.

"Yes, the woman," Abdul said. "Her number, I need it." As the clerk gave him the numbers, Abdul repeated them. His intuition had been right. Sola had changed phones.

After Abdul was finished, he gave the Hunter the receiver and he put it one the base. "Do you need to write down her number?" Abdul asked him.

"I'm the one asking questions, but I'll grant you an answer. No, I don't need to write down her number. I have an excellent memory." *Especially when it comes to Sola*, the Hunter thought to himself.

"Question four: Did you give her anything else other than the phone?" the Hunter asked.

Abdul swallowed hard again. "No."

One lie was bad enough, but two lies were unacceptable. The Hunter had enough of the question and answer session with Abdul. He backed up, pointed the gun at Abdul's head, and fired. With the silencer attached to the gun, the shot was almost noiseless. Abdul's dead body falling to the floor made more noise than the actual gunshot itself.

He walked up to Abdul's lifeless body. A large pool of blood was forming below what remained of the Arab man's head. The wall beside him was splattered with blood and pieces of flesh, hair, brain tissue, and bone fragments from the dead man's skull.

"I don't like being lied to," the Hunter said harshly as he kicked the corpse's leg. "The answer was yes."

He heard knocking on the door and a flurry of Arabic. He

assumed it was the young clerk and told him to come in. As the door opened, he grabbed the clerk and pulled him into the room. The clerk glanced at his former employer lying on the floor and started to yell. The Hunter fired one more shot and the clerk joined his employer among the dead.

The Hunter stepped over Abdul's body and went to the video monitoring system. He rewound the tape and pushed play. All he saw were people walking in and out of the store and pumping gas. Nothing familiar, as in the Recluse herself. That meant Abdul had changed the tapes. *And for what?* he thought as he kicked Abdul's corpse again. He ejected the remaining tape from the recorder. He would have to take it with him. He turned off all of the monitors and studied the room quickly before walking out the office door.

He noticed a woman at the counter. He walked past her briskly, not even taking the time to get her description. He didn't want her to catch a glimpse of his face. He knew the police would be coming to the gas station soon. Although he knew eyewitnesses were notoriously unreliable, he didn't want to linger around long enough for the woman to even think that she knew what he looked like.

"Do you work here?" he heard the woman ask as he walked through the automatic doors.

Typical, the Hunter thought, ignoring her and continuing the path to his car. He drove off quickly, heading back towards the freeway. All of the pieces were almost in place. He had his bit of fun with Sola, made her think hard, made her run. He drove east towards downtown. It was almost time for the game to end.

Chapter Twenty

Sola's Story, Part X – 1993

A fourteen-year-old girl should not know the power of her pussy. The strength of the magic between a woman's thighs can cause wars between nations and bring down empires. Once a man catches a whiff of the wonderful essence of life, and knows he has to have it, a woman can get anything she wants.

Most chicks never realize their true pussy potential. They waste it on men who don't want them, don't respect them, or don't appreciate them. But for those of us who understand what we have, we wield it cautiously. Good pussy is like a drug. Men can become addicts. They become controlling, and they won't let the pussy go willingly. They will steal for it, beat a woman for it, and threaten their mommas and their families. And truth be told, good pussy will make a man kill, not only himself, but anyone who stands in the way of his sweet stuff, even the woman it belongs to.

I discovered my power and in the end, that was all I had to

use to get Rocky right where I wanted him. I waited until the time was right, until his defenses were down. I knew he wouldn't be able to stay away.

Momma was the key, of course, although she didn't know it. She remained ignorant and I remained silent. I knew I couldn't do it without her, and I didn't care if I had to use her to get what I wanted. I blamed her. It may not have been right, but I did. Not for everything, I mean, I knew she didn't make Rocky do the things he did to me. But I blamed her for not being there. I blamed her for not believing me. I blamed her for continuing to maintain contact with him. And I blamed her most for choosing to be ignorant. She should have known the type of man he was after what he did to me. A part of me wanted her to pay too.

After three months, she started mentioning Rocky's name every now and then. Then she brought home some books about chess, but I knew the source. Momma was into "love-everlasting" books, not kings and pawns. Something told me Rocky got those books for me, and I accepted them with a smile on my face and hate in my heart.

When I was alone, I would take out my gun and hold it in my hands. I was scared at first, but then I got used to feeling the steel with my fingers. I didn't want to practice with it because I was afraid I would accidentally pull the trigger and put a hole in the wall. And all of the bullets in my gun had been reserved for Rocky.

Since I couldn't practice firing my gun, I used other tools to help me with aiming. Everything from a screwdriver to old dolls became training tools. *You better be sure when you aim it,* Truth told me. I wanted to be sure I was.

One day, I decided to walk over to Trina's. As I reached the corner of my street, I saw Rocky's Cadillac near the curb on Terrace Gardens Way. It was in the opposite direction of

Trina's house, so I altered my course and walked towards his car. My heart started beating faster and I felt my hands getting sweaty. I couldn't believe how shaky I was. If I got nervous just from seeing his car, how would I be able to take him out?

My question was answered when I saw him, leaving out of one the brick townhouses on the Way. He was flashy as ever, bling shining, looking like he could rule the world. I stared at him, and all the hate that I felt in the world rose up. I thought of running back to my house, grabbing the gun, and unloading it in his body right at the moment. But something told me it wasn't time.

Instead, I walked towards him, willing myself to smile. He finally noticed me, his eyes narrowing as he looked at me. I kept smiling, winked my eye, then turned the corner back towards Trina's place. I put a switch in my step as I continued to walk down the pathway, sure that Rocky was looking at my ass.

After I was sure he couldn't see me anymore, I backtracked and ran back to my house. I stormed into the living room, breathing heavily as I closed the front door. I ran upstairs to my bedroom and pulled out my gun. My hands were shaking and I felt tears sting my eyes. I wanted to get him then, but I didn't have the strength to. I hated Rocky more than anything in the world. I had to rid myself of him.

I saw him a couple more times in the next few weeks. I actually sought him out. I needed to steel myself against the emotion I felt when I saw him, and each time, I felt better. Or to be more precise, I felt nothing.

When he finally got the nerve to step to me, I was ready. I was on my way to Kelli's Deli when I saw his car turn onto the long road leading to the Gardens. I waved and he honked his horn. The passenger side window was open. I heard him yell my name. I stopped walking and thought briefly about going to the car, but decided against it. He would have to come to me.

I motioned for him to come to me and then waited as he parked his car and got out. As he walked towards me, I felt my fingers curl and my nails dig into the palms of my hands. *I can do this*, I thought.

He smiled brightly. "Sola, what up?" he asked as if everything was everything.

Rocky's voice was still deep, and he still had the same scent, a mixture of alcohol, cigarettes and cologne. Nothing had changed. He didn't even look like he had the least bit of remorse for what he had done to me. The first words out of his mouth should have been "I'm sorry," but no, he was giving me the Colgate smile. At that moment, I could have put my hand through his chest and pulled out his heart.

"I'm cool," I replied, putting my hands on my hips and sticking out my chest out slightly. He glanced down but his eyes quickly returned to my face.

"I know you might not believe this, but I've been worried about you," Rocky said, almost with a degree of sincerity. I didn't believe him for a minute. He was worried about his own ass and whether I would rat him out. He grinned, showing off his gold capped front teeth.

"Really?" I feigned surprise and caring.

"Look, I know you think I'm full of bullshit—"

I interrupted him. "I don't think anything, actually," I sensed the attitude in my voice. My emotions were starting to seep through. *I can do this*, I thought to myself.

"You got to know I didn't want that to go down," Rocky said.

I bet those were the same words his used with Momma. Using his deep, silky voice to convince her he was the best thing since sliced bread and that he would never do anything to hurt a teenage girl. But his smoothness did not affect me, I knew about the roughness that really resided inside his soul.

I smiled and reached to touch his hand. My skin crawled as I grasped his bling-ringed fingers.

"I know you didn't," I said.

His eyes widened as he looked at my hand. Before I released my hold, I caressed him lightly with the tip of one of my fingers. He exhaled before he spoke.

"I'm really sorry," he said.

He said it. But I didn't feel a thing. His being sorry was only going to earn him a trip six feet underground. I was still caressing him with my finger. I thought about how Momma spoke to him sometimes, her voice was like honey. I tried to imitate her.

"I know you are," I replied.

"If I can do anything—" he began, but he stopped speaking when I hugged him. I wrapped my hands around his body to shut him up. I didn't want to hear anymore of his bullshit. I was starting to shake. I had to get away from him soon.

"Come over," I said into his ear as I released him from my hug.

"What?" He backed away from me.

"I said, come over." I walked closer to him.

I could tell he didn't believe what he was hearing. I stuck my chest out again and smiled.

"Are you sure?" he asked.

"Yes. I think we need to *talk* in a more private place," I said, hoping my voice sounded real.

He looked around. There were people walking around. I knew some of the nosy ones were trying to tap into our conversation. My point was clear.

"When?" he asked.

"Well, Momma's out of town, which I'm sure you knew, so tonight's a good of time as any," *For you to die,* I thought.

"And you're sure you want me to come?" He started to look around as if SWAT were hiding in the bushes and would come and arrest him as soon as he agreed to come over.

"I'm real sure," I responded, sticking out my chest one last time.

"Okay. I'll come by tonight," he said softly, touching my face and caressing my chin. I started to shiver and nausea rose up my throat, but I forced a smile and hoped he didn't notice my disgust.

I returned home and laid in my bed. *So, it would end tonight.* I was nervous with anticipation. I had planned for so long, but I was almost frozen. I couldn't believe I was actually going to take a man's life. Not any man, but the man who raped me and killed my son. Josiah. I had to remember why I wanted him dead.

I looked out the window and watched as the day turned to evening. I kept on my clothes, a plain white T-shirt and jeans. I thought Rocky might get suspicious if I changed clothes or looked too sexy.

I heard the knock on the door around 8 P.M. At least he wasn't bold enough to use his key. I thought about how easy it would have been to shoot him as he was entering the house. I could have tearfully claimed that I thought he was a burglar, and with me being all alone, I had no choice but to shoot because I was afraid for my life. I think it could have worked. But I had already planned for it to end in the same place it began . . . my bedroom.

I hesitated before I left my bedroom, making sure everything looked okay. I had put the gun beneath my pillow. I walked down the stairs and touched my stomach. *I can do this,* I repeated in my head over and over again. There was no turning back.

I walked to the door and opened it. Rocky was standing there, smiling. I opened the door wider and motioned for him to come inside.

At first, we stood there, staring at each other. I thought I would be nervous, but I was calm. Rocky came closer.

"I knew you'd want me back," he said assuredly, touching my hair.

"I knew you had me all figured out," I responded. He moved closer and my stomach started to churn. *I can do this,* the thought kept repeating over and over again in my mind. *I can do this. I can do this. I can do this.*

He tried to kiss me on the lips, but I turned my head. His lips landed on my neck. I let him play with me for a couple of minutes, kissing and caressing me. When I couldn't take it anymore, I pushed him away. I thought about my baby. My son. Josiah. I knew it was time. "Let's go upstairs," I said, grabbing his hand and leading the way. Leading the way to Rocky's demise.

Chapter Twenty-One

Pawns can become the most important pieces of your match.
Use them wisely.
—The Qualities of Chess Masters # 317

March 31, 4:30 P.M

B.L. drove to the iron gates of Monchats's mansion. A guard stood in a makeshift station near the gates. B.L. nodded at him. The guard pressed a button and the gates creaked open.

The large two-story brick behemoth stood on top of a small hill in a revitalized part of Columbus on the city's Near East Side. Neglected for years due to the migration to the suburbs and the influx of drugs, the neighborhood had once been a haven for crack addicts and prostitutes. Monchats felt right at home.

B.L. helped Monchats form a development corporation so Monchats could use government money to rebuild his home. Monchats also restored the other homes in the area, each with square footage of seven thousand to ten thousand square feet. Monchats's home was the biggest on the block, sixteen thousand feet of pure elegance.

After finishing the homes, Monchats refurbished a nearby park and built a neighborhood playground. City administrators thought Monchats was a caring man dedicated to the improvement of his community. The administrators turned blind eyes to the drug dealers still in business only a few blocks away from the booming East Side Mecca. Of course, the dealers were under orders from Monchats and his "personal assistant", B.L.

Monchats was proud of his accomplishments. He had learned that the best way to keep the city officials off his back was to champion the needs of the poor and disillusioned, even if he had a hand in some of their misfortunes. B.L. had been with him every step of the way, from the rat-infested canals of New Orleans to the ghettos of New York, and now, the biggest country town in America, Columbus, Ohio.

In all of their years together, they only had one disagreement—Sola. B.L. was against her from the beginning, back when Monchats saw her potential at an early age. B.L. thought she was too young and impressionable, but Monchats saw the coldness of a female scorned.

For a time, as Sola honed her skills to become one of Monchats most useful weapons, B.L. was almost willing to admit hc was wrong. But then, Sola made mistakes that made him question her loyalty. Monchats would never allow himself to believe that Sola was flawed because he felt that he alone had built her. It was true that the transgressions were infrequent and rarely significant, but the absolute devotion Monchats showed her was unnerving.

When Monchats gave B.L. the okay to take Sola out after Denise's death, he smiled with satisfaction and tried to remain solemn even though he felt like jumping for joy. Sola's time had already come and gone, and B.L. had been more than willing to lead Sola to her eternal resting place. She already had reserved seating in a special place in hell. And finding the man to do the job was an easy task.

A man had come to him two years before, after the incident involving Abdul and Smith's gas station. At the time, many in Monchats's organization thought he would send Sola packing, and the man offered his services to do the job. B.L. didn't trust him at first, so he sent the man on a special mission to deal with some fools on the West Side trying to challenge Monchats's turf. The man's skills were extraordinary. The deaths even made front-page news. The man could rival Sola in her best years. B.L. never doubted him again.

B.L. thought things were going smoothly until he received Sola's phone call. He was surprised to hear her voice. He thought she would have been taking care of before noon. Even more surprising was Sola's apparent ignorance of her actions.

B.L. called her bluff, setting up the meeting at Timken and it turned out just as he suspected. Two of Monchat's men took Sola's wrath. She was trying to take out as many as she could. And then the bitch called him and tried to threaten him. She always thought she was better than what she actually was. Wouldn't she be surprised when she truly understood what was haunting her?

B.L. walked into the foyer and headed towards the large library that served as Monchats's office. He opened the large mahogany doors. Monchats was sitting behind his ornate wooden desk, staring at papers. When he looked up, B.L. could tell he had been crying. Monchats's eyes were red-rimmed from his tears.

The men nodded at each other. B.L. walked to the gas fireplace and turned it on. He sat down on one of the chairs near the fireplace. At the same time, Monchats pulled out a writing pad and walked over to the other chair facing the soft, glowing flames.

Since the Feds came down on Monchats's businesses, he and B.L. operated under almost complete silence. Writing notes had become the preferred mode of communication. Monchats held up his pen to B.L. and started writing on the pad. When he finished, he gave the pad to B.L.

"What's the news?" Monchats wrote.

B.L. took the pen and scribbled his response that read, "She took out Sizzle and Pepe at Timken. We had to leave them there. She definitely knows." B.L. paused for a moment, thinking about Sola's phone call and her idle threats. He didn't think it was worth mentioning, so he handed the pad back to Monchats.

Monchats read the message and closed his eyes. He took the sheet of paper, balled it up with his fist and tossed it into a metal trash can.

Monchats started writing again. "And your man you hired to do the job, what's his angle?"

"I met with him and he told me it's under control. He was glad we didn't get her first. He said he has plans for her. It will be over by morning."

Monchats looked at B.L. before writing again. "Do you trust him?" He wrote.

"I don't think trust has anything to do with it. He is driven by emotion, which should help him succeed. Basically, he wants Sola on a personal level."

Monchats threw another sheet of paper into the trashcan. He began writing again. "Don't you think personal feelings can cloud his judgment?" He wrote.

Instead of writing his answer, B.L. spoke. "No."

Monchats grabbed the pad. "You understand how I feel about this. I want it taken care of."

"I understand." B.L. responded with his pen.

A third sheet of paper went into the trashcan. After a couple of minutes, B.L. got up, took a match, struck it, and threw it into the trashcan. He watched as the flames engulfed the paper. He then started to turn off the fireplace, but Monchats stopped him. "Leave it," he said.

Monchats closed his eyes and lay his head against the back of the chair. Sensing his boss's need to be alone, B.L. walked slowly to the office doors. Before B.L. left, Monchats called his name.

"Yeah, boss," B.L. responded.

Monchats motioned for B.L. to return to his chair. He had written something more. B.L. took the pad and read Monchats's words. "You know, she knows how to contact me. She didn't even say she was sorry."

B.L. put his hand on Monchats's shoulder and spoke. "Would you?" B.L. asked.

The men understood the nature of the game, as did Sola. Apologies would not have been accepted. Monchats shook his head and wrote "I almost feel like I'm losing two daughters this week."

B.L. didn't know how to respond, so he squeezed Monchats's shoulder and left the office. He would never truly understand why Monchats cared so much about the project brat. As he walked to his own office on the other end of the foyer, B.L. smiled as he thought about receiving the call that Sola was dead. He almost couldn't wait.

Chapter Twenty-Two

Sola's Story, Part XI – 1993

When we got to the bedroom, Rocky commented on my new bedroom furniture.

"It looks really nice in here. I like the changes—in the bedroom, and in you," he said, grabbing me again and caressing my tits.

I knew I had to act fast. Rocky was still bigger and stronger then me, and if I made one mistake, I could be the one with a bullet in my brain. My skin was crawling and I could feel chill bumps rising on my skin. I pushed him away.

"Let me take off my clothes," I told him.

I walked backwards to my bed. My heart was starting to pound. *I can do this.* I took off my T-shirt, exposing my plain black bra. Rocky started walking towards me, but I stopped him. "Let me strip for you," I purred.

Rocky groaned. "Damn, baby," he said. He put his right hand underneath his black pants and started rubbing himself. "Hurry up and let me get to that good stuff."

I threw my T-shirt at Rocky. He took his hand out his pants and caught my shirt. He sniffed the white printed cotton before letting it fall to the ground. He then put his hand back in his pants and started rubbing himself again, this time his hand was working harder.

"C'mon baby, I want you bad," he said.

I started to undo the button on my jeans when I heard a sound that startled me. Someone was opening the front door to my townhouse. I stared at Rocky, but he didn't appear to hear the door. He was in his own world, still rubbing himself with his eyes closed and his head tilted back. He froze when he heard a woman's voice calling my name. *Momma was home.*

I jumped on my bed and grabbed the gun. No one, not even Momma, was going to stop me from carrying out my plan. I pointed the gun at Rocky. "Don't move," I told him.

Momma called my name again, but I didn't answer. I was staring at Rocky. He tried to come towards me but I waved the gun. "I said, don't move," I commanded.

"What the fuck do you think you're doing?" Rocky said. "Put that piece down before you hurt somebody."

I got off the bed slowly and stood in position. "Oh, I plan to do more than hurt *somebody*," I said coldly as I aimed the gun in his direction.

Rocky tried to play his trump card. He called out for Momma. I guess he foolishly thought that she would save him from his fate.

"Synthia! Get in here quick. Your daughter has lost her mind!" he yelled.

I heard Momma running up the stairs. "You mutha fucka. You think calling my Momma is going to save you?" I spewed out all of the hate I held inside of me. I knew I was ready.

Momma opened the bedroom door. Everything seemed to slow down. I remember Rocky lunging at me. I remember squeezing the trigger. I remember hearing the deafening sound as the bullet discharged from the gun. I remember the sound of Rocky screaming in pain as he fell to the floor. He grabbed his leg. Blood was spurting from his leg onto the floor. I thought about Truth's warning, *You better be sure when you aim it.*

Momma screamed. "Sola, noooo! What the hell is going on in here?"

I kept my gun pointed at Rocky. "Momma, get out of here," I said.

"Sola! Put that gun down!" Momma commanded.

Rocky was groaning. "The bitch shot me. Don't you see I'm injured over here? Call 911."

I thought about shooting Rocky again, but hesitated. "Fuck you," I spat out in Rocky's direction.

Momma was crying now. She looked at me and then at Rocky. "Please, Sola," she begged. "Please put that gun down."

I felt my own eyes water. "It's too late for that, Momma, I have to do this." Momma came towards me. "Don't move another inch, Momma, or I will have to kill him."

"Sola, honey child," Momma tried to speak calmly. "Listen to your Momma. Give me the gun."

"Yeah," Rocky said gruffly. "Listen to Momma."

I felt a tear run down my cheek. "You have a chance, Rocky." My voice was cracking. "Tell Momma what you've done."

Momma slowly turned towards Rocky. "Tell me what?" she asked nervously.

A small pool of blood had formed on the carpet where Rocky was sitting. Rocky was holding his leg, attempting to stop the bleeding. "I don't know what she's talking about," he moaned.

Momma turned toward me. "Is this about the fall? About

the baby?" She asked, starting to walk in my direction. "You don't have to do this," she said, attempting to get closer to me.

"Momma, I said don't move another inch," I repeated. My hands were starting to shake. I turned my attention back to Rocky. "Rocky, tell Momma what you've done," I commanded, each word coming out of my mouth slow and filled with rage.

"Tell her what? That you some crazy bitch who just shot me?" Rocky screamed.

"Don't talk to her like that," Momma said, trying to move in between me and Rocky. She was facing me as if she were trying to shield Rocky.

"You would try to protect him, huh?" I asked sarcastically. Momma's eyes were red. She was shaking, too. "Your man who raped me when he was sending you off to wherever. Your man who got me pregnant then killed my child. Your man who doesn't deserve the breath God gave him."

Momma's eyes widened and her mouth opened in surprise. "What?" she asked.

Rocky screamed, "She's lying, Synthia. She fuckin' crazy."

I looked in Momma's eyes. She knew I was telling the truth. "I didn't—" She started to speak.

"It don't matter now, Momma," I said, moving back into position. "Rocky is going to pay for his sins."

I moved closer to Rocky and unloaded the gun. I heard Momma screaming, and then felt my own body hit the floor. *For you*, I thought as a familiar darkness covered my world again.

Chapter Twenty-Three

A good memory and quick reflexes are your best allies.
Both skills will prove vital to achieving victory.
—The Qualities of Chess Masters # 345

March 31, 6:00 P.M.

Sola opened her eyes and stood up straight in the driver's seat of the Honda. *Damn,* she thought as she looked at the time. She couldn't believe she let herself go to sleep. She took a minute to gather herself and shake her sleepiness, then looked around to make sure the coast was clear.

Sola waited inside the Honda for a couple of minutes until she felt confident that it was safe to get out. She gathered her belongings and stepped out the car. It was starting to cool down, and she welcomed the chilled air because it refreshed her senses.

She walked down the brick pathway of the Polaris Park Executive Apartment Complex. She still felt slightly light-headed, so she concentrated on the rough, reddened brick patterns beneath her feet to keep her head clear.

She had only visited the Complex once before, but she didn't have the opportunity to view the entire compound. It was truly a sight to behold. It was funny what people could do when they had enough money to make and keep things beautiful.

She reached the last building in the Complex. The large five-story brick structure held at least seventy apartment suites in various sizes and designs. Tall, thin evergreen trees greeted her at the entrance to the building.

Once inside, Sola walked to the elevator and pushed the button signaling "up." Normally, she would have taken the stairs, but her destination was the fifth floor and she didn't know if she could make it in her current condition. She waited patiently for the large steel doors to open and kept her head down as people exited from the elevator.

She was glad she didn't have company as she rode up to the fifth floor. *Thank God for small blessings*, she thought. She looked at her wrist and had to make sure the bleeding was contained. No blood. The Juicy Couture was holding its own against the blood.

Sola's destination was a large suite at the end of the hallway. She didn't have a key, but locked doors never were a true barrier. She gained entrance to the suite in less than a minute.

The inside of the suite was an interior designer's dream. An expensive brown, leather sectional was the focal point of the living room. It faced a state-of-the-art smoked glass fireplace. There were white orchids in full bloom on the coffee table and on the table in the dinette that was located next to a sliding glass door that led to the balcony.

Sola walked through a tiny hallway leading to the bedroom. The room was neat, bed freshly made. It was almost hard to believe anyone lived there. But she knew better. She went to the large master bathroom. It was like heaven on earth, with marble flooring and tile, a glass-encased shower with multiple showerheads, and a Jacuzzi bathtub.

She placed her belongings on the floor and sat down on one of the small stools located by the bathroom door. She only had a short time to relax. She inhaled deeply. She didn't have many choices, and this seemed like her best option. She grabbed a towel and laid it on the floor. She opened the gift box and sifted through its contents. She was only interested in two things, a mini-cassette player and a small case that held seven mini-cassettes. She placed the items on the towel and moved it near the Jacuzzi.

She fingered through the box one last time before closing it and placing it beside her. Then she walked to the marble sink and prepared to take care of the wound. The pain struck her hard as she removed her top. She winced in pain. Her arm and shoulder were covered in blood, and her white tank top had turned red.

She turned her shoulder toward the mirror to inspect the wound. Just as she suspected. It was a flesh wound. The bullet didn't penetrate her body. The wound was ugly, and would normally require stitches, but she didn't have time for that. Instead, she took a small towel from a rack near the sink and started to clean the wound.

Sola turned on the water and waited until the temperature was warm. She started wiping blood from the end of her arm and watched as the clear running water ran red down the drain. She hesitated before cleaning the wound, she really didn't want to feel the pain, but it was necessary, and it would clear her head.

She walked back to the chair, picked up her bag, and prepared to take out the rubbing alcohol. Then she heard the front door the apartment open. All of her senses went on alert. Instead of the alcohol, she placed her fingers around her nine-millimeter gun and pulled it out of the bag. She tiptoed back to the sink and slowly turned off the water. She listened for footsteps, but she knew the soft carpet would muffle any sound of feet. She thought she heard breathing by the door. She raised her gun and waited.

The bathroom door burst open and a tall black man holding a gun walked into the room. He aimed his gun at Sola.

"Put it down," the man said, his voice deep and commanding.

"I don't think so," Sola said, aiming for the man's head.

The man's eyes widened as he glanced at Sola's shoulder and the blood-stained T-shirt.

"Looks like I have the advantage," he said as he stepped further into the bathroom. "Put the gun down," he commanded.

Sola stepped back to maintain the distance between them.

"You know what they say about the wounded in the wild," she said mockingly.

He chuckled. "Oh, you're more dangerous, huh?"

"Try me," Sola responded.

The pair kept their guns trained on each other. Neither party was willing to yield. The man finally broke the silence. "Are you going to stand down, or what?"

Sola was getting weak. Her shoulder injury was getting the best of her. However, she refused to show any chinks in her armor.

"That totally depends on you," she replied.

It was a silent duel. A game they had played before. Neither party was willing to back down, neither one willing to take chances. The man finally had enough. He lowered his weapon and placed it on the floor. He extended his arms outward and said, "I'm only doing this for you, nothing more, you need help."

Sola kept her gun raised. Her arms started to shake. There was a time when she would have killed him without a second thought, but now, things were different. She lowered her gun and knelt down to put it on the floor. The man rushed to her and kicked the weapon out of Sola's reach. Then he knelt down beside her.

"Soledad Nichols. I should take you into custody now. It would be good for you," he suggested.

Sola looked up at him. "Campbell Donovan, it will never happen," she declared.

Campbell stood up, walked over to the sink, and turned on the water. "You need to consider your options, Soledad. You've been busy with your body count, and I'm assuming from that wound that Monchats has put the word out that you're wanted, and preferably not alive. You and I both know that Monchats is not going to stop until you're dead." He wet a small towel and returned to his position on the floor. He began wiping Sola's arm.

"I can take care of myself," she said.

Campbell looked at the wound. "Yeah, I can tell," he said sarcastically, continuing to clean Sola's wound.

Sola grunted when Campbell began to clean a sensitive part of the wound. "You need stitches," he commented.

"Well, unless you have a medical kit here in your apartment, that's not going to happen. Just get me something to wrap the wound."

Campbell began to walk out the bathroom.

"Stop," Sola said as she rose up to follow him.

"You don't trust me?" Campbell asked.

"I don't trust anyone."

Campbell and Sola went to his bedroom together. Sola stayed close behind him as he opened the top dresser drawer and pulled out a couple of white T-shirts. He began to tear them.

"We can use these for your wound," he said.

After the wound was sufficiently wrapped, Campbell reached into another drawer and pulled out a sweatshirt. He handed it to Sola. "Put this on," he directed. "You don't need to have that bloody T-shirt on."

They walked back into the bathroom. She started to pull off her T-shirt. He stared at her.

"Do you mind?" Sola asked, wanting some privacy as she changed.

"I don't trust you, either," Campbell responded.

"Could you at least turn around and look at the door?" Sola asked.

Campbell laughed. "I never figured you had a sense of modesty." He turned toward the bathroom door.

He heard the ruffle of clothing, and then heard the snap of Sola's bra. She turned on the water again.

"I know you did the job last night, Soledad," he said seriously. "I know you killed Monchats's daughter."

"You think you know so much, don't you?" Sola responded.

"Well, what you don't know is that you also killed a federal agent."

"Like I said, you think you know so much. I know what I've done and who've I've done it to," she said.

Campbell turned around. Sola was still wiping herself down. Her damp skin glistened under the light. Campbell felt himself getting warm. He had to maintain his composure.

"And do you know why, Sola? Did you know the only reason Denise Ann Monchats and Kenneth Washington are in a morgue is because they were in love? How does that make you feel?" Campbell was shaking.

Sola closed her eyes and bowed her head. "I don't have time to question the reasons why people die."

"I can't imagine you're that cold of a bitch. That you lack remorse over killing two people that didn't have to die," Campbell said coldly.

"Don't imagine anything about me, Campbell. And don't assume you know what I'm feeling."

Campbell leaned against bathroom door frame. "Just why are you here, Soledad? If not to turn yourself in, then why?" he questioned.

Sola stared at him coldly, holding up the towel to cover her breasts. Anderson turned back around. "I have my reasons."

"Well, you need to speak now. If you think I'm going to harbor a criminal, you're wrong."

"Don't act like you're so fucking straight-laced. We both know you're not. You want to lecture me when you're life is dedicated to lying and deceiving people." Sola turned off the water. A small groan told Anderson that she was attempting to put on the sweatshirt. "You can turn around now." He did.

She kicked a wrapped up towel in his direction. "That's for you, Campbell Donovan, or, should I just call you by your real name, Agent Anderson?"

"You're really pushing it now, aren't you? Just call me Campbell. It keeps me focused." Campbell looked at the towel curiously. "What is it?" he asked.

"The answers to all of you questions," Sola replied.

He picked up the towel and opened it. Inside were a mini-cassette and tapes. "What's this?"

"You wanted to know why I'm here," Sola said. "I want my mother."

Chapter Twenty-Four

Sola's Story, Part XII — 1993

The first thing I remembered when I woke up was the gun shots. I was frozen for a minute, but I caught my bearings quick. I found myself in a familiar place, with the standard tile ceiling and the antiseptic smell. I knew I was at Children's Hospital. There were no tubes this time, only me in a lonely old hospital bed. I remember the television set sitting on a stand attached to the opposite side of the wall tuned in to some cartoon show. I figured some nurse left in on to make me feel better. I would never recommend television as good medicine.

What happened? I thought to myself. I recalled shooting Rocky, all of the blood, and Momma screaming at the top of her lungs. *But was he dead?* My mind couldn't reveal it. I felt a presence in the room. "Momma?" I called out, knowing somehow she wasn't there.

A woman came from behind the plastic hospital curtain. She was dressed in a dark suit. She smiled at me. Maybe she was trying to calm me. But I knew her angle even before she spoke. Her dress and look told me she was a cop.

"How are you doing?" the woman asked, continuing to display her straight, white teeth.

I nodded. I didn't want to speak. The woman came closer to the bed. "My name is Samantha Coleman," she said with a smooth, soft voice. "But you can call me Sam."

It was a classic trick, trying to make me feel comfortable—to set me up so I would be open to give her whatever she wanted. It was also the classic mistake, because even though I was young, that past year had given me the wisdom to know what she was dishing. In other words, she wouldn't get anything I didn't want her to have. I would play her game, but only to my satisfaction.

"I want my momma," I said in a soft voice.

Sam took my hand and caressed it. "Your mother's not here right now," she said.

I looked her up and down. "Are you from Children's Services?" I asked. "Are you here to take me away from my momma?"

Sam continued to stroke my hand. "I'm here to take care of you, Soledad."

"How are you going to take care of me?" I questioned. "You don't even know me."

"I don't have to know everything about you to want to help you. You've been through a lot—"

I tuned her out, watching her mouth move, but not hearing a word she was saying. I couldn't muster up any tears, so I thought about my Josiah until I felt the familiar sting in my eyes and the wetness on my face.

"Please get my momma," I pleaded. "I need her." Maybe I did, on some level, but I wanted information even more and I knew the tears would help me find out what I wanted to know.

Sam grabbed a box of tissue. I let her wipe my face. "You're a big girl, Soledad, so I'm going to be straight with you. Something terrible happened. Your mother is in trouble and the only way you can help her is to tell me what happened at your home last night."

My eyes widened. "Please, tell me what happened to Momma," I pleaded.

My pleas were weakening Sam's resolve. Her eyes began to shift between the door and my bed. I was getting close.

"Look, I don't want to upset you further. You need to get some rest," she said.

I grabbed her hand and looked straight in her eyes. "Please. Tell me about my momma."

Sam sighed. Her eyes were watering. I knew then she was broken. "Someone died in your home last night and your mother was involved. Maybe when you get some rest, you can tell me what happened.

I closed my eyes. I had gotten the information I wanted. Rocky was dead. "I don't want to talk anymore," I said.

"Hopefully, you'll be ready to talk once you've had some rest. If you're up to it, I'll ask you a couple of questions. Anything you tell me may be able to help your mother." Sam's voice was filled with concern, as if she were wondering if she revealed too much. "I'll leave you alone now." I kept my eyes closed and listened as soft footsteps told me Sam was leaving the room.

Rocky was dead. I thought I'd feel some relief, but I didn't feel anything. My thoughts turned to Momma. *She's in trouble.* How could that be? Sam said that Momma was involved. *What was she talking about?*

I couldn't find out much from just laying in the bed. I looked at the small clock on the nightstand next to my hospital bed. It was almost 6:30 in the morning. I wondered what the television stations were saying about Rocky. I pressed on the button calling for a nurse. After a couple of minutes, a young brown-skinned woman in a nurse's uniform came into the room.

"Everything okay?" she said in a soft, caring voice.

"Almost," I responded.

The nurse looked around the room. "What can I help you with?"

"I'm not really into cartoons," I said. "Could you turn the TV to channel 10?" I knew the early morning news would be on channel 10.

The nurse walked to the bed and held up a small TV remote. "It looks like someone moved your remote. Let me change that for you," she said. "And you can use this to change the channels or change the volume yourself after I leave."

"Thanks," I said as she handed me the remote.

"No problem," she said, smiling. "Breakfast will be coming soon."

I nodded my head and she left the room. After a couple of commercials, the 6:30 A.M. news report came on. The perky reporter on the TV screen tried to look serious as she relayed the news. As always, crime was the top story, only this time, the news hit close to home.

Murder in Sullivant Gardens Federal Housing Project. That was nothing new. *Victim killed by gunshots.* Also the norm. Then a familiar face appeared on the screen. I recognized the woman almost immediately, even though my mind didn't want to accept the truth of what I was seeing. It was my mother, looking like I had never seen her before. Her eyes were red-rimmed and her hair was all over the place. I sat up in the bed as another picture flashed across the screen. This time it was a side view of Momma's face. I had seen enough of those types of pictures to know they were head shots. *What the hell is going on*, I thought to myself. I turned up the volume on the TV. Then I heard something I almost couldn't believe.

Thirty-six year old Synthia Nichols has been arrested for the murder of Roland Underwood, a reputed drug dealer. She is expected to be charged with first-degree murder.

I screamed out and couldn't stop. The nurse returned to the room, followed by Sam. They tried to hold me down, but I fought them. I kept screaming, telling them it wasn't her, that they had the wrong person. I heard the nurse mention a sedative, I felt a prick in my arm, and soon, I didn't feel like screaming anymore.

Chapter Twenty-Five

Rare are the moments you have for reflection.
Use idle time to plan for your victory.
—The Qualities of Chess Masters # 360

March 31, 8:00 P.M.

Campbell turned up the heat on the stove before placing a non-stick skillet over the burner. He then turned his attention to a bowl filled with eggs, peppers, and onions and began stirring the mixture vigorously. As he stirred, he looked up at Sola. She watched him intensely.

"I'm glad you like omelets," Campbell said as he continued stirring. "Eggs are pretty much all I have in this place."

"You like to go out, huh?" Sola chewed on a thin piece of carrot, the only other food Campbell had in his apartment.

"It's not that. I'm usually at the Dollhouse and I just eat there or I grab some fast food or something."

"Fast food?" Sola wrinkled her nose. "I thought you'd be more of a health food nut," she said.

Campbell stared off into space. "In my other life, the one that matters, I do like a more healthy diet. But the thugs and strippers have cramped my style."

"And the killers, too, I take it," Sola said sarcastically.

Campbell frowned. "Let's not talk about that now." He poured the egg mixture into the skillet.

"I guess we can live in a fantasy world for a couple of hours." Sola took a sip of Arizona Green Tea.

"We have before, remember?" Campbell flipped the omelet.

"Did you think I'd forgotten?" Sola asked.

"How would I know that, Sola?" Campbell flipped the omelet again, and then grabbed a plate to put it on.

"Kind of seems logical that I'd remember. Even though you don't want to talk about reality, you could assume our past, although short, is directly related to my current presence here, Mr. Anderson."

"Hey, remember, it's Campbell to you," he said, putting the finished omelet on the plate and holding it up, inhaling deeply and moving his head back and forth in an exaggerated motion. "Now that's what I call perfection," he said as he placed the plate in front of Sola.

Sola stared at the food in front of her. "Okay, Campbell. You didn't put any sleeping pills in this, did you?" she joked.

"Ha, Ha, *muy* funny," Campbell responded.

"I see you still don't know any Spanish."

"Only because you wouldn't teach me."

"After the first lesson I taught you, I thought you wouldn't want me to teach you anything else," Sola pointed out.

"Hmmm," Campbell paused for a moment as he thought reflectively, "I liked the preparation for that first lesson. Can we have more of that?"

Sola scoffed, "You and I both know that wouldn't be wise."

"I vote for stupidity." Campbell began working on a second omelet.

There was an awkward silence. Sola wanted to change the subject but didn't know what to say. Instead, she began eating her omelet and stopped herself from humming in delight. Her taste buds were singing because of the flavor. Campbell really could cook. She looked up and saw Campbell staring at her.

"You like it, don't you?" Campbell asked.

Sola wasn't giving anything away. "It'll do," she responded.

"You are cold, you know that?" Campbell flipped his omelet onto a plate and sat on one of the bar stools beside Sola.

"You got me all wrong." Sola ended the conversation by diving back into her plate.

Campbell walked around that kitchen counter and prepared to eat. Before he could sit down, a phone began ringing. Campbell and Sola began looking around. "That you?" Sola asked.

The ringing was coming from the table located near the apartment entrance. "I guess so." Campbell walked toward the table.

He picked up his cell phone and grimaced when he saw the phone number in the caller ID display. He glanced at Sola before answering the call. She was eating, and didn't appear to be paying attention, but her ears were perked up. He knew she would be listening to every word.

"What up? This is like two calls now. You're really messing up my flow." Campbell tried to sound hard.

"Why do you sound so funny?" the caller asked.

"It's been a hard day, and I want to relax. You've called me when I asked you not to, we met and I didn't want to, and now you're calling me again. You're really starting to concern me."

"I wouldn't call if it wasn't absolutely necessary," the caller cleared his throat. "The stakes are rising in this little Monchats game."

"What's going on?" Campbell instinctively lowered his voice.

"A shit storm of cosmic proportions," the caller summarized.

"What does that have to do with you calling me?" Campbell looked at Sola again. She was staring at him now, her fork transfixed in her hand and hovering over her plate.

"I need to know something. Has Soledad Nichols contacted you?"

Campbell felt a lump in his throat. Sola seemed to sense his concern. She started to get up from her chair, but he raised his hand to stop her, silently mouthing the words, "It's okay, just chill."

"You still there?" the caller asked.

"Yeah, I'm here," Campbell replied cautiously.

"You didn't answer my question."

"I haven't heard or seen anything."

"You sure?"

The doubtful tone in the caller's voice made Campbell nervous. His eyes moved around his apartment, his gaze lingering on the furniture and the walls. He wondered if there were listening devices in his apartment. His eyes returned to Sola. He knew they would have already come after her if they knew where she was.

"Wouldn't I tell you if I had any information?" Campbell asked.

"I don't know if you would, that's why I asked," the caller explained. "But I want to warn you to be careful. You know about yesterday, but today she's been even more active. Four grown men in the span of a couple of hours. A couple of thugs at an old Timken plant and some Arabs at Smith's Gas Station. Bullets for all of them."

"What?" Campbell blurted out in disbelief.

"Amazing, isn't it?" the caller continued, "and one of

them was an old associate of hers." Campbell gripped the phone as the caller gave him detailed information about the deaths. "She's out of control. Consider her armed and dangerous."

Campbell tried to mask the worried look on his face but he couldn't. Sola could read him like a book. He watched as Sola got out of her seat and started walking toward him.

"I'll stay on my best guard," Campbell told the caller.

"And you'll call me if she makes contact?"

"You'll be the first to know," Campbell replied. "I've got to go, something's about to burn in the kitchen." He ended the call without saying goodbye.

Sola was in front of his face. "What's going on?" she asked.

Campbell brushed past her and started walking towards the kitchen. He started to lie, but decided that telling the truth was his best option.

"You're what's going on," Campbell began. "You and your murderous ways. If you're going to take out half of the thugs in Columbus, don't come here and use my apartment as your base." Campbell grabbed his plate and threw his food in the trash. He didn't feel hungry anymore.

"Can I by a vowel?" Sola asked. "Because I need a clue big time."

Campbell recalled the locations where the caller told him the deaths occurred. "Did you go to a place called Timken today? Or maybe Smith's Gas Station?" Campbell asked.

Sola folded her arms across her chest and regarded Campbell carefully. "Don't ask me questions you don't want to know the answers to."

"I'll take that as a yes."

"Take it anyway you want it."

"And your friend Abdul, did you visit him today to give him a lead gift to the head?"

Sola looked puzzled. "What are you talking about?"

"Oh, you can ask questions, but I can't?" Campbell paced around the kitchen. "I hope you didn't come here to try anything foolish, Sola."

Sola turned toward the door leading to the bedroom. "I told you why I came," she pointed towards the bedroom door. "You saw the tapes. They're yours. And in exchange, I want my mother."

"I don't know if I believe you."

"Believe what you want, but if you want me to leave just say so." Sola walked toward the bedroom.

"Stop." Campbell commanded. "Stay where you are."

Sola turned around. "What the fuck is up with you?"

"Sola, you leave here, and I know someone else is going to die. You need to stay."

"Someone will die whether I'm here or not."

"You need to stay. The cops are after you. The Timken incident is one thing, but killing men in lily-white Hillard is totally different."

"What about Hillard?" Sola asked.

"Smith's Gas Station on Hillard-Rome Road. Two dead. But I'm sure you know more about it than I do. Look, I don't have to put in you handcuffs or read you your rights. We can just get in my car and go downtown. If you turn yourself in, I can protect you."

Sola wasn't listening to him. She was staring off into space. "Abdul." Sola whispered the name softly. She walked to the couch, sat down slowly, and put her head between her legs.

"You okay?" Campbell walked up behind the couch.

Sola lifted her head slowly. Tears filled her eyes. "Are you saying the person on the phone told you Abdul is dead?"

Campbell nodded and walked around to the back of the couch. He reached for Sola's shoulders and started massaging them in an attempt to calm her. She froze and groaned in pain, pushing away from him. He had almost forgotten about her injury.

"That bastard," Sola said angrily. "He did it to get to me."

Campbell was confused. "This Abdul, he did something to you?"

Sola shook her head. "Not Abdul, but the one who did this to me," she replied, tapping her injured shoulder lightly.

"Who is it?"

"I wish I knew. My guess is some fucker B.L. hired to kill me. He missed. But Abdul didn't have to die. I shouldn't have—" Sola stopped speaking.

"Shouldn't have what?"

Sola was staring off into space. "Nothing."

"Are you saying you didn't kill Abdul and the others?" Campbell asked.

Sola looked around the room before focusing on Campbell. "I'm not really saying anything, except that if the person who's after me knows about you, then you should be prepared."

"For what?"

Campbell's heart sunk as Sola batted tears from her eyes before she spoke. "For anything and everything."

Chapter Twenty-Six

Previous experience can enhance anticipation.
Draw on your memories for strength.
—The Qualities of Chess Masters, # 388

April 1, 12:30 A.M.

Campbell Donovan watched Sola as she lay on his bed, her eyes closed, her body relaxed. It took a monumental effort to convince her to get some rest. After her omelet dinner, Sola stared out of the windows for a couple of hours, not saying a word. Campbell tried to make idle conversation. He told her about the Dollhouse being shut down for a day and about Mr. Fogelman's dumb ass, but she remained silent. He peaked her attention when he mentioned that he visited her house.

Sola told Campbell that the person after her was bold enough to come to her house and shoot her. He put his hands up and exclaimed, "Not me."

"I figured that out," she said wearily. "I concluded you wouldn't play with me like this guy's doing. You'd have probably capped me in my sleep."

"I could never hurt you, Sola," he said sincerely.

Her cryptic response chilled him. "The folly of men will

lead to their destruction," she said coolly, her voice calm and distant as if she were thinking of something that required a great deal of concentration. *Was Sola saying that she would, in fact, hurt him?* Campbell thought to himself.

Sola resisted when Campbell told her she wouldn't be useful if she was tired. She finally relented and laid down on the bed. As she rested, Campbell's eyes traveled over her apple-shaped, caramel-colored face, framed by her thick shoulder-length hair. His eyes traveled further down her body. She was a work of beauty.

He thought briefly about calling his superiors and telling them she was there. He was risking a great deal to harbor her there, even if it was for a short time. If anyone from the department found out, his career could well be over.

He glanced at the telephone on the nightstand next to the bed. Sola shifted in the bed and her hand tightened around her gun. Her eyes opened slightly before she closed them again. *It was almost as if she could read his mind.* Then again, he didn't know if he could have gone through with it even if he did make the call. *One good turn deserves another,* he thought.

When Campbell first laid eyes on Soledad Nichols two months ago, he questioned his resolve to complete his assignment. It had taken him almost two years to infiltrate Monchats's criminal organization. As an undercover agent from Washington, D.C., he entered Monchats's dark world with the name Campbell Donovan. He started in Cleveland, doing small jobs but making enough noise to make Dennis Monchats take notice. Within ten months, he received orders from the man himself. A summons to Columbus was an offer he couldn't refuse.

Collecting evidence against Monchats proved difficult. His night clubs, restaurants, and music stores were as clean as bleached socks. His work in the community made it especially difficult to get information from the locals. Monchats christened him with the name Soup as a play on his "first name" and made him a manager of the Dollhouse, a gentleman's club on Livingston Avenue on the city's East Side.

After nearly a year of drug deals, Campbell wondered why Monchats would allow him to head one of his legitimate operations, but he knew better than to ask too many questions. Despite his calm and smooth demeanor, Monchats was one of most dangerous men in America. Campbell knew better than to test Monchats's instincts by being curious. And after his first night of viewing some of most beautiful bodies on earth, and getting a lap dance that made him almost explode in his pants, he decided his job wasn't so bad after all.

When he received Monchats's invitation to attend the Colette Monchats Foundation Benefit Dinner nearly two months ago, he couldn't wait to attend. Colette Monchats had died of ovarian cancer when her last surviving son was still a teenager. Monchats held the benefit each year to raise money for cancer research. Campbell marveled at how a man could systematically destroy communities with his drugs and various criminal activities, but still have enough heart to try and save lives. It was a sickening irony, of course.

The benefit dinner was a black tie affair, and none of the seedier members of Monchats crew were invited. But the power brokers would be there. It was the perfect opportunity to meet other players in Monchats's game.

As the taxi cab drove up to the entrance to the Franklin Park Trolley Station Event Center, Campbell cursed the fact that his Navigator had broken down, but rejoiced in the fact that he could enjoy the liquor at the benefit and not have to worry about driving home. As he stared at the building in front of him, Campbell marveled at Monchats's ability to combine evil and good. The Trolley Station was once a haven for crackheads and other drug addicts, but Monchats had transformed it to a state-of-the-art meeting facility. No expense was spared.

"Fancy place, is it not?" the taxi driver asked. He was an African man with a thick accent.

Campbell stared at the large glass entrance. "You got that right," Campbell responded.

He got out of his taxi and stared at the enormous glass panel doors leading into the facility. He handed the fare to the cab driver along with a generous tip. He wondered what Monchats would be like if he hadn't chosen a life of crime— the possibilities were endless.

Campbell followed the red carpet to the large banquet hall. Before he entered the hall, he stopped at one of the large mirrors in the hallway. He briefly studied his appearance. He was tall, almost six-feet, four inches tall, dark skin, dark eyes, and a clean-shaven head. The tailor had done an excellent job on his tuxedo, taking into account his broad shoulders and long legs. He straightened his tie and smiled to check out his teeth. *Those whitening strips worked wonders,* he thought. *Not bad for a man who spent his teenage years with braces and a high-top fade.*

When he entered the large airy room, his heart almost stopped. In the midst of Columbus's elite, she stood out in the crowd; she being Soledad Nichols. The black and white surveillance photos he had seen didn't do her justice. She wore a simple black dress that molded onto her athletic body, exposing every curve. Her stilettos made her appear statuesque. Her hair was loose and curly, flowing just past her shoulders.

He couldn't stop staring at her, even when she caught his glance and looked at him strangely. *God, she is beautiful,* he thought. He shook his head to regain his senses. He had to remember who she was—Monchats's most lethal assassin, the Brown Recluse.

When Campbell was briefed on Soledad Nichols, he refused to believe she was so deadly. According to FBI records, she had worked for Monchats at least ten years, although in reality, the time period was probably longer. She was known on the streets as the Brown Recluse, and her exploits were the stuff of legends. Unfortunately, there was no hard evidence linking her to any of her crimes. She was more slippery than her employer.

Tall and extraordinarily beautiful, Soledad could have been a model. Campbell remembered asking, "You mean this woman is taking out grown able-bodied men?" He didn't even try to mask the disbelief in his voice.

The response was "yes," and sometimes more than one at a time.

"How can anyone who looks like that do what she supposedly does?" he had asked, pointing at the large black and white image of Soledad Nichols projected on a screen in the FBI briefing room.

That question was harder to answer. She was in foster care during her teenage years, but her state records had mysteriously disappeared. I.Q. tests and grade records from her elementary and middle schools suggested that she was highly intelligent. Additional information had been even harder to gather. According to the IRS, she made her money as an administrative assistant for Monchats. On the outside looking in, she appeared to be clean and legit. But Campbell had been warned. "Stay away from her."

Campbell turned away from Sola and went to the bar, taking advantage of the free champagne. He leaned against the bar counter, trying to take his mind off of the woman who had just blown him away. Someone tapped his shoulder and he almost spilled his drink. He turned around. Sola was standing in front of him, her light brown eyes studying him slowly.

"I don't know you," she said. Her voice was smooth and sexy.

Damn, this is too good to be true, he thought.

Campbell had to regain his composure. She continued to stare at him, waiting for him to respond. He took a sip from his drink and let the bubbles clear his throat before he spoke.

"I don't know you either," he replied.

His response made Sola smile, and as she beamed, he thought about slinging her over his shoulder, taking her back to his apartment and showing her what he could do.

"Looks like we have something in common," she said, laughing softly.

He put his drink down and extended his hand. "Well then, let me introduce myself. I'm Campbell Donovan."

She reached for his hand. Her hand was soft, nails neatly manicured. Her touch made his insides stir. "Soledad Nichols," she said.

She tried to pull her hand back, but he held onto it a bit longer. He finally released it.

"Latina, huh?" he asked, although he already knew the answer.

Sola looked down to the floor. He could tell the question bothered her. She wasn't used to answering questions about herself.

"I'm more like a half-breed," she responded flatly. "Most people just call me Sola though." Her eyes were cloudy, but then brightened up. Were the investigators right? Did Sola have weaknesses?

"So are you lonely?" Campbell asked. He suddenly wanted to know Sola's life story, beyond what he learned at the briefing.

She looked at him strangely. "What?" she asked.

"You said to call you Sola," he replied. "Isn't that lonely in Spanish?"

Sola chuckled. "You might want to brush up on your Spanish. Actually, Sola means 'alone.'"

"Hmm. I can't imagine you being alone." He stepped closer to her, catching a hint of her soft, earthy Issey Miyake perfume.

Sola smiled again. "Looks can be deceiving," she said.

Campbell nodded in agreement and took a sip of his drink.

There was an uncomfortable silence. He noticed she didn't have a glass in her hand.

"Something to drink?" he asked.

"No, thank you," she responded. "I don't drink alcohol anymore, and I've already had enough water this evening."

"You look like you have a little something every now and then," he said, smiling wryly.

Sola frowned. "Like I said, Mr. Donovan, looks can be deceiving. To be honest with you, I don't even like the smell of alcoholic drinks. And alcohol clouds your judgment."

"And you like having a clear head?" Campbell asked.

"That's the only way I survive."

More silence.

The room was filling up fast. The noise of hundreds of voices was reaching a fevered pitch. Campbell moved closer to Sola.

"So, what are you doing here?" he asked. Another question; known answer.

"I work for the Man," she responded, and pointed towards Monchats.

Monchats was standing between two Amazonian blondes. He was dressed in a black Valentino tuxedo, topped off with a black bowtie. The blondes were dressed alike, in twin strapless blue dresses that barely covered their asses. The blondes were both laughing, presumably about something "witty" Monchats had said. Their laughter made their huge breasts giggle.

Monchats seemed to know that Sola had mentioned him, and looked in their direction. Once Monchats caught Sola's attention, he turned his head and looked at each blonde before squeezing them closer to him. They all laughed. Sola rolled her eyes up in the air.

"Looks like he's having fun," Campbell said, slightly envious of Monchats's current position.

"I'll bet," Sola said. "And you, what's your angle?"

"Seems like we have something else in common. I work for the Man, too."

Neither Campbell nor Sola had to elaborate further. They both knew to answer the question asked, but not to give too much information.

The band started playing a slow jam. Luther Vandross was bellowing out, *If Only for One Night.*" Campbell shook his head. "I can't believe he's gone," he said sadly.

"Yeah," Sola agreed. "I was hoping he would recover from his stroke. I love his music so much. I mean, do you know anybody who didn't get married to '*Here and Now*'?" But at least he has a legacy and tons of songs his fans will love forever."

How can a cold-blooded killer be so profound, Campbell thought as he finished off his champagne. Well, maybe his perception of her profoundness was stemming from the effect of the champagne on his brain. *Or maybe it was stemming from the effect of Sola's body on his brain,* Campbell thought, stifling a groan.

Campbell held out his hand. "Dance?" he asked. He wanted to be close to her, to feel her in his arms, to live the dream that they were two different people in a different time, if only for a moment.

She took his hand and he escorted her to the dance floor. She stiffened as he took her into his arms.

"Relax," Campbell whispered softly in Sola's ear.

They started moving slowly to the music. He held her around her slim waist at first, but couldn't resist letting his hands travel lower. She backed away from him, but he pulled her even closer.

"You know you like it," Campbell whispered seductively.

Their bodies moved together in a perfect mold. He felt himself getting hard and knew that Sola could feel his arousal. He had to have her.

Sola stopped dancing but didn't push him away. She reached up and whispered in his ear.

"I want to take you home with me," she said.

He didn't know what made him harder, Sola's breath against his ear or the words she spoke.

"You're kidding me, right?" he asked in disbelief.

"One thing you should know about me Campbell is that I'm a woman who knows what she wants and isn't afraid to get it." She grinded against him and he groaned. "And from what I'm feeling, you want it to. Let's not waste time with pretenses."

At first, Campbell had a weird feeling that he was the featured fool on an episode of *Punk'd*. He would open his eyes and Asthon Kutcher would run into the room and everyone would laugh at him. After dismissing that scenario as totally ludicrous, he thought about his assignment, wondering if saying yes would jeopardize it. But as he stared at Sola and thought about what she was offering, he knew he had to throw caution to the wind. There was no way he could say no.

"You're sure?" he asked just to make sure he wasn't dreaming. "You want me to go home with you?"

"Definitely," Sola responded.

"Well, the only thing I can say is lead the way."

A sudden noise brought Campbell back to the present. He had drifted off in the memories of his initial encounter with Sola and the mini-cassette player and tapes had fallen out of his lap. He glanced at Sola. Her breathing was labored. The fact he wasn't staring at the barrel of her gun told him she was asleep. He picked up the player and tapes and walked into the living room. He sat on the couch and pondered his options. But just like the night he first met Sola, he didn't know exactly what he would do.

Chapter Twenty-Seven

Sola's Story, Part XIII – 1993

When my social worker, Delia Daniels, told me I could see Momma, I almost jumped for joy. I hadn't seen or talked to her in over a month. I wondered why they were being so hard on her, but I knew just seeing me would make her feel better.

I still remember the day I first saw Momma behind bars. It was a Tuesday, and the sky was gray. I dressed in a nice outfit Delia gave me. It wasn't Donna Karan or anything, just a black skirt and tan cardigan she probably picked up at The Express. I had to have something new because I didn't have any clothes from home. I hadn't returned to the Gardens since Rocky died.

The Franklin County Jail was located on the edge of downtown Columbus on High Street. On the outside, it looked like any other skyscraper, but the large gray building didn't have any windows. They made sure the prisoners didn't have a chance to see the outside world. Inside, there were prisoners from every walk of life, black and white, lowlife and rich, and innocent and guilty.

Once I entered the jail, I was scanned, felt up, and looked over. *I should be here*, I thought. Delia held my hand as we walked down a long dark hallway.

"Aren't you excited?" she asked in her high animated voice.

"Yeah," I said, telling the truth for the first time in a while.

After Rocky's death, I was questioned for hours by cops, brain docs, and social workers. And I told them all the same thing in the most convincing voice I could muster, "I don't remember what happened."

Some brain doc finally said I was suffering from post-traumatic stress, but I knew better. So much for the worth of his university degree.

I didn't know why I couldn't convince anyone I killed Rocky. While I remained silent, the State had charged Momma with first-degree murder. If Momma was found guilty, she would serve an automatic sentence of life without the possibility of parole. Why I was letting Momma rot in jail while I sat on the outside world?

Me and Delia walked into a large room with steel tables and chairs. Two female guards stood at opposite ends of the room. The guards were so still and silent, I thought they were mannequins until their eyes blinked. There were other inmates there, talking with each other and guests. All of the inmates wore orange jumpsuits with large black letters on their backs—FCCF, which stood for Franklin County Correctional Facility.

Delia directed me to sit at one of the empty tables. "Wait here," she said, squeezing my shoulder and smiling. "I'll be right back."

Delia walked up to one of the guards and spoke. The guard then pointed toward a thin door on the other side of the room. Delia walked to the door and went inside. After a couple of minutes, she walked out. Momma was with her.

Tears started welling up when I saw her. She walked slowly behind Delia. A guard stood behind her, watching her every step. Her hands were bound with plastic cuffs.

The jail had gotten the better of her. Her face had aged. She had tiny wrinkles around her eyes and mouth. She lost a lot of weight, too. She was never really big, just thick in all the right places. Now she was so thin she looked like she was on crack.

I got up from my chair and ran to meet Momma. I started crying and hugged her. Her hands were bound so she couldn't hug me back.

"Momma, I'm so sorry, I miss you," I cried.

Momma started crying too. "Honey child, I miss you, too."

I kept hugging her until the guard told us to sit down. We did as we were told, touching each other's hands while Delia and the guard stood over us. Momma looked up at them.

"Can't we have some time alone?" She stammered out through her tears.

"We really aren't supposed to leave Soledad with you alone," Delia replied.

"I haven't seen my girl in such a long time. Please give us a couple of minutes," Momma pleaded.

I added my own tear-filled two cents for emphasis. "Please let us have our private moment," I said.

Delia and the guard looked at each other. They backed away from us and began whispering. Me and Momma kept staring at them. They looked at us again and Delia stepped back towards us.

"I really shouldn't do this," she said, "but this in an extra-ordinary circumstance. We'll let you talk, but only for a few." Delia raised one of her hands up to her eyes. "We'll be watching, so please don't make me regret giving both of you this opportunity."

"Thank you so much," Momma said.

Delia and the guard looked at each other one more time before walking to the opposite end of the room. When I thought they were far enough away, I wiped my tears away and moved closer to Momma.

"Momma, we have to tell the truth, you can't stay here," I said, keeping my voice low so no one else could hear me.

Momma raised her bound hands to my lips. "Don't say another word. The walls here can talk and they don't have our best interests in mind," she warned.

"But Momma."

"Be quiet, Sola. You have to let it go."

God knows I wanted to know why she was trying to take the fall for me, why she took the gun from my hand and wiped off my prints and put the gun in her own hand. She even washed my hands. She called 911 and told the operator that she shot Rocky. Tears started to fall down my cheeks.

"But why, Momma?" I asked. I still wanted to hear her answer from her own lips.

Momma sighed, using her hands to wipe my tears. "I deserve to be here, honey child. I should have known what Rocky was doing to you. My instincts should have told me what kind of a man he was. What kind of mother lets her child suffer like you did?"

"I'm sorry, Momma."

"You don't have anything to be sorry for. I did what I had to do." She spoke louder, maybe so the *walls* could hear her.

"We don't have a lot of time, Sola. And I don't want to waste time talking about things we can't change. Instead, we'll talk about you. So, tell me, you staying at Children's Services?"

"Yeah, up on Mound Street. I hate it, but Delia's nice."

Momma smiled. "The woman over there?" she asked, nodding her head in Delia's direction.

"Yes. She's the social worker," I relied.

"And what you been doing?" Momma asked, grabbing my hands and caressing them.

"Reading, mostly. Playing a little chess. Nothing too big."

Momma sighed. "And how are you?"

"I'll be better when you get out of here." I touched her hair. "The prison salon definitely ain't The Art of Beauty Hair and Nail Salon," I joked, trying to make Momma, and myself for that matter, feel a little better.

Momma stopped caressing my hands and looked at me seriously. "I'm going to be real with you, Sola. I may not get out of here anytime soon."

"But why? It could be self-defense," I pleaded. "I mean, he was raping me, Momma."

Momma closed her eyes and shook her head. I knew she was trying to block out the images of what Rocky had done to me.

"Sola, it's more than just Rocky keeping me in here. The cops think I know something about Rocky and his boss's business. Even the Feds have been in here trying to rake me over the coals. I don't know nothing but that doesn't stop them from asking endless questions. They've kept me up for hours at a time. It's like they don't care that I have a lawyer." Momma was speaking loudly again. "They keep telling me that if I give them info, they'll make sure I get paroled."

"But can't you tell them something?" I asked.

"If I knew anything, and I don't, I wouldn't risk your life or mine by talking about something that ain't going to change a thing," she said. I understood her perfectly.

Momma looked over my shoulder. "They're coming," she said.

I turned around. Delia and the guard were walking towards us. I turned back to Momma. Tears were welling up in her eyes.

"I'm so sorry," she said.

I touched her face. "It's not your fault."

Momma smiled. "When did you get so grown?"

My eyes watered. I looked down at my stomach and touched it with my hand. "Since—" I couldn't finish the sentence.

Momma buried her head in her hands and cried. Delia and the guard arrived at the table. It was time to go. Momma looked at me as she rose from the table. She sought forgiveness in her eyes and I gave it with my eyes.

It's funny, you know. No matter how your parents treat you, you still seek their love and approval. And even if they kick you down, if they reach out a finger to lift you up, it seems at that moment the world is okay. That's kind of how it was with Momma.

The guard walked Momma back to the door. She looked at me one more time before she walked through the door and it closed behind her. At that moment, my last bit of humanity told me I had to save her. I would do anything to make sure she didn't spend her life in jail.

Chapter Twenty-Eight

Never let emotion control your actions.
Feelings will cloud your judgment.
—The Qualities of Chess Masters # 409

April 1, 3:40 A.M

Campbell Donovan continued sitting on the couch, fiddling with the mini-cassette player. He opened up the small box containing the tapes. There were fifteen in all. He wondered how much information Sola recorded on the tapes; how much of herself she was willing to share.

Two months before, she had been willing to share her body, and she taught him a valuable lesson.

He lay back against the couch and closed his eyes, finding himself lost in the memory of his and Sola's initial encounter again.

Campbell and Sola had left the party quickly, not even bothering to say goodbye to their host. And seeing as how the blondes were keeping Monchats occupied, he probably wouldn't notice their absence.

Campbell was surprised that Sola offered to take him to her home. He thought with her "profession," she would be much more guarded. But as he stood behind her as they waited for the valet to bring her car, his thoughts drifted to being inside her.

The valet pulled up in a shiny black BMW sports car. Campbell noticed the license plate—SASS N. He moved closer to Sola, rubbing himself against her ass.

"So you're sassy, huh?" he growled.

Sola laughed, opening the door for Campbell before walking to the other side to tip the valet and get in on the driver's side of the car.

"Something like that," she responded.

Sola drove to Broad Street, turned right and then headed east. She shifted the gears of the car as she increased speed. As her hand gripped the gearshift, jerking it into position, Campbell felt aroused. He couldn't help but ask, "Are you going to ride me like that shift?" His voice was deep, made heavy by his lust.

"I guess we'll have to see," Sola replied.

Sola kept driving east until she turned right onto a small narrow neighborhood street. Street lights gave the road an eerie glow. Sola turned again, this time onto a winding road. Campbell kept thinking of her, he almost couldn't contain himself, but he wanted to maintain some sense of control.

"It must be nice living in a neighborhood full of old folks," he said, trying to lighten up the nonexistent conversation. "I bet they're all nosy as hell."

Sola slowed down the car and looked at him. She reached down between his legs and rubbed him gently, making him moan with pleasure.

"Too bad they won't see what I'm going to do to you."

Less than a minute later, they arrived at Sola's house. It was a nice-sized ranch home. Sola drove up the driveway and behind the house. "Let's go," she said as she parked the car and turned off the engine.

Campbell's heart started beating faster. He had never felt this much sexual energy for a woman. He watched her back as she unlocked the door, admiring her back, her slim waist, shapely hips, and her long, smooth legs. The back door led to the kitchen. Sola turned on the light. She walked over to the wall near the stove and pressed a button. Campbell noticed the lack of beeping.

"No alarm?" he asked.

"You're the curious one, aren't you?" Sola smiled and walked past him, purposely bumping him on the way. "I have a silent alarm with a fingerprint-activated system."

"Wow, that sounds expensive."

"It's necessary," she said. "Follow me."

They walked through the kitchen into the den. Campbell noted the simple, classic furniture. As she turned on the light, something caught his eye.

In the middle of the coffee table was an elaborate knife. It was long, about fourteen inches, and had a gentle curve. The knife was engraved with some sort of calligraphy, which added to its mystique.

"Now this is interesting," Campbell said, walking toward the coffee table. "You don't look like the type that would like playing with knives." He chuckled and then reached out to touch the engraved handle.

"Don't touch that," Sola's warned. Her tone was serious. "It's very sharp."

He snatched back his hand. "Thanks for letting me know. What kind is it?"

Sola looked at the weapon nonchalantly. "It's a Japanese Samurai sword—well, a replica of one, even though it was made in Japan."

"It's kind of small for a Samurai sword, isn't it?" he asked as he admired the intricate design of the sword's blade.

"That type of sword was used for a special purpose." Sola walked up behind him. "Rather than be dishonored, a Samurai would choose death by taking a sword and disemboweling himself." She started caressing his shoulders. "Look, the last thing I want to talk about is the death rituals of ancient Japanese warriors. Right now, I'm only worried about another type of sword."

Campbell turned around and looked at Sola. Her eyes were beckoning him, her lips full, her body sure. He could tell she liked to be in control. He would have to show her what a real man could do.

He closed the short distance between them and grabbed her chin. She continued to stare at him and he bent down to kiss her. He tried to be gentle, but the taste of her soft lips made him hungry for more. He thrust his tongue in her mouth and pulled her closer. She returned his passion, meeting his tongue with her own. Campbell groaned when Sola began sucking on his tongue gently. After a few minutes of almost pure ecstasy, she pulled away from him. "Not here," she said, her breath ragged. "In the bedroom."

At that moment, Campbell would have followed Sola to hell if she asked him to. They walked quickly down the dimly-lit hallway into Sola's bedroom. She turned on the light. Her bedroom was immaculate. She had a large decorative wood bed with four ornate posts. Thin silk white banners were wrapped around the posts. The bed was topped with an expensive covering and four large pillows. A matching armoire and dresser completed the suite. The carpet was white and thick, almost like fur.

"Wow, this is nice," he exclaimed.

"Thanks," she responded. "I like to always feel good when I go to bed."

Campbell walked behind Sola and started caressing her

shoulders. He followed his hands with his tongue, delighting in the taste of her skin. "And how do you feel now?" he asked.

"I think you know," she replied.

He turned her around and kissed her deeply. This time, it was his turn to suck on her tongue. He pushed her gently backward until her back was against the wall. He tore himself away from her exquisite lips, knelt down and took off her shoes. He started kissing one of her legs, moving his tongue slowly up her leg until he reached her dress. She was moaning slightly, and he could tell she enjoyed what he was doing. And there was more in store.

He took his hands and lifted up her dress until he felt the soft silk of her panties. He didn't even bother pulling them down, instead he ripped them off, letting the torn fabric fall to the floor. He then positioned his shoulders under her knees and lifted her off the floor. He could feel the heat emanating from her.

She was so soft and supple, and when he tasted her between her legs, she melted like warm butter. As he used his tongue to pleasure her, to taste her, to move in and out of her, she started to quiver. He sucked her clit until she started vibrating. When he knew she was near the edge, he lowered her to the ground.

"Not yet," he whispered. He wanted to be inside her when she exploded.

He pulled off her dress, kissing her stomach, nibbling on her breasts, caressing her as she lifted her arms so he could remove her final barrier.

When she was naked, he stepped back and admired her body. She stood in front of him with her eyes closed. She was a work of art. Da Vinci couldn't have created a more beautiful sculpture of the female form.

She reached for his shirt but he stopped her. He was in

total control. He lifted her off the floor again and took her to the bed, laying her down before he started to unbutton his shirt.

They stared at each other the entire time—as he fumbled with his buttons and threw his clothes to the floor. When he was finished, he stood before her, letting her study his naked body and the power it held.

He joined her on the bed and touched her essence. She was hot, wet, and ready. His own body yearned for their union.

"You want this?" he groaned.

Her eyes were closed, as if she were in her own world. He had to bring her back to him. He took one of her nipples in his mouth and rolled the hardened flesh between his lips. At the same time, he stuck two fingers inside of her. She moaned in pleasure, opening her eyes to look at him. Her gaze was passion-filled, smoky.

"You want this?" he asked again.

She still didn't respond.

He knew a part of her would never totally yield to him, but he wanted to hear her voice, inviting him, accepting him.

He moved on top of her and positioned himself to enter her. He grinded against her slowly and she moaned again.

"You want this?"

"Please, yes. Please." Her voice was almost a whisper. He heard exactly what he needed.

He entered her and almost exploded right then and there. She was so tight, so warm. "Damn, you feel so good," he muttered. He couldn't help himself.

He started moving inside her, in and out. He felt himself swelling, her juices surrounding him, getting hotter.

He turned her around and moved her into his favorite position. She yelled out when he slapped her backside. When he entered her from the back, he slid in so deep he couldn't stop himself from shouting out her name. He had truly felt nothing more pleasurable before than being inside her.

He flipped her back around on the bed. He gripped her legs and spread them farther apart. He wanted to dive deeper into her, to consume her with all he had. Her hips responded to the call, and she started to match him stroke for stroke. It was almost too much to bear.

He let himself go in the passion. He felt the heat rising from his own body. He quickened his pace and she moaned louder with each thrust. He couldn't take it much longer.

Her muscles contracted around him and her legs began to shake. Her release signaled his own. With one final thrust, he erupted, pouring his essence into her. And at that moment, he wished he could live in that emotion forever.

Afterwards, Campbell lay in the bed basking in the aftermath of the most exciting sex he had in years. He was intoxicated by her smell in the air and the taste of her in his mouth. The thought of taking her again made him groan.

He felt Sola stir in the bed. He opened his eyes. Sola was staring at him.

He reached out to caress her face. *Damn, she is so fine.* He thought. She yielded to his touch, but stared at him the entire time. He knew she was studying him, trying to figure him out.

"Have you ever heard of the saying 'keep your friends close, but your enemies closer?'" Sola asked. It was an interesting question to ask, especially in their current state.

He leaned back. "Of course," he responded.

Sola's smile disappeared. Her hand moved from under her pillow. Campbell felt a cold piece of steel against his chin. On instinct, he reached down for his gun, but in his naked state, she had him exactly where she wanted him.

Chapter Twenty-Nine

Tread lightly when the battle is not in your favor.
Make your opponent beat you with skill.
Never allow yourself to be beaten because of your
weaknesses.

—The Qualities of Chess Masters # 421

"Don't move," Sola said in a stern voice. She continued to hold the gun to the side of his face while using her other hand and feet to remove the pillows and sheets from the bed. After she completed her task, she got out of the bed, still holding the gun in his direction. He tried to get up.

"I said don't move," Sola repeated her command. Campbell heard the gun click. "Don't think for a minute I won't blow your brains out."

"What the hell are you doing?" he asked. He couldn't believe the tables had turned so quickly.

"Turn around and lay on the bed, spread eagle." She waved her gun across the bed for emphasis.

"Sola, don't do this."

"Campbell Donovan, if that's your real name, you don't know what the fuck I'm going to do. Right now, you need to heed what I say, listen to my questions, and give me the answers I like."

Campbell hesitated before lying on his stomach and spreading his legs and arms across the bed as far as he could. He heard Sola searching through his clothes.

He remained silent, still stunned by Sola's actions. How had she known? He felt the steel on his ankles.

"You want my opinion?" Sola said as she started moving the gun slowly up his left leg. His nerves tingled from the sensation. Campbell felt like he was being stabbed with icicles.

"I think you're a cop, probably Fed," Sola continued. "You underestimated me—thought your dick would turn me into a parrot. You thought wrong."

Campbell thought briefly about remaining silent, but as he felt the gun against his back, he had to say something, anything. "It's not what you think," he said.

"Once again, you try to assume. Try giving me some answers." The gun stopped at the base of his neck.

He thought about lying, sticking to his cover story, but he knew his life would be over if he did. He wasn't going to beg Sola to spare him, but at least he could try and help himself in other ways.

"Yes, yes, I am a federal agent. I've been working undercover," Campbell confessed. "You got me." He tried not to sound harsh. He didn't want to upset her even further.

"But, Sola," Campbell continued, "you have to understand. What just happened between me and you, it wasn't planned. I didn't know I'd want you—"

Sola interrupted him. "That's where you're wrong. It was planned. Monchats wanted to test you, and you failed. Looks like your cover's blown."

So that's what it was. Campbell thought he had got his foot in the door, but it had been shut the whole time.

"So Monchats knew?" he asked.

"He didn't, but he will. You let your emotions get the better of you and you slipped."

"What?"

"You probably didn't even realize it, knowing my neighbors were old and being stupid enough to mention it. I'll bet you've been scoping out my house for months. The Feds definitely need to train their pigs better."

"So you brought me here to fuck me and kill me?" he asked.

"Don't question what I do and how I do it," Sola replied coldly.

He thought about ways to keep the conversation going and wondered if he could play a trump card with her.

"Look, Sola, Monchats is going down, and soon. You can either stay onboard a sinking ship or grab a life raft and save yourself," Campbell reasoned.

"It's so simple, isn't it? You think you can come in and talk a good game?" Sola asked.

"I'm not trying to talk a good game, Sola. We're close. It's only a matter of time."

"And what in the hell would make you think I'd do anything to help you?"

"We can get your mother out of prison."

There was an awkward silence. Then Sola pressed the gun down on Campbell's neck. The pressure made him want to scream.

"You're a fucking liar," Sola said angrily.

He tried to remain calm, not really knowing if his next breath would be his last.

"Sola, I'm not lying to you. If you give us information, testify against Monchats, I can guarantee you would see your mother free before the end of the year."

"I can't believe you'd think I ever be a rat," Sola spat out.

"It's not like that. Look, I know your mother got a raw deal. Her sentence was way too harsh."

"Because the Feds wanted to her be a rat."

Campbell could feel one of his legs cramping up and he wanted to move into a more comfortable position, but he didn't know if Sola was wavering. He decided his best bet was to remain spread eagle on the bed.

"Look," he began, "I don't deny that the FBI did and still believes your mother has invaluable information concerning major drug rings in Ohio. But she was convicted and sentenced for first degree murder, nothing else. She's been in prison for fourteen years, and she's had the opportunity to speak, to set herself free. Now you have that opportunity, too."

"What makes you think I don't want her to rot in jail?"

"I just don't think you do," Campbell shifted on the bed. "I'm not asking for much, and what you'll gain from testifying, your mother, it would be well worth it. Just think—"

Sola interrupted him. "I don't know what you think I know about Monchats's businesses. If you think my knowledge of his affairs is great, then you are sadly mistaken. As I'm sure you know, I'm only familiar with Monchats for one purpose only."

"But that's what we need. Someone from the inside. If you would tell your story, it could do so much," Campbell begged.

"You marked the wrong person, *Campbell Donovan*." Sola stressed his name.

"Sola, I'm just asking you to think about it." She didn't respond, so he continued with his plea. "You have to be tired of the life you're living. Being alone, letting some thug basically pimp you out and do your bidding."

"You don't know a fucking thing about my life," She lifted the gun off of the base of his neck. Campbell didn't know if she was letting him go or getting ready to shoot him.

"Just think about it. It won't hurt anything to just think about it. If you decide to let me go, I won't tell my superiors about tonight. You can have the address to my apartment. Anything. Look, you don't trust me, I know, so I'll even give you my real name. Maybe you can Google me or something. It's Josiah. Josiah Anderson."

He heard Sola gasp. He turned his head. She was leaning against the wall, her eyes filled with tears.

"Sola?" He started to get up from the bed. She raised her gun.

"How'd you know?" She asked with an almost childlike voice.

"Sola, what are you talking about?"

She shook her head. "You're lying to me. Trying to get to me. Mess with my brain."

"I'm not lying to you, Sola. My name is Josiah Anderson. You could blow my brains out at any second. Why would I lie?"

He couldn't believe the vulnerability Sola displayed. Before his eyes, he could sense the ice was melting from Sola's soul. *But why*, he thought to himself.

He watched Sola as she touched her stomach and slid to the floor. She appeared to be in her own world. She was looking beyond him, her eyes lost in time. He thought about getting up from the bed. He wanted to comfort her. But she was unpredictable, something he hadn't expected.

After a couple of minutes, Sola's eyes cleared and she stood up. She walked over to his clothes and pointed her gun down at them.

"Get your clothes," she said. "We're leaving."

"Where are you taking me?" Campbell asked, wondering if Sola was taking him to some dense woods on the outskirts of the city to finish him off.

"Wherever you need to go," she replied quietly.

Within fifteen minutes, Sola and Campbell were headed North on I-71. At first, Sola looked at him strangely and asked him what he drove to the benefit dinner, but her face relaxed when he explained that his Navigator was in the shop and he had taken a taxi to the dinner. They didn't speak to each other again during the drive, even though Anderson wanted to talk. He wanted to ask her so many questions. *Why did my name affect her?* He thought.

When they reached the Polaris Exit on the highway, he directed her to take the exit and told her to drive West on Polaris Parkway. Although the Polaris roads were usually difficult to navigate because of the huge mall crowds, it was late, and traffic was light. Soon, they reached the Polaris Park Executive Arms Apartment Complex. He then told her where to park.

"You know, Sola, the offer is real. I can help you with your mother. It's your decision."

"Don't ask me to rat out Monchats."

They sat in silence, the BMW's engine idle.

"So, my cover is blown?" Campbell laughed nervously. "I guess I'll have to sleep with one eye open, never knowing what you're going to do."

"You know my decision."

Campbell raised his eyebrows. "I do?"

"You're still alive."

Campbell smiled. He had almost forgotten, or, at least, he wanted to forget. "Sola, I'm sure you could get this information anyway, so I'll just tell you. I'm in the building on the edge of the complex." He pointed to one of the brick structures. "Fifth Floor, Apartment 5122. You can come to me anytime."

Sola didn't respond, so he continued speaking. "I'm not going to lie to you. I'm not going to pretend that I understand what just happened between us, and this may sound totally crazy, but I think it was something special. I know what I am and what you are, and that anything in terms of a future is implausible. But what we shared, I haven't responded that way to any woman, ever." Sola kept staring straight ahead, looking at the night sky through the windshield. "Sola, think about it. For some reason, you couldn't kill me, even though everything you've learned should have put a bullet in my brain. I just want you to think about everything. I want to help you. To save you." He heard a small click that let him know she was unlocking the passenger side door. It was time for him to go.

Campbell got out of the car, saying goodbye. Sola turned to look at him, but didn't even smile. Before he closed the door, she said, "Don't ever look for me again. Don't seek me out, don't come to my house and don't even ask for me. If you do, I won't be responsible for my actions."

He nodded slowly, closed the door, and headed to his apartment building, not quite sure if he wasn't still due for a bullet in his back. But when he turned around, Sola was already gone.

The next day, he pondered over how to tell his superiors that his cover was blown. What could he say? That he had mind-blowing sex with a woman he just met and then she forced him to lay spread eagle with a gun aimed at the base of his neck? That he could actually see himself falling for a cold-blooded killer? He was already the subject of merciless teasing for his current *assignment* at the Dollhouse.

Around noon the next day, he received a call from B.L.,

Monchats's assistant, asking him why "his black ass wasn't keeping the black booty in check at the Dollhouse."

Campbell decided to go to the club, requesting extra back up because "something could go down." But nothing was out of the ordinary. Days passed, but nothing changed. *Sola hadn't said a word.* And neither would he.

The sound of a phone ringing jolted Campbell out of his dream of the first night he spent with Sola. It was a cell phone—not his. It rang again. He was about to walk into the bedroom when he heard Sola's voice.

"Speak," he heard Sola say.

He was still holding the mini-cassette player in his hand. He opened the small box and looked at the tapes. Sola had written *Sola's Story* on each tape and a series of Roman numerals. He heard water running in the bathroom. *You don't have much time*, he thought.

He took out the tape with Roman numerals I through V printed on it and inserted it into the player. He pressed play and Sola's silky voice filled the room: "*If someone wrote the story of my life, I wonder how they would describe it. On the outside looking in, some writers might say I'm a stone-cold killer undeserving of any sympathy. And that's cool with me. It would be easy to paint the lines of my life in black and white, but truth be told, my world is full of gray.*"

Chapter Thirty

Sola's Story,
Part XIV – 1993

I tried to help Momma. I tried to get her out. After visiting Momma at the Franklin County Jail, I told Delia that I shot Rocky. Then there was another trip to the police station. Another board-certified brain doc told the cops and Delia I was making up stories to help Momma, so she stayed behind bars.

When Momma wrote me and told me she decided to plead guilty, I stayed in bed all day crying. I wanted her to change her mind, but it was already made up.

One the saddest days of my life, the saddest one being the death of my son, was seeing my mother plead guilty to first degree murder in a Franklin County Courtroom. I screamed out hysterically, "She's lying! Take me!"

A couple of bailiffs took me out of the courtroom.

Later, I heard that the judge told Momma her sentence wouldn't be lenient. He had to send a message that no one could get away with murder. Her guilty plea may have saved her from a lethal injection, but she was still looking at life without the possibility of parole.

I tried to free Momma a couple more times, but I failed. No one believed that a fourteen year old girl would purposely kill another human being. After Delia was promoted to Director of Teenage Services, Children's Services moved me to a group home for teenage girls on East Main Street. Most of the girls were runaways and druggies and I couldn't relate. I stayed to myself mostly, trying to figure out what I was going to do.

My answer came quickly, of course. As I was walking down Main Street one day, a white Lincoln Continental started following me and then stopped a couple of feet away from me. I couldn't help but look at it, I always had a weakness for nice cars.

As I walked by, the back window slid down. A voice called my name. I wanted to break out in a run, but I couldn't. I just stood there, staring at the car.

I heard the voice again. It was deep and smooth. "Sola. Come here. I wanted to talk to you."

The door opened. I couldn't see a face, only a pinstripe suit and a blinged-out hand.

"I don't talk to strangers," I responded, and started walking down the street.

The Lincoln followed closely.

The voice. "I'm a friend of your mother's."

"Ain't that what all perve's say?"

"Just get in the car."

"I don't want to end up on the back of a milk carton."

I kept walking. The Lincoln kept following.

"I can help you get your mother out of jail," the voice said.

I froze and turned around. The voice said the magic words. The door opened again, but I wasn't ready to get inside.

"We can talk like this. Then I'll decide if I wanna get inside," I said.

The voice. "You are strong-headed, aren't you?"

"What about my mother?"

"Just like I thought. You like it straight and simple. No massaging, no bullshit. We will get along perfectly."

"I don't even know you."

I saw the outline of a man's face shielded by a Fedora hat. "My name is Pierre-Henri Monchats. But I am known as Dennis," he said.

"You French or something?" I asked. Even though I was a bit scared, I was also interested.

The man who called himself Monchats laughed. "I'm Creole, and something. From New Orleans. Louisiana. In the big ol' U.S. of A. Now are you ready to talk?" The blinged-out hand reached out for me. I accepted.

My heart started beating fast as I stepped into the car. I smelled fresh leather and cologne. After I sat down, there was a flash of pinstripes as an arm reached over my legs and closed the door. My head jerked back as the Lincoln sped off down Main.

I couldn't look up at first. I felt stupid for getting into the car, but it was too late. If the voice wanted to take me out to some field and leave me for dead, there wasn't really anything I could do.

"Are you going to leave me hanging or what?" Monchats asked. I noticed an extended hand.

I took the hand and shook it, raising my eyes to see the voice's face. He was high yellow with a slight mustache and light eyes.

"Your name is Pierre?" I asked. It was all I could think to say.

"Actually the first name is Pierre-Henri. But you can call me Dennis or just Monchats. It doesn't matter to me."

"So, how can you help me with my mother?" I asked.

"Like I said, straight and to the point. I like that." He nodded toward the front seat, where a large black man was driving. "Right, B.L.?"

The large man nodded. "Sure thing."

"That's my personal assistant and best friend, B.L." Monchats said as he took off his hat and laid it on one of his knees. He had thick, dark wavy hair. "Now, he usually doesn't do the driving," Monchats chuckled. "And he's probably cursing me out in his mind, but my main man is sick and I needed B.L. today. I've been wanting to meet you and I knew today would be the perfect opportunity for me to introduce myself." Monchats reached over the seat and squeezed B.L.'s shoulder.

"Okay." I was beginning to think Monchats was playing with me. Dead in the field seemed like a certain reality.

"Before I get to talking about your mother, I want you to know a few things." Monchats voice got deeper and more serious. "I don't like to serve bullshit or have any on my plate. I keep it real and I expect everyone I deal with to keep it real with me. Do you understand?"

I nodded my head, not knowing quite what to say.

"Good. Next, I expect everything I say to you to stay with you and only you." I nodded again. "If you agree to my terms, there is no turning back. I don't like failure."

Wait a minute, I thought. "I don't know your terms," I said to him.

Monchats chuckled. "Quick thinker," he said, holding up his hand. "Just wait."

"Fine." I said.

"Lastly, we are about to have a serious conversation. Assume I know everything."

"Get on with it."

"Your mother is looking at a lifetime behind bars. I've heard about your antics and your extreme desire to see your mother free again. Now, I can't help you get her out immediately, but I can give you a chance to help reduce her sentence."

I raised my eyebrows. My interest was piqued. "And how can you pull something like that off?" I asked.

Monchats pulled out a manila folder from his black leather brief case and opened it. "Before I show you this, I want you to know who I am."

"I think I figured that out."

"Oh, really." Monchats moved closer to me. "Indulge me."

"I figure you deal drugs, a pretty heavy player too with the looks of this Lincoln."

"Well, well, perceptive too." Monchats tapped B.L. on the shoulder. "And you thought I was wrong about her."

I was starting to get irritated. "Look, could you tell me what you want or let me out of the car. I don't have time for all this," I said, sucking my teeth.

"You might do good to learn some respect for your elders, Soledad," Monchats said.

Monchats was really pissing me off. "Could we please just get on with it?"

Monchats pushed the folder in front of me. "As you wish."

In the folder was a black and white picture of a black man. "What's this?"

"That's who I need you to take care of."

I couldn't believe my ears. "What?" I asked. "What do you mean take care of him?" My cheeks were burning. "Do I look like some ho or something? Do you actually think—"

"I want you to kill him, do you understand that?" Monchats said, cutting me off.

I jumped in my sit, my heart was racing. I paused for a moment, not knowing if his clarifications were better or worse than my own assumptions. "You can't think I'm going to go around killing somebody."

Monchats took the folder and picture off of my lap. "Sola, like I told you. Assume I know everything . . . about your mother, about Rocky. About who really blew his head off, literally."

How did he know? I thought.

"I make it my business to know everything," he said as if he heard the question lingering in my mind.

"I can't do it. Let me out." I was starting to shake all over.

"Oh, I think you can do it," Monchats said confidently. "I know what it takes to kill."

"Why don't you kill him yourself instead of trying to get some teenage girl to do it?" I asked angrily.

Monchats laughed again. "Being young makes you what? Only a better weapon. Don't try to kid yourself or me. You lived in the Gardens. You know bangers younger than you who've done their share of reducing the population."

"What makes you think I can do it?"

"You have to understand, Sola, I know talent when I see it. I sense you have a gift. Didn't you plan? Didn't you think about it? How you would do it?"

I looked out the window, watching the buildings blur before my eyes as the Lincoln sped by them. "You want me to be a murderer."

"But you already are."

I felt tears welling in my eyes. "You don't know what you're talking about."

"Like I said, I don't serve bullshit and don't like any on my plate. Be real with me, Sola. Didn't you enjoy it?"

Tears were rolling down my cheeks. "You don't know anything," I cried out.

"Oh, but I do, Sola. I can imagine you there. Leading

Rocky into your bedroom, letting him play with you, and allowing him to take your clothes off. Now he's comfortable. You have him where you want him. You get your gun. Maybe you had it under the pillow, that would be my choice. Now you're holding the gun in your hand. You fire the shots. Your hand is hot. He's begging for his life. You had control over whether a man lived or died. I know you enjoyed it, reveled in it. That seductive power. Believe me, I know the feeling."

Monchats leaned back in his seat and continued speaking. "You got your gun from that Jamaican pothead, Truth, four months before you shot Rocky. You planned for it to go down in your place. And now, you're letting your mother sit in jail for you. Now I'm not blaming you for doing what you did. I have a daughter, and if a man did to her what Rocky did to you," Monchats paused for a minute. "Damn, I'd slit that man's stomach open and watch him die, slowly. I understand the need for revenge. I lost all my brothers while I was still a teen and I didn't know what to do. But you, you took control of your situation. You decided, 'I'm going to handle this.' And you handled it well. Oh, Miss Sola, you're good. No, scratch that. You're great. And what's so amazing is that you're only fourteen years old."

I felt like my life had been displayed on MTV's *Real World* or in a movie or something. I hated the fact that Monchats knew me better than I knew myself. I wiped the tears from my face. "I don't want to kill nobody else." I muttered.

"Not even for your mother? What's one more piece of scum off the earth for you to have a chance to see your mother free again?"

I looked at Monchats. He had a gleam in his eye, like a car salesman trying to seal the deal.

"Your mother is looking at a lifetime behind bars," he said. "You have a chance to reduce her sentence."

"I can't believe you'd come to me for this."

"My reasons are my own, Sola. But now you can decide." He put the picture back in my lap. "Do this and your mother will see parole in about twenty-one years. You'll be what? Thirty-five or thirty-six years old? She'll be out in time to see her future grandchildren grow." He said, grinning like a used-car salesman about to seal the deal.

"I can't." I shook my head.

"Just think about it Sola. Your mother free. I can set you up so you won't have to be up under Children's Services any more. All for a thug who likes to play with young girls."

I felt a lump forming in my throat. *A thug that likes to play with young girls . . . just like Rocky,* I thought. "What did you say?" I asked.

"You heard me," he said, pointing at the picture. "He likes girls, the younger the better."

"What's his name?" I asked.

"It's always best not to know the name of a person you have to take out. It makes it personal, messy. You speak Spanish, right? I know a little bit myself. I'll just call him *viejo verde.*"

"A dirty old man?" I translated.

"Yes, that's how I'd best describe him," Monchats responded.

I couldn't believe that I was still in the car. I should have been cursing Monchats out for asking me to kill a man. But I stayed there silent, listening and learning. I was seriously thinking about doing it.

"You do this, and I'll make sure you have everything you need to do the job. One thing though, you'll have to ride the bus," Monchats said.

"What? You want me to kill somebody then get on the bus?"

"Yes." Monchats was actually serious. "People notice getaway cars, but they won't pay attention to a teenage girl getting on a COTA."

"And if I do this, take him out," I stuttered, "my mother won't get life without parole?"

Monchats smiled again. The diamond-encrusted gold cap on one of his front teeth sparkled. "I am a man of my word."

I didn't know what to say, so we all rode around with no one saying a word. Monchats told B.L. to drop me off a couple of blocks away from the group home.

"I don't want anyone at your little group home to think you're out here turning tricks," Monchats said. "They'll put your ass on lockdown and that would mess everything up."

As we pulled up to the corner of Wilson and Main, Monchats told me to think about what he said. I told him I would. His last words were, "Remember, what I told you is for you and only you."

I couldn't believe I was really thinking about it; killing someone else. But then I thought about what Monchats told me, that the *viejo verde* was messing around with little girls—girls like me, maybe younger. I wanted to believe what Monchats told me, that the man was just another piece of scum who deserved to die; a man just like Rocky.

Chapter Thirty-One

Confidence is a trait of a warrior;
But cockiness is a quality that leads to defeat.
—The Qualities of Chess Masters # 439

April 1, 4:15 A.M.

B.L. always woke up early, a habit of a man with too many things to do and not enough hours in the day. If he could pay God to add two or three hours to the twenty-four hour day, he would. But as it was, God would probably give him a one-way ticket to hell, so he just had to play the hand he was given.

B.L. stirred slightly in the bed, trying to be careful. He didn't want to disturb Ruben. His new "apprentice" looked so good sleeping beside him, he almost wished he could keep him there. He thought back to their night together. It was truly amazing.

Even though Ruben told him he had been "opened up" during a six-month stay in jail, B.L. was gentle the first time they were together. He knew he could be forceful because his sexual drive was hard to restrain, and he didn't want to scare Ruben with his lust.

But yesterday, B.L. was stressed. There was Monchats,

Monchats's dead daughter, making sure Sola was taken care of, Sizzle and Pepe's untimely demises, and keeping Monchats's businesses, both legal and illegal, in order. He didn't like feeling out of sorts, and he needed to relieve himself. Ruben was a perfect outlet for relaxation. This time, B.L. didn't hold back, driving himself into Ruben and taking pleasure as Ruben took the brunt of his frustrations.

Ruben was up for the challenge, and B.L. appreciated his zeal. By the time they were finished basically assaulting each other's bodies, they both collapsed on B.L.'s California King-sized bed and went to sleep.

When B.L. was younger, he struggled with his sexuality. In the slum called Florida-Desire, all his boys bragged about their exploits with girls like badges of honor. He didn't want to be left out, so he tried to get with a girl. He still remembered her name, Maria Canford. He felt so awkward kissing her and touching her that he couldn't even get it up. She laughed at him and he bitch-slapped her, threatening to kill her if she ever said a word. She never did.

For a long time, B.L. thought something was wrong with him, maybe he had some disease. But he discovered his true nature when he turned eighteen years old.

Back then, he and Dennis Monchats were working for Moth, mainly making runs and pickups. B.L. went to Bourbon to make a run at one of the local gay clubs, a place called Paradise Lost. Monchats was supposed to go with him, but Monchats said he was sick and begged B.L. to cover for him. They had already been through so much together, so B.L. agreed.

When he entered the club, he felt like he was right at home. He couldn't believe he was attracted to men. He felt so nervous that he made the drop quick. He ran out of the club so fast, he almost stumbled onto Bourbon Street like a drunk on Mardi Gras.

A month later, he was back at the Paradise Lost. He wasn't there to work. He was curious. And scared. He sat at the bar and drank Hurricanes until he felt buzzed. That night, he met Tommy, an older white man who gave B.L. his first real sexual experience. After that night in one of the back rooms at the club, there was no turning back.

B.L. rarely worried about anyone finding out about his lifestyle. He had to be discreet, because there was no telling how people would react if they found out, especially Monchats. Sola did know; the result of her snooping around. But she used her knowledge to leverage her meaningless existence. He hoped that he would soon find out he no longer had to worry about her mouth.

B.L. had seen the consequences of brothers who decided to leave their closets behind or were forced out because of circumstances within and beyond their control, and it wasn't pretty. His decision to live a quasi-DL lifestyle was all about survival—nothing more, nothing less.

B.L. kept up the pretense, taking out ladies from time to time and going out to strip clubs. He treated bitches like shit because that is what everyone expected of him. As far as his real partners, he chose them carefully. He usually found men who acted hard on the outside, turned into little bitches in the bedroom. And his partners almost always had something to lose. Maybe it was a family, friends, or a job. And pride was a great silencer. There was also a threat of a bullet in the brain, but he couldn't even remember the last time he had to threaten a man's life due to his sexual lifestyle.

Ruben was different. From the first time B.L. saw him, there was a spark he couldn't explain. B.L.'s "gay-dar" was always on, and Ruben was setting off a three-alarm fire. B.L. approached him cautiously, but Ruben sensed B.L.'s interest right away, and B.L. began courting him. He told Ruben he could see them hooking up for a long time, and he gave him the position to keep him happy. Ruben rewarded him with his body, and it satisfied—immensely.

B.L. jumped when the clock alarm started going off. He reached over to shut it off. Ruben started moving, the noise from the alarm must have awoken him. B.L. cuddled against Ruben, delighting in his warmth.

"Good morning," B.L. said.

"Morning, baby," Ruben responded softly. He caressed B.L.'s hand.

"Did I tell you how much I enjoyed last night?" B.L. asked, holding Ruben tighter so the younger man could feel his arousal.

"In more ways than one," Ruben said as he moved against B.L.'s hardness. B.L. groaned.

"You want some more of this?" B.L. asked.

"Of course I do. I'm all yours," Ruben said, pushing the covers away from him. "But I want to wash up first."

"You just like a woman, always wanting to be fresh and shit."

"There's nothing wrong with that," Ruben said, getting out of the bed. "'Cause my dragon is roaring and my funk is rising. So I hope you don't mind."

"What do I say to that? Feel all dirty and return to bed? Do your thing. I'll be waiting for you." B.L. patted the bed and smiled.

"Oh, I'm betting on it."

B.L. watched as Ruben walked to the master bathroom. Before walking through the door and turning on the light, Ruben picked up the duffle bag he brought with him. As Ruben closed the door, B.L. yelled out to him, "Hurry back."

B.L. reached down and started rubbing himself, anticipating Ruben's return to the bed. He was already aroused, but he wanted to be at full attention when the bathroom door opened. He closed his eyes and savored the sensations he was giving himself, and yearned for the pleasure he would get when his lover returned.

B.L. was so caught up in his groove, he didn't hear the bathroom door slowly open. The man on the other side of the door didn't come out, instead choosing to peek outside. He smiled as he watched B.L. He liked to watch. But time was of the essence. Others would be waking soon, and he hoped to be on a plane headed for New Orleans before anyone took a good look at his handy work.

Ruben aimed his gun at B.L.'s mouth, which was slightly open. He only wanted to shoot twice, one bullet for the head and one bullet for the heart. B.L. was groaning softly. Ruben had been taught never to hesitate, so he fired. The silencer on his gun made the shot sound like a puff of wind. B.L.'s head exploded and his blood, brain, and skull spread out in a colorful display resembling fireworks.

Ruben fired again, this time aiming for B.L.'s chest. The visual effect was less dramatic, but Ruben couldn't help but smile as B.L.'s lifeless and somewhat headless body slumped over. Sola would be proud. But he wondered what she would think of the extra job he had planned.

Ruben couldn't resist getting some sexual satisfaction from his prey. Sola told him that using his body to get what he wanted was a unique and indispensable gift. And as always, she had been right. B.L. fell right into his arms, oblivious to the sinister plan percolating around him. But Ruben also knew the end result of his sexual selfishness—evidence. He had to get rid of as much as possible.

Ruben dressed quickly and ran to his car, throwing his duffel bag into the back seat. He opened the trunk and pulled out a plastic orange container, which held almost a gallon of regular unleaded gasoline. He returned to the

B.L.'s house, and took out the batteries to all of the fire alarms before returning to the bedroom. He began pouring gasoline on the bed, on B.L., on the floor. He saturated the carpet and kept pouring until he reached the bedroom door. He was glad B.L.'s first-floor master bedroom was located in the back of his house, because he had more time to get away before anyone would notice the flames.

Ruben pulled a long flammable string out of his pants pocket and laid it on the ground. He used his lighter to ignite it, then watched as the flame picked up and traveled slowly toward B.L.'s bed. The smoke was rising. It was time to go.

He walked slowly and deliberately to his car. He didn't speed out of the driveway, instead choosing to coast at a leisurely pace. He didn't increase his speed until he reached the main road.

Sola told him not to contact her, that she would know when the deed was done. And he almost couldn't resist. A southern kid had taken down one of the biggest names in the drug business, but he couldn't tell a soul.

"Never brag about your work," Sola told him, "Let your work brag for you."

Before Ruben returned to his motel room to pack and prepare for his trip back to New Orleans, he went to an ATM to withdraw some cash. He took out the max, four hundred dollars. He stared at the receipt after he completed his transaction. Sola was a woman of her word. She had trusted him to do a professional job. He had been paid in full.

Chapter Thirty-Two

Prepare for victory wisely.
—The Qualities of Chess Masters # 464

April 1, 4:35 A.M

The Hunter decided to wait before returning to Sola's house until it was late enough that any prying eyes would be closed. He parked a few blocks away from her street, deciding it was best to jog the short distance to her house. A short run would get his juices flowing. And in Sola's neighborhood, jogging also wouldn't arouse much suspicion from any night owls or early-risers.

He strapped a small backpack on his back, checked the tightness of his shoelaces and began running towards Sola's house. He reached his destination quickly and without incident. He didn't even break a sweat. He jogged to the back of the house and then slowed down. Before going to the back door, he took off his backpack and took out his cell phone. He dialed a security code that could disrupt Sola's wireless security system. He didn't know if she had a chance to activate it before she left during his last visit, but it was better to be safe than sorry. Her back door was easier to open than a Christmas present.

Not having to worry about any alarms, the Hunter entered Sola's house and walked straight to the bedroom. He walked to the bed, traveling the length of the bed while feeling the sheets. There was a small bloodstain on the bed sheet near the pillows. *Sola was here after he shot her*, he thought. He smiled as he imagined her rolling around in pain.

The Hunter pushed the bedsheet back and lay down on the bed. He grabbed a pillow, held it to his nose, and inhaled deeply. He put the pillow down and reached for her bedsheets, covering himself in the cotton that surrounded Sola less than twenty-four hours before. He could smell her scent everywhere. It was intoxicating.

He had wanted Sola for so long, but she was always just out of reach. At first, it seemed he would never get to her. But he found hope in the most unlikely place—prison.

At the Orient Correctional Complex, during his eleven-year stint for attempted murder, he met James Johnson. James was a mid-level thug known on the streets as Chance.

Even then the Hunter had been studying Sola intensively, reading the papers, knowing when she had killed. He trained for the day he would see her again. He lifted weights and ran to strengthen his body, and exercised his brain by reading books. He got stronger.

Chance became his cellmate during his seventh year behind bars. Chance was a total thug, born and bred to be a menace to society. Like most inmates, he claimed he was innocent. He laughed at Chance's claims. "Aren't we all?" the Hunter told him.

As the months passed, Chance's lips got looser and he told his tale. Chance had worked for Pierre-Henri Monchats,

Dennis the Menace, since he was a teenager. Although he started out in the game just dealing, he started doing enforcement work when he filled out and became a man. Chance was six feet, three inches tall and weighed at least three hundred twenty pounds. His work included breaking the arms and legs of dealers who didn't meet their quota, among other things. No excuses were ever accepted.

Chance thought he was riding high until, out of nowhere, he was arrested for the murder of some guy he didn't even know, an execution-style murder on Columbus's East Side. As he listened to Chance describe the murder, the Hunter knew exactly who did the crime, the Brown Recluse—Sola Nichols.

Needless to say, Chance was pissed. He sought Monchats out for help, only to be stopped by B.L., who told him coldly that "things fall apart" and to "take it like a champ." He finally copped a plea for manslaughter so he could have a chance of being free again. Chance started tearing up as he told him that he had to make a plea for the chance to be free and live to see his girl and babies again. As it was, Chance would only be able to see his family on visitation days.

"Man, I'm going to be here for at least fifteen years because Monchats wants to protect his bitch."

The Hunter became closer to Chance, getting him cigarettes and weed, and some liquor every now and then. He showed Chance the ropes of Orient. He told him about the gangs, from the White Supremacists Groups to the prison versions of the Bloods and the Crips. He also told him who he could trust to get things not considered to be the normal prison issue, including weed and other "illegal substances." In the pen, you could get pussy once in a while if you knew who to talk to.

The Hunter also warned him of the Back Door Alliance, the fuckers who could turn regular men into jail bitches on threat of death. These weren't punks, didn't even look feminine, but they were determined to fulfill their needs by any means necessary, including being with unwilling men. Chance accepted the information with gratitude, but never realized that the knowledge he gained wasn't free.

As time went on, the Hunter got more information about Sola, and it fascinated him. While he was doing his time, Sola had become more skilled than he imagined. Monchats thought she was so special, he even sent her to other states to do his bidding. She had killed so many men that no one really liked her, or trusted her, except Monchats.

"Man, if she stepped into a room, you would never know if your head would get blown off," Chance cackled.

One day, when the prison was on lockdown because of rising tensions between white and black inmates, he asked Chance if anyone had ever tried to kill Sola. Chance didn't stop laughing for at least ten minutes.

"Nobody would even think about it," he said, gulping for air as he tried to contain his laughter." Even if you got close enough to do it, and if she didn't get you first, Monchats would have you dead by sundown. She's like a slave to him, man. I wouldn't be surprised if she didn't have 'Property of Dennis Monchats' branded on her ass," Chance said.

"But I mean, if you did it, how would anyone know?" the Hunter asked nonchalantly.

"Are you serious, man?" Chance asked, raising his eyebrows, "Monchats got ears in places where the sun ain't never shined. He would know who it was before the bitch took her last breath."

He would not be deterred by Chance's warnings. The Hunter knew he would be the one to kill Sola. It was only a matter of time.

As the time for his parole hearing got nearer, he trained harder, longer. Runs on the prison grounds to strengthen his legs, and push-ups in his cell to strengthen his arms. Never one to cause too much trouble, he became a model prisoner, even helping to set up a prison outreach program with a focus on reading and chess. It was all a part of his plan. When he went to his parole hearing, the three members of the board smiled brightly as they reviewed his prison record. He played to their emotions and sensitivities.

The Hunter told the parole board what they wanted to hear, that he was a son of the unforgiving father named The Ghetto. That blood-sucking bastard didn't take prisoners, just made him blind and misguided. He even shed a few tears as he reflected on the life he almost took, telling the board he prayed to God everyday for forgiveness because he regretted his actions. He was even more thankful that the teenage victim, Dacari Mays, didn't die and had healed completely. He even showed the trio two letters Dacari sent to him. Dacari had forgiven him and was now a young, up and coming pastor at one of Columbus's biggest churches. After his moving performance, the Hunter knew his release was virtually guaranteed.

Once he got out, it was so easy to return to the Game. Former inmates were always prized possessions in the underworld of Columbus and beyond. In the 'hood, doing a stint in jail was like a badge of honor. He earned a lot of respect. Even though he did a little slinging here and there, it was almost like a part-time job; his main focus was taking out Sola.

The Hunter left Columbus for a while, seeking out two men, one in Cincinnati, and the other in Los Angeles. Both men were well known for their skills in ending human lives. He was surprised and grateful that they were willing to answer his questions and allow him to learn. They understood the nature of revenge. Once again, his life in prison gave him the opportunity to meet his goal. He wouldn't have been able to find them had it not been for his stay in Orient.

The Hunter's perfect chance came only ten months after he'd been paroled. A prominent Columbus businessman, Clifford Roberts, had been killed on the East Side. Initial news reports claimed that he had been robbed, but the story didn't smell right. What would a person of his stature be doing on Miller Avenue at midnight?

As the weeks passed, news began to trickle out that Roberts had been with a prostitute; quite an embarrassment for his uppity suburban wife and kids. Then the rumors began that it was a professional hit. In Monchats's close circle of associates, everyone knew the truth, Sola had killed Roberts, and without Monchats's blessing.

Monchats found out that Sola killed Roberts for an Arab man named Abdul to help him straighten out a business deal. The police got word that someone from Monchats's crew had killed Roberts and started putting pressure on Monchats's legitimate and illegitimate businesses. Monchats's money wasn't flowing right. He was in a foul mood for months. Word was that Sola was marked. It was the perfect time for him to introduce his services.

Through his connections, the Hunter arranged a meeting with B.L., Monchats most trusted assistant. He didn't hesitate telling B.L. that when the time was right, he wanted the call to take Sola out. He even told him how he knew Sola and why he wanted her dead.

B.L. told the Hunter he didn't know him and didn't trust him, but he gave him a chance to prove himself. B.L. gave the Hunter an assignment, warning him that if he didn't like the results, the grim reaper would be paying him a visit. The Hunter scoffed at the notion that his work would be anything less than professional. Within a week, the Hunter killed two men on the west side. He didn't ask their names or the reasons they needed to die. He just did what he was told. B.L. showed him well-deserved gratitude.

Just when he thought he would have his chance to meet Sola again, he learned that Monchats sent her to New Orleans for two reasons—to get away from the heat the Columbus Police Department was putting on the crew, and to redeem herself. She did her duty, and once she returned, Monchats forgave her. All bets were off. And he had no option but to wait. Until now. Now the Hunter was ready. He had wounded Sola, and it was time to put her out of her misery. He sat up in Sola's bed, taking his cell phone off of the clip attached to his sweatpants and checking the time. It was almost 5 A.M. Perfect. He recalled the number Abdul had given him the day before. He pressed the numbers slowly and pushed send.

The phone kept ringing. He was disappointed. *Where is she*, he thought to himself.

He was about to end the call when he heard Sola's sleepy voice on the line. "Speak," she said.

And he did.

"I'm waiting for you," the Hunter said.

"Who the hell is this?" she asked, the sleepiness still in her voice.

"They say you never really forget a voice, Sola," the Hunter said as he traced the lining of the bed pillow next to him with his fingers. "I remember yours. Do you remember mine?" There was silence. "Are you there?" he asked, thinking she had ended the call.

"Who the fuck is this?" Sola asked. He could hear the irritation in her voice.

"I once told you that if you know the game of chess, you can figure out most things in the world. I have figured out it was our destiny to meet again—and to settle accounts."

He could hear her clear her throat. *She knew.*

"What do you want?" Sola asked.

"To meet you again," he said. He was getting aroused at the thought of her with him in her bed, dying by his hands.

"Where?" Her voice was solemn.

"At the place I first let you know I returned."

The Hunter ended the call, not waiting for Sola to respond. He reached down into his pants and grabbed his hardness, stroking himself fast so he could achieve a quick release. And as he felt the heat rising in his body, and the pressure in his loins grew to a fever pitch, he knew she would come.

Chapter Thirty-Three

Sola's Story, Part XV — 1993

The choice to kill or not to kill wasn't easy. But looking back, I guess I never really had a choice. It took me two weeks before I called the number Monchats gave me and told B.L. I would do it. Momma was going to be sentenced in a month. I didn't want to take the chance she would be locked up forever. And something told me that Monchats could somehow get her sentenced reduced.

Once I agreed to do the job, everything fell into place. The instructions were simple. The *viejo verde* lived in a double on the east side off Livingston Avenue. He lived alone. He didn't have many visitors, except for the girls he brought home. I would go and do the job after dark. Monchats told me it would be best to go to *Viejo*'s house and tell him I wanted to be a ho.

"Tell him your Momma is on drugs and you need some extra cash," he said. "Once you get in the house, don't give him time to relax. Aim for the head, then fire. If you really want to be sure, give him one in the chest, too."

I took the COTA a couple of times to get used to the trip. I only had the nerve to walk down *Viejo*'s street one time. I looked over my back every step of the way. I didn't want anyone to notice me.

When I asked Monchats about my appearance, he told me a disguise would be best. One of his *girlfriends* took me to one of the Asian wig shops to pick out something short to put over my wild, thick hair. Monchats told me to wear baggy clothes.

"You'll want to put on some extra layers," he said.

"Why would I want to do that?" I asked. "Won't extra clothes slow me down?"

"Well, there are two reasons. First, the bigger you look, the more people ignore you. When is the last time you looked in the face of someone chubby?" He was right. I couldn't even remember. "Second," Monchats continued, "You might be a little close when you shoot him. Things will be bloody. You might have to take your first layer of shirt and pants off."

I nodded, understanding his logic.

"Now remember," Monchats warned, "if you do take some clothes off, make sure you take them with you. Stuff them in your pants or something. Never leave anything at the scene. Investigators are getting good with their shit now days and I would hate to see you get pinched on your first run."

On my fifteenth birthday, two days before I was supposed to take out *viejo verde*, Monchats picked me up in the Lincoln and gave me a special gift, a nine-millimeter gun in a medium-sized, black gift box.

"I guess I should say thanks," I said.

Monchats laughed. "I know it's not your standard birthday present, but I knew you'd need it."

"I said thanks."

"Always the smart one, aren't you?"

He took me out to eat a good meal at Ryan's, an all-you-can-eat buffet. I piled my plate with everything from macaroni and cheese to fried chicken. I ate so much I could hardly move and I was sleepy by the time he dropped me off at the group home.

"Are you ready?" he asked after his driver stopped the car.

"As ready as I'm going to be," I replied.

"Good," he said as he handed me another box. "Open it."

I fumbled with the box. There was a beeper inside. "What's this for?" I asked.

"When you get done, walk seven blocks on Livingston until you reach the Livingston Medical Office. There is a payphone there. Call B.L., but don't speak. Just hang up once you hear his voice. Do you understand?" I nodded. "Good. You will receive a page with a number to call. When you call the number, I will pick up the phone. I want to you say yes or no, that's it. Then hang up the phone. Okay?"

"I got it."

"Walk five more blocks to the bus stop on Champion. And it's all done."

"Okay."

I started to get out of the car. Monchats put his hand on my shoulder. "I have complete faith in you, Sola. I know you won't let me down."

"Thanks."

"Happy Birthday."

I got out of the car and went into the group home. When I got inside, I hid the gun underneath my pillow and hoped no one got in my stuff. Most of the girls were scared of me, but I couldn't take any chances. So I acted like I was sick so I could stay around my bed as much as possible.

When the day came, I almost lost my nerve. But I knew it was too late to turn back. I laid in my bed all day, *still sick*, and tried to get myself ready.

I took the COTA bus downtown and then transferred to the Livingston Avenue Bus going east. I was sweating hard. The bus rumbled to my stop quick.

I jumped off the bus at the corner of Livingston and Kelton Avenue and walked a couple of blocks to Seymour Avenue. *Viejo* lived three houses away from where I was standing. My heart was racing. *I can do this.* The sky was dark and the dim street lights were on. The street was empty; no kids outside. Since most of the homes were boarded up, I guess there wasn't any reason to think there would be.

I walked slowly up the street. When I reached the blue house, I really got nervous. *I can do this.*

I walked up the stairs. My stomach was starting to hurt. I could hear the blood rushing through my ears. I stood at the door before ringing the bell. I touched my stomach. *I can do this.*

I heard someone fumbling on the locks. The door opened. The man in the picture was right in front of me. *Viejo Verde.*

"What do you want?" he asked.

Viejo slightly resembled the picture I saw. It was him, I was sure, but his face looked more aged and his hair was grayer. I tried to look him straight in the eyes when I spoke to him.

"I need some help. I heard you help girls like me," I said, trying to sound sincere.

I remembered what Monchats told me about how *Viejo* helped girls. I tried batting my eyes and sticking out my chest, hoping my feeble attempts at looking sexy would fool the old man.

He looked around, his eyes shifting left to right. "What makes you think I can help you?" he asked.

I had to sound good. "Look, man, I know you can help. I can do some work for you, and you can give me some money." I lifted up my baggy shirt to show my belly button. I couldn't lift my shirt too high, because the gun was at my side. He stared at me. I didn't think I was getting through. "C'mon man. I need to get a fix for my Momma," I said desperately. "If I don't, I don't know what she's going to do to me."

He opened the door wider. "Look, girl, I don't know who the fuck you are, but you need to go home."

Monchats had told me to look inside myself and find the thing that made me kill before. I put my hand on my stomach and closed my eyes. He was right, I could still go there.

I stepped on the doorframe and put my hand on his chest. He backed up at bit and I stepped further inside.

"C'mon baby," I purred. "Let me inside."

"I told you to go home," he said forcefully.

Time was running out. If he shut the door in my face, I would fail. And I was not going to fail. I had to take the initiative. I kicked him between his legs and he grabbed himself, howling.

"What the fuck?" he yelled.

Viejo was in a vulnerable position and I took advantage. I pushed him into the house and kicked him again. I felt a rush of excitement and fear. I didn't want to think about what I was doing. I pulled the gun out and fired. I kept firing until the man was lying in a pool of blood. I wanted to scream, but I couldn't. I had to get out of there. I didn't want to walk back out the front door, but I didn't have a choice. I didn't know what was in the man's house, and I wasn't going to find out. I was shaking like crazy, so I took a second to breathe. I had killed again.

I stuffed the gun back into my pants, securing it against my side as I opened the door. The gun was warm against my skin. I looked up and down the street. I didn't see anything, so I walked out of the house and down the steps.

Once I hit Livingston. I couldn't walk anymore. I ran. My muscles protested and my lungs screamed bloody murder, but I kept running. I wanted to run away from myself, but I couldn't. I reached the Medical Office and could hardly breathe by the time I got to the payphone. I reached in my pocket for a quarter and called B.L.

When he answered the phone and spoke, I waited a second before hanging up. A couple of minutes later, I felt the vibration of the beeper. I looked at the number and dialed it. When I heard the phone pick up, I knew Monchats was on the other end and I broke down. I couldn't help it.

I heard him breathing. I was sobbing into the phone. I couldn't speak. Monchats finally spoke to me.

"What's your answer?" his voice was cool and direct.

"What?" I asked, gasping for air and sobbing uncontrollably.

"Your answer?"

I cried harder. "Yes."

The phone clicked. Soon, I only heard the dial tone.

I wiped my eyes and started walking down the street. I did what Monchats told me. I kept walking five blocks to the Champion Avenue bus stop. When I reached the stop, I sat down on the bench and tried to forget about what I had just done, but the images of the *viejo* were seared into my brain. His eyes wide and his mouth open in a state of shock as the bullets slammed into his body; the blood pouring out of him like a river. My conscience was working overtime, nagging me and telling me that what I did was wrong, that I would pay for my crime. And as I waited for the bus, it took all of my might to hold back my tears.

When the bus did come, I got on slowly, not looking at the driver as I put my dollar in the fare collector.

"You all right?" the driver asked. I looked up. The driver was a middle-aged, black woman. I nodded slowly, still avoiding the driver's eyes. "Well, you might want to check yourself out, honey," she said. "You got blood on your pants."

I looked down and saw four spots of blood on my pants. The largest one was the size of a quarter. I almost broke down right there. I wanted to confess; to tell someone what I had just done. "I just murdered a man!" I wanted to yell out. *Put me in jail now and release Momma*! I thought. Instead of confessing my sins to the driver, I nodded again and told the driver, "thanks."

I rode that bus downtown, and then I transferred to another bus that drove me to a stop right in front of the group home.

Outside of the iron gate leading to the entrance of the group home, I took the bulky shirt outside my sweatpants to hide the blood spots. I also took off my wig and ran my fingers through my hair. I wiped my eyes and hoped I didn't look to crazy, even though I knew the resident advisors were used to seeing teenage girls looking wild.

After I signed in, I hurried to my room and put the gun back under my pillow. I grabbed a towel and my body shower gel and went to the shower. I took off the clothes and wrapped them in a ball. I turned on the hot water as high as I could stand it, then I rubbed my body until my skin felt raw. I thought I could wash away the memory of the *viejo's* death, but he stayed with me; on that night and for many nights ahead.

Chapter Thirty-Four

When all of your pieces are in place, strike hard and fast.
Don't give your opponent a chance to recover.
—The Qualities of Chess Masters # 475

April 1, 4:50 A.M

The sound of a phone ringing woke Sola. She slowly opened her eyes. The phone rang again. It was the cell phone she'd gotten from Abdul. She reached for it.

"Speak," she said groggily.

After the chilling phone conversation, she felt stunned. A cold wave flowed through her body, chilling her spine. *It was time.*

She went to the bathroom to check on her shoulder. The bleeding had obviously stopped, and she didn't feel like changing the makeshift T-shirt bandage. She took it off anyway, along with the rest of her clothes. She decided to take a shower.

As the warm water and soap suds drained down the sink, she thought about him, the man who had been hunting her. She should have known it would be him. One of the few people she knew that had to live a life of hell for reasons entirely not of their own doing. And she knew he blamed her.

She should have known he would come for her one day.

She hadn't seen him since they were both teenagers, after he healed significantly and she became a killer. She had returned to the Gardens to visit Trina and the rest of her PICs, LaKisha, Dee, and Netta. She was sixteen, and didn't have a license yet, but she was already driving around in her first car. Monchats had bought her a red Toyota Camry for her birthday.

Sola had avoided the Gardens, choosing to spend most of her time on the east side under Monchats's watchful eye. But after so much time, she thought she could handle visiting the place where she grew up.

When she drove down the long street leading to the Gardens' townhouses, everything felt different. The Gardens was a place she didn't know anymore, and maybe that was a good thing. She parked in front of Trina's townhouse, honking the horn and yelling, "Hey, girl! Get your ass out here so you can see my new ride."

While waiting for Trina to come outside, Sola stared in the direction of her old townhouse. It was just out of sight. She knew she wouldn't be able to go there, in fact, she didn't want to.

Sola felt a lump forming in her throat as she thought about her life in the Gardens and her eyes started to sting. She was almost thankful when Trina ran out of the door and started yelling about the Camry. Sola knew she had to bury her memories, for they brought nothing but pain.

As for Trina, for the most part, she hadn't changed. She was still with Chris, who was still dealing, and her bulging belly let Sola know that Trina was expecting a child.

"Hey, girl, this is sweet," Trina said, praising her new car.

"I'm so glad to see you doing okay. For a while, I thought you felt like you were too good for the Gardens."

"Never that," Sola said.

"No, I understand, girl. With all that happened to you, I understand why you couldn't just come back. Knowing me, I would have never came back," Trina said, trying to sound reassuring.

"Yeah, well, I still got a lot of stuff to work out," Sola said, "I came today, but I don't know if I'll be getting around here much."

"Hey, like I said, I understand," Trina said sadly, "but that's what phones and cars are for. We'll always stay in touch."

"Definitely," Sola agreed.

Sola hugged Trina, embracing her like a long-lost sister. Trina started crying, but Sola's tears were long gone. Instead, Sola looked towards her old townhouse again. That's when she saw him. He was standing still, returning Sola's stare. Sola remembered his eyes. If looks could kill, her heart would have stopped right at that moment. Sola had never seen so much hate coming from anyone, especially him.

Juan Chela Martinez.

A couple of months after she saw Chela, she remembered hearing that he beat some thug to a pulp in the Gardens. Even though he was seventeen at the time, they charged him as an adult. He was convicted of aggravated attempted murder and received a sentence of sixteen to twenty-five years.

She hadn't heard much about him since he'd been in prison. And until she decided to tell her story, she hadn't much thought of him at all. *It's funny how things work out*, she thought as she stepped out of the shower and dried off. *Fate is a muthafuckin' bitch.*

After she dressed, she walked back into the bedroom. She heard the sound of her own voice filling the room. Campbell was listening to her tapes. She smiled. She guessed he couldn't help himself. She straightened out the bed sheets and returned to the bathroom. She cleaned up as much as she could. Before she turned off the bathroom light, she looked at her backpack, which was sitting in a chair. She decided to leave it there. She wouldn't need it anyway.

When she returned to the bedroom, she opened the drawer to the nightstand. There was a writing pad and pen inside, along with other knick-knacks. She took the pen and scribbled on the pad. She went back to the bathroom and laid the pad onto the gift box.

She walked through the bedroom and down the small hallway leading to the living room. Campbell was sitting on the couch, staring at the player as it played back her story. She crept up behind him and grabbed his shoulders.

"You like?" she asked playfully.

Campbell jumped and the player fell out of his hand onto the floor. "Damn, Sola, you scared the shit out of me," he said.

Sola laughed, walking around the couch and sitting down. "I didn't mean to 'scare the shit out of you.'"

Campbell shook his head. "I'm fine, but don't give me a heart attack," he said, grabbing his chest like Fred Sanford and lifting his head in the air.

Sola sat back on the couch and began thinking about Chela. Her mind drifted to her past.

"Something wrong?" Campbell asked, breaking Sola's concentration.

Sola turned to look at him. "Why? Do I look like something's wrong?" she asked.

"You look refreshed, but worried. What's up?"

"Just wondering if you like the tapes," she lied.

"I really haven't had a chance to get through much."

"What part were you listening to?"

"You were saying something about the first guy you made out with."

Fate is a muthafuckin' bitch, Sola thought as she stared off into space.

"You okay?" Campbell asked.

"Yeah, I'm cool."

Campbell put the cassette recorder on the table next to the box of tapes. "Can I ask you something?" he asked.

"What?" Sola turned to look at him.

"Why did you decide to make them—the tapes."

"I'm beginning to feel like an old 45 vinyl record," Sola sounded as if she were teasing Anderson, but she didn't smile. "Like I said, I want my mother. You told me to tell my story, and I did. A deal's a deal."

"But it had to take some time to record all of this," Campbell said as he fingered the tapes.

"Yeah, it took time."

"So when did you decide to make them?"

Sola sighed. "I don't know. After we met, you know, I thought about my mother. What she sacrificed. She wasn't perfect, but she still gave birth to me. She didn't deserve the hand she was dealt." Sola blinked back tears.

"I always felt responsible," Sola continued, "for Momma going to jail. It seems only fitting that I'd be responsible for setting her free."

"But what about Monchats? You'll testify against him?" Campbell asked.

Sola pointed at the tapes. "You have all the testimony you need right there."

"It may not be enough."

"Are you trying to fuck me, Agent Anderson? Let me

know now, because if you can't guarantee my mother's freedom-"

Campbell interrupted her. "No, no," he shook his head, "I haven't even heard enough of the tapes. I mean, if Monchats directed you to murder people, is that in these tapes?"

"You'll have to listen to find out." Sola rose from the couch. "I mean, with the info I've given you, along with all the evidence you claimed to have gathered, I can't believe you Feds don't have enough to take Monchats down. But don't ask me to do anything more. I just want my mother out. And soon."

Sola started walked toward the entrance door to the apartment. Campbell got up to follow her.

"Where are you going?" he asked.

"You don't want to know," Sola responded.

"Sola." Campbell walked quickly to her and grabbed her uninjured shoulder. "You don't have to leave. I can protect you. There's all kind of things we can do for you."

Sola saw the yearning in his eyes. "What can you do? Witness protection? I don't think so. What's the point of living in a place where no one knows you if you still feel like you have to look over your shoulder all the time? Where's the safety in that? I'll never live like a dog. What else? Police custody? Monchats has so many cops and inmates in his pocket I wouldn't know where the knife was coming from. If I'm going to go down, it will never be behind bars." Sola put her hand on Campbell's cheek. "You can't protect me. It's time for me to go."

Campbell shook his head. "I can stop you right now, Sola. I can restrain you. Call my superiors and have you arrested."

"Me and you both know that wouldn't be wise."

"Sola, you're not being rational."

"I'm not trying to be rational, I'm trying to be me. And you have to let me go." Sola turned around and reached for the door handle. "You know, Anderson, I mean, *Campbell*, when I was younger, I liked to read. But I was kind of impatient, you know? I would read the end of the story first and then go back to the beginning. I liked going through the story knowing what was going to happen at the end." Sola opened the door. "I suggest you grab the last tape and listen to that one." She started to walk out the door.

"Don't go, Sola." Campbell was almost pleading. He grabbed her arm. "Don't you wish—"

"I live in a reality-based world," Sola interrupted. "I don't want to waste time in a dream world."

"God, Sola!" Campbell hit the door with his fist and the frame shook from the impact, "You don't know how this feels. To meet someone and wish you lived in another world where the past didn't matter."

"Josiah Anderson," Sola reached up and began caressing his face. "One day, you're going to meet a woman who's going to blow your mind and be right for you. You will spend your life showing her all the reasons she is your one and only." Sola stepped into the doorway. "You and I both know whatever you think you feel is an illusion. Maybe you think you need to protect me, but you don't."

"Sola, you have to let me help you. You can remain here. Let me help you," Campbell begged.

"I can't stay." Sola walked down the hall toward the red exit sign leading to the stairs. She disappeared through the stair hallway and never looked back.

For Sola, it was hard to leave Campbell at the door, but she knew it was the right thing to do. She walked to the Honda quickly, not knowing if he would follow her. She jumped into the car and drove off fast. There was no turning back.

She headed South on I-71. Her mind was swimming. She turned to the classical music station. Beethoven filled the car. For the first time ever, the music didn't help. She turned it up louder. Maybe she could at least drown out her thoughts.

She merged onto I-70 East traffic. She would be home soon. The sky was starting to lighten up. She looked at the clock on the Honda's dashboard. It was twenty till six. Basically morning.

She wondered why Chela hadn't killed her yesterday morning. *Only yesterday*, she thought. The past day felt like a year. She figured Chela was playing with her, letting her know what it felt like to be hunted, to be on the other side of the aisle.

She took the Hamilton Road exit off I-70 and drove down the main road until she reached her neighborhood. She drove slowly as she approached her house, not knowing how Chela was going to act. But she wasn't going to back down, she was driving straight into her driveway.

She let the engine idle for a minute while she collected her thoughts and assessed her options. Chela was obviously in her house, waiting for her. She would give him the meeting he wanted.

As she got out of the car, she heard a voice call her name. She turned around. It was her neighbor, Mr. Johnson. He was dressed in a long, blue robe. He wore slippers on his feet.

"I thought that was you," Mr. Johnson smiled. "When you didn't come right back yesterday and I didn't hear from you, I got worried. I was going to call the police. Then I saw this young man, named Donovan something, and he told me you were alright. He was the second man to visit yesterday. The first one came right after you left. He was a weird one. Something about him made me uneasy."

On any other day, Sola would have loved to listen to Mr. Johnson give her the full report on her house, but today was not the time, and being outside, exposed to the elements, and being exposed to someone who wanted to kill her, was definitely not the place.

"Mr. Johnson. I hate to be rude, but I think you should go back to your house and go inside." Sola started walking to the back of the house. Mr. Johnson followed her.

"Well, I need to know about my car. You said you would bring it back to me, but now you come up in a blue car that isn't mine. And then this man comes by yesterday saying he wants to talk to you about some windows, but I think he wanted something else."

Sola put up her hand. "Mr. Johnson, please, go home." She continued walking.

"Look, if there's something wrong, maybe I can do something to help. If there's some trouble, you know."

Sola stopped walking and looked at her neighbor. "Yes, Mr. Johnson, there's some trouble, but nothing I can talk about now. I just want you to go home."

"If you say, so. Just remember, I'm here—"

Mr. Johnson's head exploded. His body then flew back into the back of Sola's BMW and he tumbled over the edge onto the ground. He didn't even have a chance to scream. Sola gasped and tried to get down, but then felt the sharp pain in her back as a bullet ripped through her. She fell face down to the ground.

She could feel the blood flowing from her body, but she could still breathe. She moaned loudly and looked for Mr. Johnson. But she already knew he was dead.

"You didn't have to fucking do that," she whispered into the air. "He had nothing to do with it. He didn't deserve to die." She kept repeating herself, trying to maintain her consciousness. *You didn't have to do it, you didn't have to do it, you didn't have to do it.*

She stopped speaking when she heard footsteps behind her. A hand grabbed her shoulder and twisted her around. She yelled out in pain. She stared in the eyes of her nemesis. There he was. He smiled at her.

"And so we meet again." Chela said as he pointed a gun to Sola's head.

Chapter Thirty-Five

Sola's Story, Part XVI – 1993

I thought it would take me longer to recover, but it didn't. I killed a man I didn't even know, but I got over it. Maybe I blocked the murder out, I can't pretend to know. What really mattered to me was that Monchats was a man of his word. Momma got life with the possibility of parole after serving twenty years.

I later found out the sentencing judge in Momma's case had an appetite for black booty even though he had a wife of thirty years, six kids, and three grandchildren. The judge had the perfect white picket fence American family, well, at least on the outside. Monchats had pictures and video of the judge with one of his ho's doing things his wife had never even thought of, let alone done. But hey, whatever it takes.

Monchats took me under his wing and trained me. I moved out of the group home less than two months after the second death and into one of Monchats's apartments. A white woman with long, blonde hair and big breasts claimed she was my foster mom. But after the paperwork was processed, and I started living in that east side apartment complex, I never saw my blonde foster mom again. I was living on my own. And I only had Monchats. He was basically like a father to me. I had his entire arsenal at my disposal. And yes, I killed again and again.

I won't lie. At first, the killing really used to get to me. Every time I would take a life, I would shiver and cry and pray I wouldn't have to do it again. But after a while, the deaths didn't bother me anymore. I became numb to the bloodshed I caused.

Eventually, I convinced myself I was a soldier in a street war. I knew it wasn't the typical war between nations, but the reasons for the battles were basically still the same. Lives were lost, property destroyed, entire families left in ruin. And for what? Territory, respect, political gain, bad deals, and broken promises? War is war whether a country is fighting another country or a crime boss is fighting his enemy in the city streets. I trained for battle like any soldier would—mentally and physically. Monchats wanted me to be all I could be—and I was.

I strived for perfection. I studied my prey. I tried to cover all the bases before I struck. My work was top-notch, and I was appreciated. How many people have died by my hands? I stopped counting after sixty. I think of those dead as pawns in the game of life.

Some years later, I found out that Monchats, despite his claim that he didn't dish bullshit, had served me a full plate. I met a man named Abdul, an Arab guy from Palestine. He told me that Monchats lied to me from the beginning. The man Monchats had me kill, the second death, wasn't after young girls after all. At least not in the way Monchats made me think.

The man's name was Colin Lee. He was just some old

pimp thinking he still had some game. Abdul had heard of Colin Lee from his brother, Khalil. Lee had hooked Khalil and some other Palestinians up with some housing when they first came to Columbus. Because of Lee's generosity, Khalil began living the American dream. Even though Khalil eventually moved to Michigan, he had never forgotten Colin Lee.

I explained to Abdul that I knew nothing about the man I knew as *Viejo Verde*. I warned Abdul that details were dangerous. The less I knew the better. But Abdul had his own agenda. He wasn't trying to convince me that killing Colin Lee was wrong, he just wanted to inform me of how low Monchats would go to achieve his goals.

Abdul told me that Colin Lee had made his ends, but like anyone who has tasted the sweet treat of power, he wanted more. He couldn't accept his retirement. Like I said, Colin Lee was a pimp. He missed the old days. He was having a sort of weird late-life crisis. Since Lee didn't even have any ho's under his belt, he told some of Monchats Main Street ho's he could treat them better. He tried to get them in his corner. Monchats found out about Lee's shadiness and decided to teach him a lesson.

Monchats was making his mark on the city and Lee had disrespected him. Lee had to die, as an example to anyone else who might have designs on Monchats's territory for any reason. It was a respect thing, nothing more, nothing less.

I felt betrayed in a way I don't think I can express. I know I wouldn't have killed Colin Lee if Monchats hadn't told me that Lee messed with young girls. It was at that moment I realized how much Monchats had manipulated me over the years. I thought seriously about killing Monchats, making him pay for what he had turned me into. But I couldn't. Like I said, he was like a father to me. The part of me that was loyal to him controlled my actions.

Did Abdul's revelation make me stop killing? No. I was in so deep that I didn't even imagine trying to change my life. I knew Monchats wouldn't let me go, and his dog, B.L., was gunning for me. I convinced myself that living under Monchats control was my curse for killing Rocky and Lee, and letting Momma stay in jail. The bottom line is that it was too late for me. I buried Monchats's treachery deep in my mind and moved on.

As for the rest, I moved into my own house by twenty and had a fake 'office' job at Monchats's offices to keep the neighbors happy and to keep the Internal Revenue Service off my back. Of course, I didn't spend any time working behind a desk, but I did spend my days training to become better.

For an assassin, murder is an art form. An outlet of expression. An assassin kills like a painter paints or an author writes. It's not like gangbangers who just drive by and spray whoever's in the street, or even a serial killer who seeks out victims for some sick satisfaction. I accepted my role, and I accept the consequences of my lifestyle. I refuse to say I am victim. I had a choice. I made it.

As for Momma, she is still in jail biding her time until she gets out. Unfortunately, I haven't talked or written to her in years. The last time I visited her, she told me not to come again. She told me that knowing what I did and seeing me in person was too painful for her. She said she would rather have the memory of me than the reality. She knew what I had become. She always blamed herself.

I sometimes think of my dead child, the boy who would have been named Josiah, was named Josiah, my "fire of the Lord." I wonder if my son would have forgiven me for my sins. I wonder how my life would have turned out if I would have at least had my child. But I don't have moments of reflection often. You can't change the past and the future isn't certain. Really, I know I only have each day.

I don't know why I can tell my story now, after all these years. It's been so long and I know that the killing won't stop, even if I'm not the one doing it. But I do know that I won't be sitting in some jail cell for the rest of my life. I also know I can't pretend to be someone else while looking over my shoulder the rest of my life.

Once my story is told, I will become a marked woman. My life won't mean shit. I am prepared to meet my fate. I know the game and how it's played. Someone will come for me and finish me off. But, I will not go down without a fight. It's not in my nature.

So, how would someone tell the story of my life? I really don't know. But at least you have it now. Do with it what you will.

Chapter Thirty-Six

Evasion is a tactic of the weak-minded.
Diversion is the hallmark of intelligence.
—The Qualities of Chess Masters # 482

April 1, 5:55 A.M

Campbell stared at the player long after Sola had stopped speaking. Even though the tape only played for a couple of minutes, he had learned so much. He looked down at the rest of the tapes. *This is a goldmine,* he thought.

There was enough information on the tape he'd just heard to at least get murder charges against Monchats to stick. He knew the tapes were great evidence, but the real thing would be an even better catch. If he could have only gotten Sola to agree to testify. Maybe he still could.

When Sola decided to leave, he wanted to stop her, then to go after her. But he knew it wouldn't work. Whatever he thought he felt for her, he had to let it go. Sola had told him "the folly of men will lead to their destruction," and she was right. Dreaming about what might have been could jeopardize his entire career, as well as his freedom. It was time to get back to reality. If Sola didn't agree to testify against Monchats, she would have to go down with him.

Campbell looked out of the window and saw the dim light of the sun. It was almost morning. He rose from the couch. It was time for a shower, and for work. His first destination was the field office to drop off the tapes. The investigators would need to listen to and study all of the tapes. Campbell was sure Sola's every word would be transcribed and examined carefully.

He walked into the bedroom. Sola had made up the bed. He touched the sheets as he walked by the bed. He inhaled deeply, hoping to catch a soft hint of her in the air. Nothing. He would have never known she had been there if he hadn't seen it for himself.

He went to the bathroom. He turned on the shower and started to take off his clothes when the gleam of steel caught his eye. He looked over at the chairs near the bathroom door. In one chair, there was Sola's small black backpack. It was open, but there was nothing sticking out of it. On the other chair was a gift box with a lid. On top of the box was a notepad, and the most surprising thing of all, a nine-millimeter handgun.

Campbell froze for a minute, instinctively looking around. Was Sola playing with him or what? Was she planning to come back?

The steam from the shower was starting to fill the bathroom. Campbell shut the water off and opened the bathroom door to let out the steam. Then he turned his attention to the items lying on the two chairs.

He began to reach for the bag when he thought about the significance of what Sola had left behind—*evidence*. He hurried to the kitchen and found some plastic gloves. He put them on and returned to the bathroom.

The backpack was nearly empty. There was a small knife, a pocket knife, and three round silver balls. There was also a gun case. There was a silencer inside of the case. *Sola likes to travel light,* he thought.

Next, Campbell picked up the gun. He wanted to be careful with it. He checked to make sure the safety was on. He placed the gun on the vanity counter.

When he looked at the writing pad, his eyes widened. Sola had written something on the pad. He grabbed it and started reading.

I thought you might want these things. You'll find the piece most useful. And so you know, I wanted it that night too.

Anderson looked at the note. Something was nagging him, pulling on his brain. He looked at Sola's possessions. The backpack, the weapons, the gift box. He thought about the tapes and what they meant. *Once my story is told, I will become a marked woman. My life won't mean shit. I am prepared to meet my fate.* That's what Sola had said on the tape.

Anderson remembered the phone call. Sola's solemn face. He ran to the bedroom and picked up the phone. He dialed the numbers furiously. He heard ringing.

"Thomas," a sleepy voice said. Agent Michael Thomas, associate director of the Columbus Field Office, was Anderson's immediate superior.

"Agent Thomas, this is Agent Josiah Anderson. We have an emergency."

"Well, well, Agent Anderson, or should I say, Campbell Donovan. Yesterday, you chewed my head off when I called you, but now you're calling me. What a surprise."

Campbell couldn't believe a man could wake out of his sleep and be a complete asshole. He didn't have time to mince words.

"Sir, you told me to contact you if Soledad Nichols contacted me. Well, she has."

"What?" Agent Thomas asked as if he couldn't believe his ears.

"Soledad Nichols, Monchats's Brown Recluse, she contacted me and something big is about to go down," Campbell's hands were shaking.

"Is this some type of joke?"

"No, sir. Please, we've got to act fast. I believe someone is trying to kill her. Sir, she turned over some tapes." His mind worked fast. *A little white lie won't hurt,* he thought. "She may be willing to testify."

He heard shuffling. "Are you serious?" Thomas asked.

"As a heart attack," Campbell replied.

"Let's get the locals on this. They'll be able to respond faster. Where is she?"

Anderson really didn't know where Sola was, but he had to take the risk that he would be right. He couldn't lose her, not now.

"Send them to her house," Campbell said as he gripped the phone. He then told Agent Thomas the address. "Hurry, sir, we don't have a lot of time."

"I'll get right on it. You've done a great job, Agent Anderson, I knew you wouldn't let us down."

"Thank you, sir. I'm going to get dressed so I can meet the locals at Soledad Nichols' residence."

"Are you forgetting something?"

"You're undercover, Agent Anderson. You're in deep. If you go over there, you may compromise yourself."

"Sir, I get your point, but this is too important to me. I can't stand on the sidelines."

"I understand. We best get on this right away. I'll meet you in twenty."

Campbell hung up the phone and grabbed a shirt to put on. He opened the bottom drawer of his dresser and pulled out his gun. He rushed out the front door, almost forgetting his keys. As he ran to his Navigator, he thought of Sola and hoped there was enough time to save her.

Chapter Thirty-Seven

Despite your best efforts, a match may end in a draw.
If that is your destiny, rise to meet it.
—The Qualities of Chess Masters # 497

April 1, 5:56 A.M

And so we meet again, Sola thought. That's what Chela said to her. She stared at the gun, then closed her eyes. *Get it over with, motherfucker,* Sola thought. She felt her body getting cold.

"Get up, bitch," Chela said, his voice full of venom and hate. He had held it all in for over a decade and now he had his chance to release his rage.

Sola remained on the ground, her eyes closed. Chela knew the shot wasn't fatal. He could see her chest moving slightly up and down. He reached over her body and put the gun to her head.

"I said get up," Chela spat out between gritted teeth. When Sola didn't respond, Chela grabbed her by the hair and started to drag her to the house. "You're going to move one way or the other." The pain was unbearable, and Sola groaned. Chela released her after dragging her a couple of feet. "Now get up."

Sola decided to stand up. She was actually surprised she still could. Her back was pulsating. She felt her own blood on her skin. She rose up and stumbled to the already open door. Chela was following close behind her.

Once they got into the house, Chela grabbed her injured shoulder and squeezed. It took all of Sola's effort not to yell out from the pain. She didn't want to give Chela the pleasure. Instead, she grunted. She felt his breath near her face.

"You don't know what pain feels like, do you?" he asked. His breath was warm. "Do you want to know about my pain, the pain you caused. Do you?" Chela's voice rose. "It's all because of you." He squeezed her shoulder again. "Follow me."

He kept the pressure on as he led her down the hallway to her bedroom. Her head was feeling light and her legs felt like they were about to give out.

When they reached the bedroom, Chela threw her onto the bed. "I feel like I've been waiting a lifetime to do this." He got on top of Sola. His weight was suffocating.

He's going to rape me, she thought. *This bastard is going to rape me.*

Instead of ripping off her clothes, Chela put his hands around her neck.

"I know what you're thinking," he whispered. "That I want to fuck you like I did a long time ago. But the truth is, your pussy is the last thing on my mind." He tightened his grip around Sola's neck. "You want to know what'll get me off," he continued. "Your dead body."

As it became harder to breathe, Sola started to fight him, to resist the death Chela was trying to deal her. Her struggles excited him.

"I can feel your heartbeat," Chela said huskily. "It's getting slower." Chela started laughing. "Yeah, fight it, *puta*. Give it your all."

Sola struggled to speak. The gurgling sound made Chela

pause. "What are you trying to say, bitch? Do you want to beg for your life?" He loosened his grip and bent down near her face. "Beg for it, Sola. Plea all you want. I want to hear it."

When Sola spoke, it was nothing more than a whisper. "Not here," she said. Then, she raised her knee and connected with Chela's groin.

Chela grabbed himself, yelling in pain. Sola kneed him again, then used all the strength she could muster to push him off of her. She rolled off the bed and onto the floor, coughing as she caught her breath.

She crawled across the floor, then used the bedroom door handle to help her stand. She looked back at Chela, who was curled in a ball on the bed, groaning. She started down the hallway for the den.

She walked slowly, the pain making each step painful. As she reached the end of the hallway, she felt her back explode again. Chela had recovered. He was coming after her.

She used her remaining momentum to reach the den. Chela shot her again. The shot propelled her on to the couch in the living room. She gripped it before crashing into the coffee table. The glass shattered on impact and the tiny shards dug into her skin.

"You think you can get away from me, bitch?" Chela said as he grabbed her hair again and turned her to face him, pinning her arms behind her. "I'm sick of playing with you. The game is over. It's time for you to die."

Chela gripped her neck again. Sola looked at him. He was grinning down at her, enjoying his task. Her eyes traveled to the large scar that dominated most of his face, from his forehead down to the edge of his lip. She closed her eyes again.

Monchats would sometimes call her a bag of tricks because she was always full of surprises. And she had one for Chela he wouldn't like. She freed her hand from behind her and made one quick thrust with the small Samurai sword that had been displayed on the now broken coffee table. Chela gasped and released his grip on her neck. She continued her motion upward and felt his insides beginning to spill out of him. She locked eyes with Chela as he took one last gasp. She managed a final "fuck you" as he fell on top of her.

It was becoming harder for Sola to breathe, especially with Chela's weight on her chest, but she didn't have the strength to move him. Shadows were dancing across the room and her mind was telling her to let go.

Sola thought of her mother and hoped that she would be okay. She had done all she could do to make that happen.

As her breathing became more labored, she closed her eyes and prepared to dream. She heard sirens in the distance, pounding footsteps, a male voice calling her name—Josiah.

She imagined it was her child, a son who would now be a teenager. She wondered what he would look like, how smart he would be, what promise he would hold in the world.

Chela's weight was lifted from her. Sola felt light and free. She exhaled one last time. Her game was over.

Epilogue

After you've experienced the heat of battle,
it is best to seek out serenity, regardless the
outcome of your match.
—The Qualities of Chess Masters # 500

One week after the deaths of Soledad Nichols and Juan Chela Martinez, Pierre-Henri Monchats was indicted by a federal grand jury on multiple counts, including drug trafficking and murder. Even the national news covered the event. On the day Monchats turned himself in, he decided to give up his freedom in style. He took a stretch Hummer limousine to the main Columbus Division of Police station downtown. He wore one of the best suits money could buy: a black pinstriped Callini.

When he arrived at the station, the television crews were waiting for him, as well as an army of federal agents. The Feds refused to just let Monchats walk into the building like he was a king. Instead, they read him his rights as he stepped out of the limo and arrested him. The cameras captured Monchats being frisked and cuffed. The nightly news repeatedly showed Monchats doing the perp walk out of the limo and into the police station.

Monchats wasn't the only one to feel the federal government's wrath. When the Feds started picking up Monchats "business partners," his associates started running like roaches. For all intensive purposes, Columbus was on lockdown.

Among the evidence used by the grand jury was a set of mini-cassette tapes provided by the FBI. According to court documents, the FBI recovered the tapes after a search of Sola's home following her death. Agent Josiah Anderson wouldn't receive credit for his find. Anderson thought he would be able to return to Washington D.C. after Monchats' arrest, but his superiors decided to keep him on assignment. He would still be living another man's life—the life of Campbell Donovan.

As more information about Monchats surfaced, the media frenzy grew. City administrators, judges, and cops associated with Monchats tried to distance themselves from the now-revealed criminal. The governor, two members of the U.S. House of Representatives, and five state senators returned donations Monchats gave them during their campaigns. Other government officials elected by the people, secretly reviewed their records to make sure their connections to Monchats were neatly severed.

Newspaper accounts suggested that the prosecution had a strong case against Monchats. The Feds weren't playing around. They seized all of Monchats's property and businesses, and froze his accounts. Richard Archer, the Director of the FBI, held a press conference, praising his team for bringing Monchats down. He promised a vigorous prosecution.

"We should be thankful another criminal is off of the streets," Archer said. "And our mission now is to keep him off of the streets and in a jail cell."

On the day of Monchats's arraignment, the federal court room was filled to capacity. The bailiffs had to turn people away. Reporters scribbled feverously in their notepads as Monchats pleaded not guilty to the charges against him. The trial would be presided over by the Honorable United States District Court Judge Juliette Barnes-Jordan. She was conservative and untouchable. She would only be swayed by the evidence, nothing more, nothing less. Since Monchats was considered a flight risk, Judge Barnes-Jordan didn't allow bail.

The remains of Bailey "B.L." Langston were found among the burnt-out ruins of his house. Due to the extensive damage to the remains, a cause of death was uncertain, but based on the bullets and shell casings found in the near vicinity of the remains, the Franklin County Coroner couldn't rule out death by homicide.

The story of B.L.'s death appeared in the middle of the Metro section of the local newspaper. According to the papers, police investigators thought B.L.'s death was drug-related. The investigators didn't have any witnesses, and no one was talking. The chances B.L.'s killer would be found were slim to none. B.L.'s demise was overshadowed by the upcoming trial of Pierre-Henri Monchats, who received front page coverage. In death, as in life, B.L. took a back seat to his boss.

At the same time Monchats's defense lawyers were plotting their strategy, Synthia Nichols was given a pardon by the Governor of Ohio. This extraordinary action by a Governor known to be tough on crime went "unnoticed" by the media.

Any thoughts of revenge on Synthia Nichols were quickly squashed. Word came from New York that she was not to be touched. She had done a great service when it mattered most and she never told a soul what she learned from her numerous trips to Cleveland and New York. She was released in time to make sure her daughter received a proper burial.

Prison had not been good for Synthia. The years of stress and anxiety had taken its toll. At fifty years old, Synthia looked ten years older. Once voluptuous and vibrant, she was now rail thin and quiet. Her thick, black hair was now stark white. The confidence she exuded with every step over a decade ago was replaced by a slow and deliberate walk marked by sorrow. But Synthia wasn't worried about her looks anymore, she just wanted to take care of her daughter.

Sola's going home ceremony couldn't have been more beautiful. The internment at Greenlawn Cemetery was the hardest part for Synthia, who wept over her daughter's coffin before it was lowered into the ground. The Cemetery was less than a half a mile away from the old Sullivant Gardens Housing Projects, which lay in ruin after the federal government closed the complex six years before. *There are two ways out of the Gardens—on the road or in a box.*

As Synthia returned to her limousine after the internment, Campbell Donovan walked up behind her and tapped her on the shoulder.

"Ms. Nichols," Campbell said.

Synthia turned and stared at Campbell. Her eyes were red and swollen and her lips were trembling.

"Yes," Synthia replied.

Campbell held a medium-sized gift box in his hand. "Your daughter." He held out the box. "She wanted you to have this."

Synthia looked down at the box and reached for it, tears welling in her eyes. "What's your name?"

"Campbell Donovan, ma'am," he slipped.

"And you and Sola were friends?" Synthia asked with a half smile.

Campbell's eyes filled with tears. "Yes, I think we were."

Synthia took the box and held it to her chest as she closed her eyes. "She gave this to you?" Synthia asked, referring to the box.

"Yes. Her last wish was for you to have it."

Synthia opened her eyes and looked at Campbell. "Mr. Donovan, I have always believed that my daughter really died fourteen years ago." She looked down at the box. "What was left was a lonely shell of a woman."

Campbell turned and looked towards the gravesite. "I believe there was a little bit of the girl you knew still inside, Ms. Nichols." He turned to look at her and he could fill his tears spilling onto his cheeks. "I wish I had known her then. Maybe I—"

Synthia interrupted him. "I know, Mr. Donovan. We all have wishes. But at least she can rest now." Synthia started walking towards the limousine. "Goodbye, Mr. Donovan." She didn't look back.

As the limousine driver turned onto I-70 and headed East, Synthia stared at the box intently before opening it carefully. There was cash, business cards, papers with bank account numbers, and a medium-sized envelope with the word 'Momma' scribbled on the front. Synthia opened the envelope. There was a letter inside. The tears began to fall again as she read the note.

> *Momma,*
> *If you're reading this you're free.*
> *Free to do anything you want.*
> *There's money to get you started,*
> *contacts to help you get situated,*
> *and enough money in the bank to keep*
> *you well. Don't worry about me, 'cause*
> *I'm free too.*

Synthia couldn't help but think of her life choices. She knew she would begin to heal, *someday*. What she didn't know is if she could ever forgive herself.

You are free, honey child, she thought. And then she folded up the letter and sobbed.